The UNHERALDED KING of PRESTON PLAINS MIDDLE

JEDAH MAYBERRY

Published by River Grove Books
Austin, TX
www.greenleafbookgroup.com

Distributed by River Grove Books

For ordering information or special discounts for bulk purchases, please contact River Grove Books at PO Box 91869, Austin, TX 78709, 512.891.6100.

Design and composition by Greenleaf Book Group LLC
Cover design by Greenleaf Book Group LLC
Cover images:
feather ©Veer/Julja
field/tree ©Veer/Alloy Photography

Publisher's Cataloging-In-Publication Data
(Prepared by The Donohue Group, Inc.)
Mayberry, Jedah.
   The unheralded king of Preston Plains Middle / Jedah Mayberry.—1st ed.
     p. ; cm.
   Issued also as an ebook.
   ISBN: 978-1-938416-13-2
   1. Brothers—Connecticut—Preston—Fiction. 2. Minority teenagers—Connecticut—Preston—Fiction. 3. Suburban life—Connecticut—Preston—Fiction. 4. Preston (Conn.)—Race relations—Fiction. 5. Bildungsromans. I. Title.
PS3613.A92 U54 2013
813/.6   2013930629

First Edition

For the kids—

MJ, T, S, CDD, RIII, C,

MDDCME, J&J, KD, E,

JJJT, BIS, JEX, MMB, KCN

Possibility is everything.

*Love takes off masks that we fear we cannot live without
and know we cannot live within.*

—JAMES A. BALDWIN

ACKNOWLEDGMENTS

I am eternally grateful to the folks at River Grove Books for taking a gamble, for encouraging me to bet on myself. It is amazing the transformation that can occur in the hands of professional editors, proofreaders, and graphic designers, coaxing the story from my head in precisely the way I had imagined it. I thank each of you for your dedication to task, for your kind consideration in steering some piece of the project through to a place that could not have been reached on my efforts alone. Les, thank you for your unvarnished opinion *it ain't bad, mind you, but it could be better*. It is better, in part, due to your thoughtful insight and steady encouragement. To my family, who have stood by me, stride for stride, every step of the journey: I am nothing without you. No amount of success would have meaning without you to share in it. To my extended family, my people, my crew, I carry you with me every place I go. So stand tall, be your best self. In turn, I will work to be my best self, to do you proud. To the cat and dog and everyone, I thank you.

Trajan Hopkins at his brother's memorial service, November 4, 2004

You may never have been to the place that I call home. But I trust that you, too, have a home, that you come from someplace. I don't know the place you claim any more than you know mine. Yet if my someplace speaks to your someplace, if it conjures thoughts of home, then you might come to know me. To know me, you will have had to know my brother. He was my whole world.

PROLOGUE: SILENT WALLS

"Ma," Trajan exclaimed over his shoulder, hoping to send the words down the hallway and around the corner into his mother's bedroom. "Where are my white socks?"

"I don't believe I'm wearing any socks," she announced, tossing the covers aside, contented by the sight of her bare feet staring back at her.

"I didn't accuse you of wearing them," he replied, burying his elbows deeper into his top dresser drawer.

He took care to pull his voice back inside his own room. He had been left to converse with silent walls since his brother's passing. He'd poked his head inside his mother's doorway earlier that morning, asked whether she wanted some breakfast. She thanked him for being so considerate, sending a fleeting smile in the direction of the open doorframe. But, no, she didn't need anything to eat. At least she was talking today, sitting upright for a change, her pink robe adding light to the room. He didn't want to risk upsetting her with the drudgery of life's mundane little details. The likelihood that he would miss his soccer match if he couldn't find his white socks was not the conern he wished to see push his mother back into the shadows. His mother had been his brother's biggest fan, with Trajan close on her heels. She nurtured the bond between mother and sons, spending time with each in carefully measured doses to ensure that either child got equal shine. But Langston, the older by a full three years, held a direct line to her heart. The bright beam of her happiness rippled inside of him, rippled, rippled, then sank.

ONE

Trajan Hopkins lived his whole young life in Preston, a dimple of a town nestled among a string of dimple towns, lining the banks of the Thames River as the river makes its slow march into the sound, Long Island jutting like a raised index finger from the tip of New York to protect Connecticut's southeastern shore from the steady crush of the sea. The Thames River Valley mutated over the years into an oddly shuffled deck of hardscrabble little enclaves making their faint impersonation of urban strife, surrounded by the quaint veneer of buttoned-down New England sensibilities. Time marked the peripatetic crisscrossing of peoples, mixing peaceably in most instances, retreating at the end of any given day to their own neutral corners,

the melting pot amounting to little more than steaming compart-
ments, from native to all flavors immigrant, to those non-immigrants
whose arrival on these shores signifies a period of deep contradiction
in our nation's psyche, their forefathers having been dragged forcibly
to the land of the free. Together they forged a tenuous harmony of
existence comprising the only world Trajan had ever known.

TURNABOUT

The village of Preston is largely defined by the things it is not, by the things its expanse of working farms and decaying historic landmarks serve to subdivide. The town sits too far upriver to share a whaling history with New London, its neighbor to the south; is too far removed from the sound to claim a part in the seaport Mystic boasts as its crown jewel; lacks sufficient battle lore to go down in history as a namesake to the famed Colonel Ledyard, run through with his own sword for refusing to surrender his fort to the British. Instead, Preston is home to a disjoint scattering of mill roads and numbered byways named according to the places they can take you to or from, Norwich-Westerly Road providing the town's most traveled thoroughfare.

The richness in cultural diversity found throughout the region is visible solely on a microscopic level, requiring you to wander about armed with a satchel of DNA swabs, instructing people to stick out their tongues. Taken individually, everyone is in the minority, the assortment of ethnicities barely amassing sufficient numbers to warrant distinction, New England austerity casting a disapproving eye on any attempt to affix labels. Seen together, the people of the Thames River Valley represent a long and varied history, anchoring a slow blossoming in culture the same way the earth was formed, one layer at a time.

The native comprises the region's inner core, a solid center ensconced in molten lava spawning a scattering of interrelated tribal allegiances: Mashantucket Pequot, Eastern Pequot, Mohegan. Pilgrims arrived in time to form the lower mantle reshaping the core, with destructive force by most accounts. The wave of European settlers that followed imported slave labor and indentured servants—Africans followed by the Chinese—to settle the upper mantle and hardened outer crust. The rest of the world arrived in flocks—from Thailand, the Philippines, New Zealand, Guam; Brazil, Colombia, Panama, Guatemala; Argentina, Venezuela, Guyana, and the Caribbean—decorating the land's rough surface with flowering grasses and colorful plants and shrubs. The wind in the trees carries their whispers, the flow in the Thames their blood, their sweat, their river of tears.

Colonization placed the confluence of cultures in violent conflict, their respective histories rooted in the distant past, odd remnants of which dot the landscape, providing evidence of the big bang that birthed the eventual outgrowth of people. The Parke Family House sits precariously close to the main thoroughfare. Erected circa 1670 the house's wooden clapboards reflect the reserved palette of pale blues and grays that has come to represent the standard for architectural simplicity popular among local homebuyers to this day. Huge fieldstones mark property lines stacked haphazardly, held together by spit and time.

Forged four hundred years ago by the persistent passage of horse-drawn wagons, the roadway had originally been intended to transport materials and produce between plots of farmland, fenced in hand-hewn rail and post. For decades, Preston sat undisturbed by outside forces as time transformed the world around it. The casinos summoned a new Martian landing bringing unwanted bustle: New Yorkers traveling past from one direction, Bostonians heading the opposite way to patronize one or the other of the Indian-run gambling establishments. The rumbling of cars streaming past is to blame for weakening the footings of several period Colonial homes, the tide having turned, the resurgence of tribal concerns crumbling the walls of those credited with having disrupted the advance of Native American culture in the first place, turnabout constituting the fairest of fair play.

MOTHER, DAUGHTER, SISTER, FRIEND

Every community has its recognizable icons. A doctor cures things, but it takes someone who's been sick to want to sing his praises. A person will have to have been rescued from a blaze before the thought occurs to acknowledge a fireman for his efforts; a person has to catch religion before worshipping at the preacher's pulpit. But everyone in the course of their school years has encountered that special someone who endeavored to reach them.

Dottie Hopkins worked as a teacher's aid in the elementary school her sons, Langston and Trajan, had attended. She catered to boys just like them, boys who would have gone unnoticed had it not been for her keen eye. Boys whom, shown the right amount of motherly love cloaked in a heavy covering of toughness, she believed capable of meeting the same high standards she set for her own two boys. Mrs. Hopkins fostered as many good sons in that school as the school had ever produced, her own boys included.

The town of Preston crumpled in on itself—vacuum pressure collapsing air inside a soda can—upon learning that one of their own, Mrs. Hopkins's eldest son, had succumbed in the hands of the police. No one would escape the loss. Mrs. Hopkins was their mother, daughter, sister, friend—meaning each of them, by proxy, had lost a son too.

Dottie's kids were none too difficult to identify. Their clothes, invariably two sizes too big, showed ample signs of wear, of too-frequent washing. They were the kids made to stand in the lunch line holding pink and green raffle tickets: one for milk, the other for whichever hot entrée was on offer that day. That was before Mrs. Hopkins put her stamp on things. Her lot in life was not so far removed from that of anybody in her classroom. She convinced Mr. Day, the school principal, to move over entirely to a raffle ticket system. Have everyone in the lunch line look the same. The transaction to acquire meal tickets was carried out at the start of each week in the relative privacy of the school office, leaving those able to pay for their lunch with one less thing to lord over those unable to pay.

"You ever noticed," Langston observed on the drive home one afternoon, "Oscar Hairston wears the same clothes every day?"

She pondered the question, working to determine whether her

son was genuinely concerned for Oscar Hairston's well-being, or had intended the remark as idle commentary, offered in passing to fill the short ride home. Langston would start middle school in another couple of years, depriving Dottie of her daily visits with him—time spent in close proximity to her eldest son, a luxury she could not hope to keep forever.

She studied his vacant expression, the same unshakable stare that she had long envied in her father's eyes, one capable of concealing any amount of turmoil in his world.

"Oscar looks real fine in that outfit," Dottie replied, hoping to silence the possibility that pity was what sat lurking beneath her son's wispy lashes. "It must be his favorite. To wear my favorite outfit to school every day; I would find that most comforting."

Dottie recognized that those were the lucky ones. An ill-fitting set of wash-worn clothes meant they had a doting somebody at home, their own Mrs. Hopkins filling them with pride as they stepped out the doorway each morning in hopes of keeping their heads lifted throughout the course of the day—Dottie sent to watch over them in place of their resident somebody, rather than the other way around. As it was, Trajan never saw a hand-me-down, the clothes ripped straight from her sons' backs before they were too far gone to be of use to somebody else. Their father complained that they couldn't afford to clothe the whole world.

"We can't afford to let the world go around naked and freezing either, Chester," she chided her husband. "Now can we?"

That's typically how arguments ended between the two of them, the ends of her logic rooted in some benevolent cause trumping anything her husband might think to say. Dottie's father warned that she'd have nothing left to tend to her own affairs, should she continue throwing her energy into other people's concerns.

"My guys are well cared for," she assured him.

"As long as you recognize that your husband is one of your guys too," her father advised, having found himself on the losing end of a similar proposition with Dottie's mother. The solemn vows he and his wife had made, to give each other their best, adopted a different character the day their daughter was born, Dottie being the most precious thing her mother had ever laid eyes on. He had played second fiddle for enough years to recognize in his son-in-law someone caught in the same restless abyss.

Migration

Dottie came from a long line of public servants. Her mother was a schoolteacher. Her grandmother, Eloise Durant, had also been a schoolteacher. Eloise made her way to the Thames River Valley from Waycross, Georgia, her mind set on giving back in a place that seemed more appreciative of her services. Dottie's grandfather, Granville Hastings, arrived from Sumter, South Carolina, under similar circumstances. He completed a stint stationed at the Coast Guard Academy in New London, electing to remain in the river valley at the end of his tour, conditions in South Carolina having altered little in the time he'd been gone.

Granville Hastings held his post until the time of his death as head bellman at the Amos Lake Inn and Resort, his contribution to the world consisting of an immaculate smile, his voice booming to greet each hotel guest as if the two of them were family, the traveler coming home for a visit. Dottie's grandparents embodied the promise of the Great Migration fulfilled: industrious parents to a prospering baby girl, Dottie's mother-to-be.

Dottie's father, on the other hand, was a bit of a rambler, decidedly less settled in his life choices than Granville and Eloise Hastings deemed suitable, especially for someone who wished to court their daughter, Estelle. This did little to quiet Alonzo Tooker's growing interest in the object of his affections. (Having always gone by Took, he became, in the second half of his life, Grandpa Tuke, Langston's baby way of saying Took, the pronunciation spilling to the rest of the world until he became known simply as Tuke, usually introducing himself that way.) The four squares of Took's heritage included American Indian, his grandfather counted among the Native Eastern Pequot; French-Canadian, owing to excursions of the fur trade into the eastern United States from Quebec; plus two parts Cape Verdean, the African slave in him drawn to Miss Estelle's easy ways and her mother's fine southern cooking.

Took first caught sight of young Estelle, home on break from the women's teachers college in Springfield, Massachusetts, in the summer he worked as a yardman at the Lake Resort. He stood in plain view of her father and made his way toward her, first with a tip of his hat as she passed from the oval drive into the lobby, followed by an

13

upturned smile as she stepped off the back porch to take in views of the lake, where a sprinkling of daffodils was beginning to take root, making their intrepid stand above the water's glass surface, despite the promise of a short-lived stay—the swift fall of winter in New England taking few prisoners. Estelle was taken by Took's insistence. It showed his determination to know her, pursuing her despite her father's looming presence. To Granville Hastings, it was the consummate show of disrespect.

"Mr. Tooker," Granville commanded, his broad stance sending an uneasy shiver of groans along the length of wooden boat dock that extended from above Took's head to the water's edge. "I need you to arrange the canoes along the lakefront before the guests come down for breakfast." Granville held an elevated view of himself, the way a he-man lifts his full body weight above his head, looking to prove a point. He called everybody "mister," from lawn boy to resort guest. That way, he could pretend they were all on equal footing.

"As soon as I finish clipping these roses, Mr. Hastings," Alonzo responded, his full attention lost in the delicate form drifting lakeside in a floral sundress, the exposed length of Miss Estelle's proud neck fueling the daredevil in him.

Granville's Carolina instincts told him to cause a fuss, to let his voice boom with newfound purpose and wipe Alonzo's face clean of its smile. He started toward Alonzo just as Mr. Wheaton, one of Amos Lake's long-standing patrons, sauntered out onto the porch beside him. "Fine morning, isn't it, Mr. Hastings?" he asked, tilting his head in the direction of the sun, a lingering haze from the morning dew still fighting for attention along the horizon as the sun initiated its climb toward open sky.

The lake stretched out before them. When the water is still, it casts a shadow in muted shades of brown and green and blue along the opposing shoreline, painting a picture in two lines of trees: one above ground, the other hanging upside down, birds and trees, clouds and fish all dangling submerged, crowding one another for space. "The air doesn't get much sweeter than it does out here," Mr. Wheaton remarked, his thumbs pressed into his belt loops to channel a fresh breeze in the direction of his protruding belly.

Granville adjusted the slant of his smile, recalibrating the boom in his voice. "Fine morning indeed, Mr. Wheaton. Can I interest you in some breakfast?" he asked, turning his attention toward more civil matters.

Even the boss man has a boss man, Alonzo remarked to himself as Mr. Hastings escorted the man to the dining hall. *That will never be me.* He bent to take a long pull from the garden hose. He despised drinking from the hose. It suggested that whether or not Granville Hastings addressed him as mister, the man was above him, that Miss Estelle, too, was beyond his grasp.

"I expect him to get right on whatever I've asked of him as soon as the words leave my tongue," Granville complained later that evening to his wife, Eloise. "Not after he's through ogling my daughter."

"Deny them access to one another, and you'll wind up chasing her straight into his arms," Eloise warned, Estelle possessing a hand-in-the-cookie-jar mentality with which her mother was all too familiar. "Allow her to regulate consumption on her own, and she'll eventually have her fill of interest in him. Any attempt to squelch that interest is bound to garner the opposite effect."

Miss Estelle made no overt response to Alonzo's advances, though her eyes never strayed far from anyplace where her father directed him to work. By the end of her second week home, Alonzo ventured a word in her direction.

"Afternoon, Miss Hastings," he offered, nearly bending in two to greet her. "I am Alonzo Tooker, but my friends call me Took."

"Meaning that you intend for us to be friends?" she asked, using the proper, well-mannered tone that she would soon recognize as capable of driving him wild.

"Friends would be an appropriate place to start," he responded, his ability to match her proper way of speaking limited by his tenth-grade education. Took was no dummy, but two more years of school had seemed an awful waste, knowing that college was not what lay ahead for him. Plus, there was money out there to be made.

Later in life, Took described himself as having been a traveling man, only not one going for distance. The ends of his world extended little beyond the place where his grandfather's people had first set roots. He had washed dishes, carried bags, tended yards at various establishments around town, anything to make ends meet, his apparent purpose in life standing in stark contrast to the purpose

16

that Granville and Eloise Hastings had in mind for Miss Estelle. Took's flat gray eyes said they had seen things, had witnessed tremendous chaos. The long part down the middle of his crinkled hair said he had stirred up his fair share of difficulties, had caused as much ruckus as those eyes had seen.

He was on hand the night a man—someone Alonzo had worked alongside one summer packing crates of walleyes and striped bass for the trip across state—got his head busted open with a lead pipe, the attack stemming from accusations over a card game. Having never considered the man especially bright even before his skull had been split, Took fully expected to find a babbling idiot the next time the two crossed paths. The man appeared to have suffered no ill effects. If anything, he became even less self-conscious, showing off the scar across his scalp to anyone who cared to venture a look.

"You see the lump he put on my melon, Took?" the man asked, hunched over, his hands at work atop his head, directing Took's gaze to the spot of the injury. "I thought that fool was going to kill me."

"In time, he will," Took assured the man, disappointed at having missed the chance to hear him babbling, to attempt to decipher clear thought inside his jumbled chatter.

17

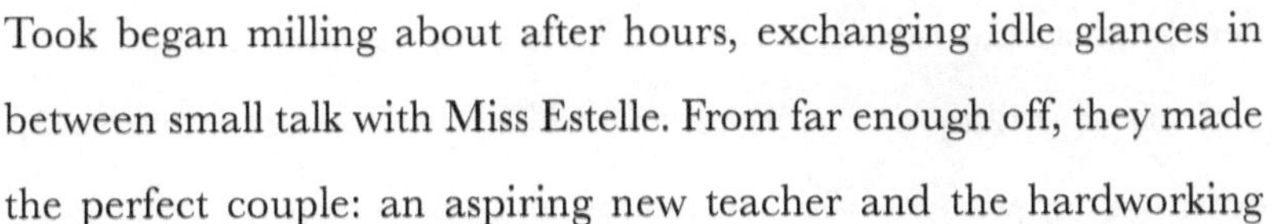

Took began milling about after hours, exchanging idle glances in between small talk with Miss Estelle. From far enough off, they made the perfect couple: an aspiring new teacher and the hardworking handyman, set to make their mark on the world. But within Mr. Hastings's resolute stare, the pairing looked like a plan intent on ruining all that he and Eloise had worked to establish for their daughter. To his way of thinking, Took was that light-eyed stranger who'd come wandering through Sumter before Granville had acquired sufficient insight to fully comprehend the intermingling that takes place between grown folks, stirring up assorted difficulties, and then getting back on his high horse before anyone could call him to account for the damage he'd done. He was the wild hair in a finely finished do, the weed sprouting at the center of a carefully manicured lawn.

The Hastings sought to distract their only daughter with every imaginable thing—tennis, badminton, bird-watching, horseback riding—to keep her outside of Mr. Tooker's reach. They encouraged her to mingle with the resort guests, to acquaint herself with the single young men lying about; never mind that no bachelors of color would visit that summer. They didn't comprehend her infatuation with Took, failed to recognize the hold his gray eyes and the part down the middle of his crinkled hair had already placed on their daughter—the cookie jar at work against a most determined will.

Miss Estelle earned her teaching certificate at the end of the ensuing school year, setting a foot on her chosen path in life, one that entailed teaching in somebody's grade school, marrying the man of her dreams, and raising a family of her own according to her own notions of order. Alonzo Tooker would be her next measured leap down that path after her period of apprenticeship in Waterbury, an assignment she felt her parents had conspired somehow to create in hopes of pushing Estelle and Mr. Tooker further apart without compromising the obligations the certificate program imposed on its graduates to teach within the public school system in their home states.

To say that I have missed you would be a colossal understatement, she wrote to him in her only letter home. She was fairly certain that he would never write back, but she wanted him to know how the thought of being in his company again had so consumed her. *I am embarrassed to say my first year's curriculum has transformed, and now includes reading, writing, and the virtues of Alonzo Tooker. None of my pupils seem to have minded. I fear their parents won't be as sympathetic.* She addressed the letter *c/o Amos Lake Inn and Resort.* She spoke regularly with Granville and Eloise by phone. The letter was her way of conveying her sincere intentions to see things through with Mr. Tooker upon her return.

"Why would she do such a thing?" Granville grumbled as he handed the envelope to Eloise, wanting to gauge her reaction. "Go off and ruin her life for the likes of him?" The venom that stirred whenever he used the term *him,* grinding his teeth on the word, had no specific target in mind. Took had, for the most part, been respectful. Showed no distaste when asked to address Granville as mister. (The two shared a mutual dislike for having to call anybody "sir." Took had never had cause to address anyone that way. Granville had left all his sirs—*yes sir* and *no sir, boss*—back in South Carolina. He was in no hurry to start any such tradition in Preston.)

"In your eyes, no one will ever be good enough for your little girl," Eloise explained. She brushed his cheek with a gentle touch of her palm. "Let them be," she advised, handing the letter back for him to see that it got to its rightful recipient.

Granville delivered the letter personally the next morning. "Mr. Tooker, I believe I have something that belongs to you."

Alonzo prepared for the worst. He had gotten the boot before. This had all the familiar signs of a firing: the out-of-way approach, the sealed envelope, presumably containing his last week's pay. He was many things, but a laggard was not one of them. He made sure to complete any task assigned him with minimal instruction or supervision. He didn't mind the heat, didn't mind the cold either. He never caused trouble with any of the resort guests. For the most part, he kept to himself, routinely doing the work of two or three men when left alone to do it. If Mr. Hastings saw fit to fire him for becoming friendly with his daughter, then so be it. He would leave with his head held high.

Took sensed other troubles brewing inside the boss man's eyes. The venerable Mr. Granville Hastings for the first time appeared sheepish, downtrodden. Even the boom in his voice was laden with uncharacteristic humility. He didn't seem angry; nor was he elated, for that matter, at the chance to at last rid himself of the thorn in his side. Took caught sight of Estelle's name scrawled in lavish script above the return address as Granville extended a hand and passed the envelope to him.

"You do right by her" is what Granville said to him as he let go of the letter, resigned, defeated, accepting of the thing that the universe, despite persistent effort on his part, had deemed irrefutable.

The cookie jar split wide open after Estelle maneuvered a transfer back to the river valley, the time she spent with Took made all the more torrid by their long separation. That time together with him eventually produced a child. The Hastings's only grandchild was born midway through the spring semester of Miss Estelle's first year of teaching in town. The soft gurgles of a baby cooing provided ample consolation for the tribulations they feared lay ahead for their daughter, having attached her hopes to the likes of Alonzo Tooker. Dottie Hopkins entered this world part Hastings and part Grandpa Tuke, each side conjuring a loyal following around Preston.

When boys reach a certain age, none of them bigger than a bump in the dirt, they test one another. Some pick up a bat and ball. Others take to the gridiron. Trajan's brother, Langston, lived to fight. Legend has it he entered the world with fists balled, one leg cocked, prepared to strike in the event the doctor attempted to swat his backside more than once. Langston's broad smile shone openly on their father's face when he told the story, his ordinarily stoic demeanor overcome with delight at the anecdote he alone could tell.

Langston trained in martial arts from the tender age of six or seven. He fancied himself preparing to compete in the 2000 Olympics in Sydney, upon learning that Tae Kwon Do would be introduced as an official Olympic sport. He walked around day and night practicing moves, punishing the air with interposed thrusts of hands and feet. He fashioned a stretching implement from a length of rope thrown across the metal support of a basketball hoop that stood in the playground unused after-school hours. He would plant a foot on the blacktop, the rope tied at one end in a slipknot, pulling his free ankle skyward until his legs performed the splits along the pole supporting the backboard. With time, he used this method to extend the reach with his left foot to match that with his right. Then he'd switch to his right side to keep pace with the left until he could control either foot in ways the rest of the world struggled to comprehend.

Never one to pick a fight, Langston pursued martial arts for the charge, the thrill of engagement: to excise another man's spirit, find his weakest point, then press hard against it. Trajan became a sounding board for his brother's budding philosophy on all things concerning war.

"You want it to be your choice whether or not to let up on an opponent," Langston explained, invoking the lessons his TKD instructor had begun pouring into his head through repeated lecture. "But you have to stay cool, requiring discipline best held inside an unfettered mind," he said, ping-ponging between his own words and those of the TKD instructor. "I mean, there's no point in continuing to press a kid after you've exposed his weakness, have broken your adversary's will to fight. The decision not to let up is reserved as a last-ditch measure called for only in the most desperate of times, on the off chance this kid has pinpointed your weakness and is looking for a reason to press hard."

Imagination eventually took hold, inspiring loose embellishment on top of the instructor's no-nonsense account. "Let a whole gang of people jump you and you're free to cut loose, a full regimen of training at your disposal." Langston twisted his hands in front of him contemplating inside his mind the moves he would make, his head on a swivel to keep multiple targets in front of him at once.

"You really think Mom and Dad are going to let you go all the way to Australia?" Trajan asked, a globe in the school library having debunked the myth inside his head that a trip Down Under would require extensive digging.

"If I'm good enough, they'll be proud to see me go. Might even let you come with me," he said, sealing the deal with a nod and a sly wink, to his brother's delight.

Trajan showed little interest in martial arts. Regarded it as something Langston and their father did together. Trajan didn't share that kind of bond with their father, his view of the world trending in the direction of their mother's way of thinking: Boys fight when they're not shown any other way to express themselves. A brother capable of taking on the whole world, though, who just might get into the Olympics, taking Trajan along for the ride, was an altogether separate matter. Their father contended that this great nation was built on the backs of men fighting.

"Boys die when men fight," their mother replied. That is not what fate had in store for her sons.

Langston shrugged off suggestions from the neighborhood kids that he was King of Preston Plains Middle School. Having been taught to respect the majesty of the sport of Tae Kwon Do, his principal aim to acquire mastery over one's body, mind, and spirit, he considered any attempt to gain prominence or reputation in someone else's eyes to be a mindless show of bravado. Still, there was no shortage of challengers to the throne, Langston their hero even if he shunned the crown.

Someone would inevitably turn up to deliver word of the latest disturbance. "Albert Chu says he's gonna catch you," the person would say—on the way home from school, after supper, before the streetlights come on, over the weekend, Tuesday after next, in the new millennium, when the moon is blue—satisfying what Langston had come to expect from Albert with his perpetual fill-in-the-blank proposition of threats.

Langston's expression remained steady, his attention fixed on a jumble of concrete further down the walkway, lifted by the silent creep of an ever-encroaching root system. A lone sycamore stood in a thin patch of new grass that led away from the schoolyard, working to appear inconspicuous.

The messenger continued in his assigned task of filling Langston's head with worry, his weight shifting back and forth between nervous feet. "Claims he saw you the other day talking with his sister again."

"We have class together," Langston explained, his conciliatory manner of speaking baffling Albert's stooge. "We're going to have to talk every now and again."

"Albert says now and again is more than he's willing to stomach," the messenger responded.

Langston adjusted his tone; any hint of apology drained from his voice. "You tell your Albert to come. I'll be outside when he gets here. *Waiting.*" This last bit he said as he leaned in, the corner of his mouth crinkling on the word for emphasis.

Langston had battled Albert Chu countless times over the years, neither gaining clear advantage, neither seeming able to let the rivalry fade. Albert's grandparents owned the only sit-down, table-cloth Chinese restaurant in town, the family restaurant having sponsored one of the Little League teams from the first fledgling steps of an organized league in Preston. The Chus' grandsons played their entire Little League careers for Chinese Kitchen, as had Langston. Soccer had taken hold in Preston by the time Trajan came along.

There was a time when the biggest controversy in the Chu family stemmed from the eldest son, Diang, having stepped outside the circle of family tradition and taken up with a brown-eyed blonde, an ex-navy wife grown bored with her husband's endless excursions to sea. So, on top of marrying outside his kind, Diang Chu married a divorcee.

Diang and his bride, in time, had three children: two boys and a girl. The brothers Albert and Alfred were staggered in age with Langston and Trajan, the Chu boys each older than his Hopkins counterpart by little more than a year. The daughter, Angelica, fit neatly between the brothers in age, placing her in the same grade with Langston. The two had been classmates for as long as either could remember having attended school, a fortuitous turn for Langston and a persistent source of aggravation for Albert, who having appointed himself responsible for protecting his sister's honor, viewed Langston as a constant menace. Tensions between the two continued to build despite (or perhaps due to) the fact that they played on the same baseball team and were even named to the all-star team together. They focused on making the best of an awkward situation, however, their association affording Langston privileged access to Albert's sister.

The Chu brothers' insistent meddling proved largely unnecessary, the lot of them ranging from just shy of ten to half a rung over thirteen. Albert and Alfred had, at best, suppressed a serious case of puppy love. Nobody's honor was in real danger for at least another couple of years. This mattered little to Albert Chu. His sister was, after all, the comely maiden, a seldom-seen mix of sweet demure spiked with in-your-face allure, from the full pout of her lips to a hint of blonde from her mother's side sprinkled throughout an overflowing lion's mane of her father's jet-black hair. Possessing his father's lanky build and fluid ways as well as his mother's even brown skin and haunting eyes, Langston was a most probable suitor. Langston knew this; Albert knew this. Even Angelica, at times, appeared cognizant of the silent pull radiating between her and Langston.

Angelica volunteered to work the concession stand any time Langston and her brothers had a game, making her easy prey in Albert's estimation. "Keep an eye on him when it's my turn at bat," he instructed his younger brother, overlooking that players weren't allowed outside the dugout during the course of a game. This was a minor inconvenience for Langston, who wound up spending the bulk of his allowance each week financing trips back and forth to the concession stand.

"Buy yourself a hot dog," he told Trajan, squeezing a dollar bill wrapped around a few coins through a hole in the cinder block partition that formed the dugout walls.

"But I already had two hot dogs plus a slice of pizza," Trajan complained.

"Then you must be thirsty," Langston suggested. "Get yourself a soda and bring me a sheet of candy buttons and a grape Big Buddy. I need something to chew." He extended the money inside the pincer grip of his fingers. "And make sure she knows it's for me," he said, checking over his shoulder for eavesdroppers.

The Chu brothers stayed on the lookout for any such exchange. It starts with bubblegum. Before long, they're sharing sips of soda, dipping hands in the same box of popcorn. Where will it end?

Camaraderie

Any on-field camaraderie ceased once the final out had been called, both sides returning to their respective individual interests. Langston's interests—wrapped in inherent warmth and charm, those unassuming good looks, his easy way with people—centered on his constant pursuit of comely maidens in town, the lovely Angelica Chu highest among them.

How things went with Angelica on any given day began to dictate Trajan's quality of life. An uneventful day left the brothers to their normal after-school routine: cereal overflowing their bowls, enjoyed to the tune of their favorite cartoons. Langston indulged Trajan, allowing him back-to-back episodes of *Hey Arnold!* with its endless string of important-to-learn lessons. Then it was *The New Batman Adventures,* its principal lesson how to take a straight punch—*KAPOW!*

But anything out of the ordinary with Angelica—a walk home together, a note slipped inside his locker door—filled Langston with added adrenaline, leaving Trajan to spend the afternoon steeped in lessons on how not to get hit—especially if things had gone well between Angelica and his brother.

"Come here, Beavis," Langston would issue as fair warning. Trajan refrained from pointing out that this would make his brother Butt-head, as that would only fuel the assault against him.

Albert Chu despised Langston to his core. Imagined him dead or at least crumpled and bleeding at the bottom of Potter's Ravine, named, at the time of their adolescence, after the family who occupied the split-level ranch sitting adjacent to the steepest slope in town. The moist earth fell away along their property line in a deep gash left over from Jurassic times, covered on either side in lush green. Its expanse alone warranted distinction, though public records make no mention of the name.

At best, Langston viewed Albert Chu as little more than another hill to climb, a post along which to measure his progress with training. At worst, Albert was an adversary bent on thwarting any advance Langston attempted in the world. They battled for starting position on the playing field. The head coach argued that, being left-handed, Albert was better suited to play shortstop. Moving Langston to second base would improve their fluency in turning a double play. He failed to comprehend the depth of their rivalry.

Chester Hopkins volunteered to assist in coaching the team to maximize time with Langston and Trajan, troubled waters brewing between him and their mother. But proceeds from the Chu family business paid for the bats and balls, the restaurant's name adorning the front of everyone's cotton jersey. In the end, the name on the jerseys won out over Chester's daily presence on the field, which did little to improve relations between Langston and his dad.

Dottie, too, had taken to spending lots of extra time away from home. She had meetings: faculty meetings, school board meetings, parent-teacher conferences. On parent-teacher night, she sat alongside the teacher's desk and wrote out name tags. She solicited in-class volunteers to serve throughout the school year, allowing the teacher more one-on-one time with each parent. Then there were her tribal meetings, a recent reconvening of the Eastern Pequot. In light of success from the neighboring tribes in winning favor with both the

state and the federal government, the tribe had set to work petition-
ing to be recognized as a sovereign nation.

Chester met her on her way in the front door one evening after
he'd sent the boys to bed early. "Dorothy, I don't want to be the one
to have to say this, but you should quit with all those meetings," he
told his wife. "It's never going to happen. What do you think? The
state is going to allow another casino on some forgotten tribal land?
There are two casinos in operation around here already. There's not
going to be a third."

"Why is it you seem intent on crushing my dreams?" she asked.
"A casino is the least of our concerns. It's about righting a wrong,
returning my people's land to its rightful descendants." She wished
she didn't have to explain.

"Baby doll, I'm not trying to place limits on your dreaming. I just
don't want to see you come away brokenhearted is all," he pleaded.

"Now you want to worry about my heart. Trust that my heart is
plenty tough." She gave him ample time to respond before turning
up the hallway to bed.

When had they grown so far apart? Reached the point where he
could no longer dial up the charm, feather it in, and pull her back
to him? "What goes around comes around to stay," she once said to
him. He began suspecting her of all the things he'd been guilty of
doing. Each PTA-sponsored event she attended turned, inside his
head, into a romantic getaway with one of the other parents, a male
teacher, the school custodian. Gatherings of the leadership council

appointed among active tribe members could only amount to more of the same. Chester soon found it easier to stay gone as well, his physical presence no longer serving to conceal his unremitting emotional retreat.

Nobody seemed surprised when Chester finally took up with the Ramirez lady on the other side of town, her only son just a grade behind Trajan in school. Even Dottie seemed relieved to no longer be the subject of rumor and innuendo. She never stopped loving her husband, though she had stopped wanting from him, believing she had already gotten the best he had to give when her sons were born. Refused to set herself up for the kind of hurt that hanging onto some part of him would require.

Dottie was at one of her tribal meetings the night Chester had the boys help him load his things into the back of his Pontiac, all his possessions piled on top of one another: a guitar neither boy had ever heard him play; green trash bags filled with clothes from his side of the closet; his record collection from the time he thought he would deejay, organized in milk crates; his stereo equipment (large house speakers consuming the backseat all on their own); a lamb's wool jacket Dottie had given him to celebrate ten years together.

He dug out the waffle iron from deep inside the bottom cupboard and left it resting on the kitchen counter. He was the only one who ever used it, waffles reserved for the man of the house to prepare.

Given as a wedding gift, he dared not be so presumptuous as to claim it as personal property.

It took half a dozen trips; Grandpa Tuke refused to let Chester borrow his station wagon. If Chester was going to leave his daughter, he wasn't going to do it with the aid of Tuke's Toyota Cressida. Langston and Trajan stayed put between loads. They pictured the Ramirez kid helping Chester unload across town, moving his possessions in the opposite direction, from Pontiac to clothes closet, a couple dresser drawers set aside to make room for his things.

"I never wanted it to come to this," Chester said into the still air that hung between them after the last load had been transported. "That I would be living apart from my boys. But it has reached a point between your mother and me that there's no other way. Something has got to give."

"If you think you're miserable," Trajan snapped at Chester, suppressing their father's urge to explain himself, "imagine how Mom must feel."

Trajan had long perceived the difficulties between Dottie and Chester, felt the weight of them dimming his mother's smile, her head hanging lower anytime she looked his way. Langston was slower to catch on. He sat stirring on the sofa next to his father, his hips and shoulders at work imagining the things he would thrust and jab and kick the next chance he got to train.

Dottie's knees went soft as she pushed open the front door to find her whole family assembled in the living room waiting for her, Chester seated between his sons on the sofa trying to look regular. She had sensed this day coming—in all honesty, for many months. Saw it in eyes no longer able to meet hers, hands that had grown accustomed to touching without any discernible intent. From the way they were all sitting nestled together, it appeared he'd convinced the boys to leave with him.

Her face quickly swallowed up its initial shock, mild surprise masking her expression as she busied herself putting away her things while Chester sent the boys off to bed. She measured his gait as he returned from the back hall, turmoil brewing inside his dull eyes.

Chester used to have a way about him that Dottie found endearing—a quiet brooding that exposed his vulnerability without coming off as pathetic. He attended to her principally as a way of satisfying his need for companionship. His mounting insecurities didn't much matter, depending on the frequency of his attempts to woo her and how agitated he became whenever she wasn't immediately receptive. Dottie recognized, now, that she hadn't been entirely fair having him dial back his need for her, space it out until she was content being close with him again. But he didn't need to leave her this way.

"Tell me you're not leaving to be with her," she insisted, genuine hurt showing in her voice, the thought of being alone crashing in on her.

Chester ventured a glance in her direction as he bent to gather the rest of his things: one last bag of clothing, a box of high school memorabilia he'd kept on display in their bedroom.

"I'm leaving because my needs no longer seem to be a priority for you."

She curled her lip at him. "I don't care to remember when last my needs meant a thing to you."

"Think what you will, but I've considered your feelings in everything I've done."

"You certainly have a funny way of showing that consideration, wouldn't you say?"

He steadied his look on her face, willing his eyes to show the emotion stirring in his head. "It's only out of consideration for your feelings that I didn't leave sooner."

She returned his stare, a full range of emotions on display. Let him pass through the doorway for the last time as a resident under the same roof with her.

Dottie organized a yard sale the following weekend—rid herself of anything that reminded her of their life together. The waffle iron was first to go. She made every effort to dispose of the entertainment center that housed his stereo equipment, a tangle of stray wires taunting her from vacant cubbyholes on either side of the television set. It was their first major purchase as a couple. She thought for a minute she had sold it, but the bulk of it—solid oak standing floor to ceiling—put the prospective buyers off the idea. Even the offer of

Tuke's station wagon to transport the thing was of no use. The buyers looked like newlyweds, the bulge of the woman's belly suggesting their union had been put on the two of them. She couldn't bear to saddle them further with a mark from her inauspicious beginnings with Chester, especially knowing how the tale ends. Instead, she had the young man help her push the thing against the dining room wall. She filled the shelves with knickknacks, forbid the boys from calling it an entertainment center. It became her new hutch.

Devil's Stew

The boys had grown accustomed to the sound of their father's feet on the floor in the morning, the scent of his aftershave lingering in the hallway, the kitchen, wafting out the front door. The force of a single one of his sneezes shook the house to its foundation, hay fever wreaking havoc on Chester's sinuses. They looked for his car in the driveway when they came in from school, listened for his key in the door at the end of the day.

Having spent his days working to earn favor with the fairer sex, his and Trajan's mother providing a live-in example of how a woman can be made to feel—what might bring a smile to her face, what would produce a frown instead—Langston was especially attuned to the effect his father's leaving would have on their entire family. Chester living outside the household only amplified Langston's propensity to fight. Having yet to learn to express the anxieties he was experiencing at home, animosities with Albert continued to stew. It was inevitable that tensions would erupt every so often between the two, heightened insecurities fueling their quarrel.

It was the last day of school—a half day affording long idle time for the brand of foolishness kids can't help but throw themselves into when left unattended for any amount of time. A dozen or so kids hung back after the final bell had rung, encircling the two combatants in a makeshift human sparring ring punctuated by gaping mouths and pairs of bulging eyes. The ring had come to witness what would presumably be the last battle in this long-standing rivalry, as Albert was continuing on to high school over in Norwich after summer break drew to a close, across the river that presented itself like the elongated cleave of a peach, splitting the valley in two.

Trajan looked despondent, Albert Chu having donned a similar expression. (Angelica refused to watch, calling Langston and her brother imbeciles and turning her back on a feud invented largely in her honor.) Trajan and Alfred had lived the rivalry firsthand. Having suffered their own share of bumps and bruises on the battle lines alongside their older brothers, the younger siblings refrained from joining in the jeers from the crowd. Each had long feared that this rift, its origin rooted in fool's logic, would never find a rational conclusion.

Chants rose from the onlookers as a taut standoff ensued: *"FIGHT! FIGHT! FIGHT!"* And the first blow found its mark. The struggle proceeded like countless before it, short flurries of activity interspersed by long periods of scheming, the boys closely enough matched to require constant recalculating to counter one another's tactics. Wrist met leg, leg caught thigh; a glancing blow went thudding against an unsuspecting shoulder; a stray hand grazed an overexposed chin.

Command of the situation shifted back and forth with even reciprocity when another flurry broke out. Albert caught Langston's leg midair as he was coming off a roundhouse kick—a purely defensive move on Albert's part, merely incidental in its intended effect. It was one of those moments that spill in slow motion from the fountain of time. Realizing the shift in fortune, Albert drove Langston's body with full force into the pavement. Langston's shoulders caught the brunt of the impact, snapping his head backward against a boulder, its granite surface shaped like a balled fist by the cruel hand of fate. A loud *crack* from the collision erased the fight in both boys, the crowd clutching chests, covering mouths to contain the horror. Trajan wished he'd left with Angelica, that he'd not been on hand to witness the fall, his brother laid prostrate in the schoolyard.

The injury sidelined Langston for the better part of the summer. He discovered he could modulate his vision by pressing a hand against the knot on the back of his misshapen head. But that only aggravated the headaches. Once the swelling subsided, he continued to find remarkable lingering effects connected to the lump that had settled permanently in the space between the base of his skull and the firm tendons of his neck. He found that closing his eyes caused the images inside his head to slide sideways. Not blurred vision. It was like he could see ten scenes at once. Rubbing the knot helped calm down the slideshow, like changing radio stations, dialing through brief periods of mixed static as you leave the reach of one station before moving into the range of the next. His mother would be midway through a conversation with him and images of Langston's father would surface. Then Trajan would come traipsing through from the day before, telling his mother what he'd given his brother to eat, how long Langston had slept. Langston wondered whether he had always been able to see this way, if everybody could.

Bit by bit, his faculties returned. His motor skills improved; his sight, blurry from the outset, started to clear, though the view between shifting radio stations remained, as permanent as the knot on the back of his head. He eventually regained command of his speech, though the slightest slurring was evident whenever he put too much emphasis on his s's and t's.

RING THE ALARM

Langston and Albert were ordered by decree of a formal settle-
ment agreement to remain a hundred yards from one another for
the balance of their school years together, which finally suppressed
the urge to beat one another senseless. The Chu family placed two
hundred thousand dollars in trust, accessible to Langston upon his
turning eighteen, in the interest of putting the ordeal behind everyone involved. Chester felt his son deserved more for his injuries, but
he conceded, wishing to avoid the added strain of a protracted court
battle. Saw boys who might have been best friends, given other circumstances; teammates who'd found themselves on opposite sides in
every other regard.

The decree also stated provisions regarding how the money was to be dispensed should Langston not reach his eighteenth birthday. Seeming superfluous at the time, this tiny clause missed foretelling the fate of Trajan's brother by a scant few months.

Cross Pond

Angelica visited Langston throughout the summer, Albert powerless to stop her. It was more likely still that Albert encouraged the visits, his sister playing ambassador on the Chus' behalf to soothe any sore feelings lingering between the families. Langston and Angelica became boyfriend-girlfriend of sorts, adopting a pet phrase coined from the stilted greeting he managed on their first visit together while Langston was still confined to the living room sofa during his recuperation: "Ith good to thee you." They continued to greet one another this way even as his speech improved, each time sending Angelica's face into a titter of blushed cheeks and gleaming eyes.

They held hands on the sofa, made goo-goo eyes at one another. Trajan had caught them kissing on more than one occasion, arms folded around one another like the stone sculpture their mother had resting on a shelf in the dining room hutch. She called it *Love's Embrace. What did love have to do with all that slobbering, tongues moving back and forth inside one another's mouths like two worms, fishing cross pond?* Trajan shuddered at the thought. If he ever had a girlfriend, he would never make her kiss him the way he'd seen Angelica kissing his brother, devouring him with her tongue.

Dottie stopped at the store on her way from work to pick up a few items for dinner on the afternoon Langston suffered his first seizure. She had sent the boys on their way that morning with clear instructions: "Go straight home and try not to get into anything I'll have to hear about later," her eyes pleading for a bit less drama in her world.

Their mother would certainly have understood that Langston hadn't tried to have a seizure, that Trajan hadn't tried to give him one, the two looking wild eyed at one another as something inside Langston took hold, shaking his pupils to afford them a look inside the back of his skull in search of the source of his latest difficulty. The entire ordeal lasted no more than a couple minutes. Langston returned to his normal self, his pupils focused again on the outside world. The brothers made a pact that night to keep the secret, hoping to spare their mother the added burden of a crippled son whose body seemed intent every so often on shaking itself to pieces.

Angelica was not as willing an accomplice after the first incident she witnessed. She went running to find Trajan once the guttural clucking sounds got started in the back of his brother's throat. Trajan leaped to action. After the first episode his brother suffered, he had consulted the bookshelf where their mother kept her reference materials, determined from stolen reads of a first aid manual what to do to lessen the possibility of serious injury in the event of another attack. He retrieved a plastic cake spatula from the kitchen to secure his brother's tongue, easing the bite of his clenching teeth. He sat his brother upright with his arms folded across his chest, then held him to steady the convulsions.

By the time Dottie entered the kitchen that evening, her thoughts lost among a dwindling trail of workaday outside concerns, Angelica's eyes were still wide with worry, her mouth shaped to utter a startled little *oh my*. She started talking before either boy could get to her, incoherent stammering rising unannounced from her side of the room.

"Mrs. Hopkins," she blurted, "we weren't doing anything. I mean, we were just sitting on the sofa, Langston and me, when . . ." She struggled for the proper words, ones capable of lending adequate physical description to the scene she'd just witnessed. "When his body went stiff, then started shaking all over."

Her eyes scanned the room for any familiar thing that could remind her of something more she needed to tell. "I didn't know what to do. But Trajan. Oh, Trajan was terrific. I'm talking calm. Efficient."

"Slow down, girl," Dottie insisted. "You're going to give us both fits." She exhaled slowly as Angelica proceeded to fill in details of the afternoon's events. She searched her sons' faces for confirmation, laboring to keep her eyes from bulging.

They dropped Angelica off in the parking lot in front of Chinese Kitchen. Left her to explain why her eyes were so wild, the reason for her incessant stammering. That night, Dottie drove Langston to the emergency room at Backus Memorial Hospital. The attending physician said there wasn't much they could do for Langston post trauma, but she arranged an appointment with a neurologist for later in the week. He attributed the source of Langston's seizures to a long-term effect of the head trauma he'd experienced earlier that year.

"I'm reluctant to diagnose his condition as epilepsy without any other indicators present," the neurologist explained. "But the treatment should be similar." He said there was nothing they could do to stop a seizure once it got started. Limiting the potential for an attack was the best way to help the patient lead an unrestricted life. He offered a thin smile, measured in duration, meant to reassure Langston and his mother.

Changing Stations

Langston was made to wear a medical alert bracelet instructing people what to do in the event that he suffered a seizure in front of them. Instead, it caused people to question how they should approach him when he wasn't curled over seizing. For the first time since he was a baby, life for Langston was being dictated to him—what he could and couldn't do, with whom he could do it.

The USA took gold at the Sydney Olympics. Chester sent away for an autographed poster of Steven Lopez, winner of the Featherweight Division. Langston would have competed at Flyweight had he continued his training regimen. Trajan helped Chester hang the poster above his brother's bed as a surprise for Langston's birthday.

45

It's the only time Trajan can remember hearing his brother crying, tortured moaning rising unrepressed throughout the night from Langston's side of the room.

Trajan hustled home from school the next day. He stashed the poster in the hall closet, tucked it behind rolls of wrapping paper left over from Christmas. The whole Steven Lopez thing had been as much Chester's dream as Langston's, an entire family bound by a common pursuit. There's no telling who took the heartbreak harder. Langston never asked his brother what had happened to the poster, knowing that hanging it hadn't been Trajan's idea in the first place. Disposing of it, on the other hand, had clearly been his doing. Langston wished the two of them had gotten to see Sydney. Trajan was, after all, a most decent little brother.

Langston sputtered through the ensuing school year, distancing himself from the few friends he had. Failing to form new associations. The stream of images sliding inside his head made it difficult to focus on his schoolwork. A math quiz from third period stood hazily between him and his sixth-period teacher, making her history lecture impossible to follow. He was given study hall in place of phys. ed., leaving him alone for an entire period while the rest of the day came crashing in on him, the scenery rushing past in a jumbled slideshow inside his head.

Mr. Hopkins, are you paying attention? a teacher would ask. *Do you understand the assignment?* asked another. *Mr. Hopkins, would you care to come to the board and complete problem number four for the class?* Questions echoed at him from every angle. *Langston, it's time to go home,* his brother interrupted, having at last crossed the street to retrieve him after school, when a new sequence of echoes would begin—mother, father, brother scenes competing inside his head for attention.

Dottie refused to enroll her son in a modified curriculum. She was perfectly equipped to augment any instruction he found difficulty with in the classroom. She had known kids with similar afflictions who came to lean on the allowances afforded them, kids who eventually came to embody their limitations. Their experience in the classroom became an ever-rising tide, stifling their abilities. The more indulgent the allowances shown them, the less capable they became, until they were drowning again, flailing in wait of the even-greater allowances that would then be shoveled their way. Dottie was intent on having her son continue his education with minimal added assistance.

Langston entered the classroom each day knowing he just needed to get through it. He listened intently for his name, prepared to cycle through the imagery circling his head for the question he needed to answer. On a good day, the circus acts synchronized inside his head to form a reasonably coherent set of activities he needed to follow. He learned ten times as much on days like this, provided he could summon the right portion of each lecture at the time that best fit. Other times, he was just there, a warm body keeping his chair from flying around the room.

He went home at the end of the day exhausted. Preferred to sit in the dark to keep new imagery from taking root, each new thought complicating the acts he needed to tame in preparation for the day to come. Trajan learned to navigate the narrow spaces between the furniture in their bedroom by way of a dim sliver of light filtering in from the hallway. He pulled clothes from his dresser drawer by touch, used the weight of the fabric to determine which tops went with which bottoms, to tell winter from summer pajamas. He went to bed some nights dressed like a fuzzy peacock. As long as he changed again before Langston woke in the morning, the image of his little brother dressed in an inside-out mismatch of pj's and after-school clothes wouldn't add to the disturbance inside Langston's head.

His diminished interest in academics drove a deepening wedge between him and Angelica. "We can study together if you like," she offered, hoping to help in any way she could. The offer was met by a noncommittal shrug of his shoulders. Did he not know or did he not care? Did he no longer know whether he cared?

"We could *not* study together," she continued to press.

Another shrug, then finally a fully uttered acknowledgment. "We're not studying now," he muttered into the space growing between them on the living room sofa.

"But we don't have to do it together."

And that's how it came to pass that the King of PPMS lost any hold he had on the comely maiden. There was no formal dissolution of status between them, as they'd never formally declared they were anything more than friends, the closest of friends who had yet to recognize the significance of putting into words the potential for much more between them. That silent pull never found its full voice. Angelica stopped visiting, having in her mind attributed the source of Langston's agitation in part to those physical encounters on the sofa together, his frustration stemming from the need to resist further temptation. Rather than fight the forces conspiring to keep them apart, she suppressed her feelings toward him, silenced the urge, turned her back on puppy love, and got on with life in middle school.

Langston attempted to do the same. Did his best to reclaim his former self from his present self who went jittery whenever he refused to take the phenobarbital the doctor prescribed. Yet, like that system of roots Langston had observed in the schoolyard trailing away from the base of a sycamore to make a break in the sidewalk, the resilience of a living spirit will eventually find its way through. If not, the whole tree will perish.

BROWN-EYED PEA

Preston Plains Middle School gave way to Norwich Free Academy once the time came to cross the river and enter high school. NFA cast a wide net, serving, in addition to Norwich proper, the surrounding villages of Yantic, Taftville, and Preston, none of which was capable of sustaining sufficient enrollment to justify a high school in its home district. Norwich extended west to include Norwichtown, the majority of whose residents lived in the sprawling Sylvia Lane Housing Project, where families of every ethnicity shared a single address; Preston had nothing of the sort to rival it within the confines of its town lines.

The handful of kids of color who matriculated together from Preston had little in common with the kids from Sylvia Lane. Sylvia Lane housed mostly kids of color, the kind of kids for whom everything was a hoot, a row, a reason to show their teeth—sometimes bubbling, other times gnashing at anything not deemed Norwichtown cool. From way up in outer space, all those brown faces must have appeared the same. The kids from Preston drew their affiliations along different lines: who had played youth soccer together or Pop Warner football; who had sat next to you since the first day of kindergarten.

Landing in NFA three years ahead of his brother, Langston found the transition jarring. He didn't mesh with the Sylvia Lane kids. He failed to comprehend their unspoken kinship, didn't fit well inside their circle. He was not their kind of cool. A couple of Norwichtown girls approached him in the schoolyard during lunch break midway through the first full week of class, scouts sent from the opposing camp to test the bounds of his affiliation: Was he black-eyed pea or blonde? Langston stood mesmerized by the sight of them: large hoop earrings dangling nearly shoulder length; the fingers of both hands covered in silver rings encrusted with various stones of indeterminate worth; hip-hugging jeans stretched tight across early indications of budding curves. Their hairstyles, cut at blunt angles, reminded him of so many video girls proffered as eye candy on *Yo! MTV Raps*.

Those hoop earrings would be a huge liability in a fight, was the thought that struck him. Tender lobes ripped loose by an errant tug of a finger, a well-placed stab sending your opponent reeling from the most superficial flesh wound. Still, it would be the swiftest way to put an end to the conflict should one arise, though Langston seriously doubted the girls were headed over seeking a physical altercation—unless it was a setup, a skillfully planned diversion meant to conceal a sneak attack from an unprotected front. He adopted an apprehensive stance, angling his chin over either shoulder to broaden his view, the brick face of the cafeteria wall covering his backside.

He put all his senses to work in an effort to gauge friend or foe, causing the girls to stop short of his position. They took turns introducing one another, having sensed the need for a bit less familiarity with their approach: Tasha Davies and Yolanda Liggins, who claimed to be cousins. Tasha made the first move, closing the distance between them. She looked like she stepped straight out of a Benetton ad, beauty as seen through the world's lens invisible to the naked eye. Her skin was flawless, the darkest Langston had ever seen on a girl, the full spectrum of colors shimmering inside her complexion depending how the sun lit her face.

She steadied him with her stare, electric eyes seemingly set on peering inside the depths of his person to uncover things ordinary eyes failed to see. Her lips parted to reveal a dazzling smile, one meant to indicate friendly intentions between them. "What's your name?" she mouthed, appearing not the least shy.

"I'm Langston," he replied, working to invoke whatever remained of his brand of cool.

53

"What kind of name is Langston?" Yolanda asked, attempting to steal the spotlight from her cousin.

"Like the poet," Tasha responded.

"Yeah," Langston confirmed. "Like the poet."

No one in Preston had ever made the connection. No one would have known that his mother had gone away to Long Island for college. Managed to complete a couple of semesters majoring in African American studies at Stony Brook before realizing she was pregnant, an unintended consequence of a visit home in between semester breaks to keep the fires burning strong with Chester. It was never clear whether Dottie held Chester or Langston responsible for precipitating the demise of her college career. "You get what life gives you," she said once it became inevitable she return to Preston for good. In the end, she got Langston, and she threw herself headlong into the giggles and laughter and joy that accompany early parenthood. Chester stood by her side, a still eager participant.

She named her firstborn after her favorite writer, having developed an affinity for Langston Hughes's indelible sense of self despite his mixed heritage: West African, European, and Native American, much like her own. Trajan was lucky to escape having been named "Simple," given their mother's fondness for the man who created the character, his most enduring, an affable everyman collected from Hughes's travels in life.

It's remarkable how legend transforms itself as the story spreads word-of-mouth across town, the teller amplifying those details that most appeal to his sensibilities, fabricating others to make the story fit until the subject of the legend no longer recognizes the origin of truth behind the lies, his story told to him like he had no part in its making.

"I heard you went nutty a couple summers ago," Yolanda interrupted.

Tasha leaned a shoulder into Yolanda, a curled lip telling her cousin to hush. "You can tell from those sure eyes he ain't nutty."

"I didn't say he *was* nutty. I said he *went* nutty," Yolanda corrected her.

"I fell," Langston interjected. "The fall brought on seizures. But I'm better now." He buried his medical alert bracelet deeper beneath his shirtsleeve.

"Word around school, you tried to hang yourself from a basketball hoop, but the rope caught on your ankle, causing you to bang your head against the concrete," Yolanda insisted, ignoring the slant of her cousin's eyes trained on her in a growing state of disbelief.

The notion produced a broad smile on Langston's face, making him appear all the more nutty to Yolanda, to Tasha even less so. He needed to fend off the urge to lean back in his stance, extend a foot over his head, and then swipe the air with it to show them why he'd adopted the practice of tying his ankle to a backboard support

55

post. If he did, he knew somebody across the yard would mistake the move as boastful and would wander over to show what he could do with his own foot, and another rivalry would take hold. Something Langston could ill afford in his present state.

"Tell you what," he offered. "From now on, anything you want to know about me, feel free to ask directly. I wouldn't want the two of you walking around confused, spreading false truths about me." He put his smile to work again, the warmth of his own hypnotic stare resting on the deep chocolate complexity of Tasha's brown skin. "We're good?" he asked.

"We're good," she replied, pulling Yolanda by the arm before something even more ridiculous could spill from her cousin's tongue.

And with that, Langston found a new way through, a break in the sidewalk toward his newfound self. He realized at fifteen that he had, in all likelihood, already experienced his one true love. Everything else in life would, at best, amount to scarcely good enough. He recognized that sometimes the most you can do is like a person, treating her the best you can, according to how you like her. If she likes that you like her, then she might treat you the best she can in return. And that's the most either of you can ever expect from the other.

Angelica witnessed the whole exchange from a tiny alcove inside the cafeteria. She stood behind a pane of mirrored glass and watched the string of emotions play across Langston's forehead, from furrowed anxiousness to flirtatious preening, fawning in front of those girls for everyone to see. She didn't consider herself jealous. No, not jealous. But she was hurting just the same. They hadn't planned to meet that day. Langston hadn't gone back on any promise made to her. That did little to ease the hurt. She had hoped they still mattered, that they might seek each other out whenever possible, offer one another a friendly face as they made their way on unfamiliar grounds. And there he was with that smile he used to reserve for her, grinning in response to something she wished she'd said, someone else grinning back at him. She was losing him in a trillion tiny pieces, grains of him sliding past her with magnificent force.

Different

Tasha and Langston began "talking," which Tasha had to explain meant that she would call him after she got home from school and they would talk until her mother came in from work. He was to call her after supper, but not too late, so they'd have time to talk before either of their mothers rushed them off the line to get ready for bed.

"So this means we're dating?" he asked, rehearsing in his head the times he was supposed to call her versus the times she would call him.

"Dating?" she complained, screwing her face up like he'd spoken in some foreign tongue, clearly not N'town cool. "You mean do we go together? That's going to depend how you do keeping up with regular phone calls," she said, feigning a coy innocence.

Langston was not a phone talker. He'd pick up the phone whenever their father called to say what time he would be by to get them.

Or he'd speak to their godmother when she phoned to wish either him or Trajan a happy birthday. Neither scenario required anything more of him than a, *See you then, Pops,* or a canned response or two in answer to their godmother's standard kid questions. *I just started ninth grade,* or *Thank you for the savings bond.* (Aunt Sherry—as they were instructed to call her, even though she and their mother were not blood relatives—always sent savings bonds for their birthdays.)

But what could he possibly have to say to a girl? He was relieved to find that Tasha had enough phone talk in her for both of them. She'd begin by catching him up on who had said what on the bus ride home. "My cousin still thinks you're odd, but Vonda Newbill says you're kinda fine. You just dress different. I told her you and me were talking, then she started looking at me all strange. I was like, *whatever*. She ain't nobody to me."

She barely took a break between thoughts to catch her breath. Then she'd ask what had happened on his bus.

"Nothing special" was his usual response.

"You-all *are* different," she said, seeming to regret that was the case as much for him as for herself. "It's like you're scared to be yourselves or something."

"Everybody's different, I suppose."

"Not that different. It's a good thing you're fine."

He told her she was fine too. Knew that's the thing he was expected to say.

"You're only saying it 'cause I said it."

"No, really," he started to explain. He indeed found her remarkable with those electric eyes and that flawless skin and all.

"Boy, I'm just playing with you. I know you think I'm fine." He was glad he hadn't said pretty or, worse yet, cute—definitely not N'town cool.

"Anyway, I was thinking of getting twists in my hair. Lauryn Hill is sporting this real tight do in their latest video," she said, primping, imagining how she might look disguised as Lauryn Hill. "You think the Fugees are gonna break up?"

He'd heard that they might but told her he didn't know for certain.

"Where do you get your hair cut?" she asked. "Hemphill's or Strong's?"

Hemphill's was the first black-owned barbershop granted a permit to do business in Norwich proper, the cleave between the separate halves of the peach showing signs of having narrowed. It took Mr. Hemphill two whole years to build up the nerve to produce a Guyanese flag in the back of the shop. It raised a big stink until one of the neighboring merchants pointed out he could pledge allegiance to whatever flag he liked so long as it hung lower than the Stars and Stripes. "Pledge allegiance to the ground beneath your feet, then your homeland," he said, pointing to the Argentinean flag hanging low in the window of his flower shop across the street.

Strong's, meanwhile, had been in operation since the beginning of time in Norwichtown, established well within the footpath on the way past Sylvia Lane. It was common knowledge that Strong was prone to drink during working hours, the smell of cheap swill resting beneath a red and white peppermint inside his mouth whenever anybody was in his chair. No matter—his skill with a pair of clippers more than offset his fondness for liquor. Besides, a persistent tremor took command of his hand when he wasn't drinking, so better a dazed artisan than a sober hack, an attitude enabling Strong to maintain a healthy clientele despite Hemphill setting up shop along Main Street.

Langston had no firsthand knowledge of either place. He and Trajan got their hair cut in the half bath, seated atop one of their mother's kitchen stools, an old tablecloth hung around their necks to catch the clippings of knotty brown hair. Chester's hand, made all the more sure by a plastic number two guard affixed to the buzzing end of a set of hair clippers, lopped the hair evenly on all sides into the same fuzzy, round ball, the variegated contours of each son's head affording the only variation in style. Grandpa Tuke had worn his hair in a long plait down the middle of his back since he was old enough to make such choices on his own, but he took care not to disrespect Chester's household. He advised his grandson to check with his father first when Langston asked to let his hair grow into a high-top fade, the teen's interest keen on making a favorable impression with Tasha—though he took pride in knowing Yolanda still found him weird. He found her weird too.

Langston and Tasha eventually settled into one another, achieving a better pH balance than outward indications might have deemed possible. Langston's homegrown cool tempered Tasha's blunt angles, honed to survive a lifetime spent battling the preponderance of negative influences blotting everyday existence on Sylvia Lane. She, in turn, encouraged Langston to educate anyone admitted into his circle about the origin of his name, to conjure Langston Hughes. Her affiliation with Langston renewed her interest in poetry, some *MTV Raps*, some Nikki Giovanni, some Maya Angelou. She indicated that her family had emigrated from Grenada when asked in social studies class to throw a dart at the map of cultural heritage. Langston insisted he was from Preston. He defied their teacher to suggest otherwise, Tasha's steadfast belief in the unabashed promotion of self-worth cementing for Langston the purpose behind his mother's struggle to have her people recognized, to prevent them from being further disconnected from their homeland.

Butterflies and Ladybugs

Rumors of the Fugees breaking up eventually proved prophetic, spelling by association the end of the road for Langston and Tasha Davies as well, her ability to hold both sides of a conversation eventually falling short. Langston soon found lots of girls to like—from blunt cuts to frizzy tease ups to loose, dangling curls—and as far as he could tell, they liked him too.

Dottie began to call everyone Hon, never bothering to remember anybody's name. "Hang on, hon," she said into the telephone anytime somebody called for her son. "I'll see if he's free."

He eventually came looking for her after he hung up the phone, trying one of his looks on her. "Hey, Ma. How was your day?"

"Hey, Ma, my foot," she shot back at her son. "You need to settle on one of these simple girls and let the rest of the flock fly away from here."

"Ah, you know you're my best girl. How'm I gonna pick someone who will treat me as good as you?"

She cursed his father's name. Cursed the example he'd left, his son coming away with the misguided notion that any woman worth having might fall for such a blatant display of baseless affection. She understood the need for her boys to grow to be men. But she was determined not to see them grow to be that kind of man.

"Why is it all the men in my life want to be gigolos? What, you're supposed to be some kind of player now?" she asked, realizing she missed the Chu girl nearly as much as he did.

"Ma, I'm not trying to play anybody. Me and those girls are just talking."

She sent the boys fishing with their Grandpa Tuke. He was the best man she knew, even if he, too, had caused his fair share of heartbreak. He'd had plenty of years to get past any wrong he'd done. Plus, he was her father. She could count on him for anything she and the boys needed.

"You want *me* to give them the birds and bees talk again?" he asked, certain Chester would have had that talk with the boys by now. He hated the rivalry, fearing the boys' father might take offense any time Dottie pushed Tuke to step inside his shoes.

"I'm not talking birds and bees," she said, wearing him down with her eyes. "I need your help to get them beyond the initial pop and sizzle of being in love with a girl."

"What are we talking, lions and tigers? Crocodiles and alligators?" he teased, his face questioning what knowledge she believed him to possess beyond the basic workings of birds and bees.

"I'm talking butterflies and ladybugs," she said, grinning at him. "I want them to understand what it means to commit to another person, to give themselves over and to expect the same in exchange. What it means to love someone, hoping for nothing more than for that person to love you back."

"And you think I'm the right person to convey all that?"

"You did okay by me," she assured him, "back when I was your ladybug."

Tuke smiled at the thought, remembered when she still fit on his knee.

When Dottie called her parents to say she and Chester were getting married, the bulge Langston made inside her belly just visible across her midriff, Dottie's mother told her to have lots of babies. Took had been the most attentive when they first had Dottie to look after, and so Dottie's mother came to view babies as an anchor of sorts, a kind of glue used to bond two people until they were capable of making a go of it on their own. Think of it like training wheels for marriage. "Pin him to you," she told her daughter. "Then pin him again before he can think to get up."

But Took had stayed with just the one child, pinned, and dispassionate for it, but steady. Peace and harmony with the in-laws continued to elude him. All Granville's agitation had quietly transferred to his wife, Eloise. Alonzo was plenty good as a son-in-law, yet he refused to play the part Mrs. Hastings had in mind for him. He and Estelle had enjoyed their whirlwind romance. So where was her daughter's Prince Charming—gallant, refined, all the things Granville was plus all the things he was not? The strain between Estelle's mother and Took eventually brought the whole thing crashing down, mother and daughter at odds, mother and son. Even Granville Hastings had gotten into the habit of speaking up on Took's behalf. But as his booming voice withered, so did any hope for peaceful resolution between his wife and their son-in-law.

Took's loyalty to his only daughter remained unshaken. The two of them would trudge into the woods together to visit with Mother Nature, talking about life and all its meaning. Took had a favorite stand of trees. They'd position themselves toe-to-toe, necks craned, staring up at the pale bark of a towering white birch.

"Dodie, would you say those trees are many you or many, many you?" This was a game they had played before. She didn't yet possess the means to estimate actual height but had come to appreciate the notion of relative measure.

"They're many, many you, Daddy," she guessed.

Took's eyes welled with pride. He took her by the hand, led her to the edge of a nearby cliff, a granite protrusion littered along its base with dead leaves and fallen tree branches. They inched forward, toed the edge until heartbeats reached high in their throats. They stood silent as the swirling of a most determined wind moved past their ears. "The wind is braver than we are," he whispered. "But we can be brave like the wind, can stand tall like the trees if we understand our connection to those things."

Come springtime, their pathway was overrun with butterflies as they made their way past fields of wildflowers before slipping beneath the dense tree cover. A ladybug accompanied them on special occasions, tagging along on the back of Dodie's pudgy little hand to rest its wings awhile. Having been cast aside most of his youth—his mouth unmistakably black, his wide nose paired with eyes no one had ever seen, hair they couldn't place—Took taught his daughter to appreciate both sides of nature. Birds and bees can be pretentious, pesky, vicious at times. He wanted Dodie to be a butterfly, beautiful in her own right, whether or not the birds appreciated her virtues; he wanted her to be nurturing like the ladybug, attending to everything around her with quiet diligence. (Butterflies inside a cocoon would later prove simpler to explain when he was asked where babies come from, a gift the spirit gods had handed him unsolicited.)

Having reached the age her father had been when they last

ventured into the woods together, Dottie asked him whether he'd wanted a little boy.

"What would I have done with a son?" Tuke replied.

"You could have taken him fishing, hiking. Taught him how to spit." She appreciated the care he'd shown in choosing his words, the parent in her recognizing that life's most pressing concerns seldom afford simple answers.

"But I did all that with you, Dorothy. Why did I need a little boy?"

"It would have been more natural."

"The fishing or the spitting? Because I've already got an expert spitter in you. And I've enjoyed many a fishing trip with your boys. They're coming along, but it has been far from natural," he said, mocking his daughter's insecurities.

Tuke assumed responsibility for imparting knowledge of life and all things living to the next generation in the continual procession of butterflies into the world. He packed the boys into his station wagon and drove out to Amos Lake. As Granville Hastings's ill-gotten son-in-law and thus the surviving heir to one of the resort's last proprietors, Tuke was afforded unrestricted access to the grounds surrounding the Lake Resort.

Having been closed a dozen years or more, the inn stood in a state of steady decline. Tuke assured his grandsons that nature would, in time, take back any mark man made on her skin, would erase the structure from existence. The boat dock under which Tuke had spent countless hours admiring the woman he would eventually make his wife suffered the worst of it. The sun beat directly off the dock's wood-planked surface. The narrow lake bed formed an alleyway directing the wind from every hurricane that had made landfall in the last half century to come crashing against the resort's back door.

"Tell me, which one of you has a girlfriend?" Tuke asked, directing his inquiry toward Trajan.

Trajan rolled his eyes, deflecting Tuke's attempt at being subtle. He tilted his head in the direction of his older brother, who came under siege now for the first time since he had stopped sparring.

Langston resented the sneak attack. He wasn't going behind anyone's back, wasn't doing anything to cause concern, yet he indulged his grandpa, knowing their mother had put him up to it. Langston had come to accept that life would no longer afford him secrets to keep, his daily routine having become a pitiful succession of strictly limited possibilities.

"I'm not talking to anyone special," Langston responded.

"That may be your problem. You need to get more particular about the things you set out to do," Tuke replied, dusting the edges of his lecture with things he felt needed to be said on top of the bit about girls. "Hard as it is to catch life by the tail, it's even harder to shake free if life catches hold of you first, carries you in a direction you're not looking to go."

He baited another hook, allowed time for the message to soak in; he feared he might have spared them all years of heartache had he and his grandsons only had this talk sooner. "The time has come and gone for you to sit back and expect random chance to make things happen for you," he continued. "Take charge of your fate, son. You'll be devastated by the outcome if you continue to let life lead the way for you."

Tuke was serious about his fishing, even though the reason for their excursion had been contrived. He dropped a half-dozen lines off the end of the boat dock, spaced reasonably far apart, the hook on each line resting at a different depth to give the fish some variety to choose from. He and the boys took turns casting into the wind, reeling the lure back to shore in an effort to lead the fish in the direction of their open hooks filled with live bait. He had the boys drop their lines in the water when it wasn't their turn to cast, instructing them to hold their rods stock-still. "How would you feel sitting down to eat with the shadow of a stick trembling restlessly above your head?"

The boys focused renewed attention on keeping their poles still above the water's slippery surface. Tuke turned the conversation back to Langston, baited lines standing guard along the teetering dock railing.

"Maybe give the girls a rest till you get yourself settled."

"But you didn't wait," Langston challenged his grandpa, the legend of Alonzo Tooker on ready offer around Dottie's household.

"Sometimes love won't let you wait."

"I'm not trying to fall in love," Langston assured his grandpa too emphatically, suggesting the opposite was closer to the truth.

"Maybe you should leave the girls alone until you're ready to try," Tuke suggested, draping another line across the railing.

Langston never made anyone his official girl, but he maintained lots of special friends, straining relations between him and anyone who had or hoped to officially have a girlfriend. With anyone who had a sister, the entire school presented itself as a giant collection of Albert Chus. That is, the old Albert. By the time high school came rolling around, Albert and Alfred had dropped the connection of As in their names. (Angelica retained the full pronunciation.) Bert Chu's and Fred Chu's affiliation became building and racing dirt bikes. If you had to take machine shop and wanted to pass, you became fast friends with one of the Chu brothers.

One and the Same

The high school years trickled past. Blink once and freshman year was over. Blink twice and they were partway through their last year at NFA. Langston did just enough to get by while Angelica, still demure and still alluring, applied herself in every conceivable direction: French Club, Lacrosse, Mathletes, Student Council, Symphonic Band, all of it keeping her at the head of the class. So on top of considerable physical charms, she possessed bona fide genius, the hand of fate at times decidedly less cruel.

A letter arrived from Princeton, a black and orange tiger scrawled alongside the return address. Angelica learned in an online chat room organized on behalf of prospective P'tonites that the admissions office used two types of letterhead: a prancing tiger for acceptance letters, a deflated tiger lounging across letters of rejection. Hers was prancing.

Angelica read the letter to her grandmother as the two prepared place settings for the midweek dinner service. That was her job in the restaurant, while her brothers were admitted inside the kitchen to chop vegetables and help maintain steady production from the rice steamer. She bit back the words when the letter finally reached the part about her having been accepted. She peered through the dim light in the dining hall to gauge her grandmother's reaction, the sun working overtime to compete against the heavy gingham window coverings.

"Gam, I got in," she whispered into the silence enveloping their movement in between tables.

"That good," her grandma replied, folding another napkin before setting small dishes of plum sauce and spicy mustard down together on a centerpiece. "You should go. Princeton be good for you."

"What about Gamps?" she asked, excitement sending her nerves in competing directions. She recognized that the news would break her father's heart a little. Would break her grandfather's heart a lot, his belief that family should stick to family even if Princeton comes knocking. Albert and Alfred had dutifully accepted their share of responsibility around the restaurant to repay their grandparents for all their sacrifice (the Al's still pronounced inside the family circle). Her grandpa couldn't understand why Angelica seemed intent on doing the opposite.

"Leave your grandpa to me," she assured her granddaughter, taking Angelica by the shoulders. "Your Gam is going to make it all right. Okay? Now back to work, college lady," she teased, an added bounce in her step as she headed back to the kitchen.

Angelica committed to telling no one outside of her grandmother. She wanted to roll around in the idea awhile, cover herself in it like feathers and make a glorious, spinning mess.

She made herself promise the next morning on the drive to school that she wouldn't look for Langston, but that she would share the news if she happened across him. A remote possibility, seeing how little their worlds intersected anymore, his side of the school confined to the machine shop, the cafeteria, and the school gymnasium. Hers extended to include the chemistry lab and orchestra hall in addition to the gym and cafeteria. Still, she held out hope, wanted to be the one to tell him, believing he still deserved to know.

By Friday afternoon, the school day dragging to a close, the news would no longer keep. Angelica posted herself outside the boys' locker room, knowing that to keep his moves sharp, Langston did floor exercises last period as a free elective, though he was no longer permitted to use those moves in anyone else's presence. Coach

Graebel let Langston work out occasionally with the team on lifting and stretching, though his tendency toward epileptic-type seizures prohibited him from competing in any sport, Olympic or otherwise. (Even Angelica wasn't permitted to saddle him with the full diagnosis. His seizures were *like* epilepsy, not the full-blown thing.)

Finally he emerged, his backpack draped across his shoulder, his free hand twirling a stick of some kind inside his cheek.

"I have some news," Angelica said, beaming.

His eyes begged to hear more though his mouth remained disinterested. He had learned to wait before speaking, especially when in the company of comely maidens. That way he'd have something useful to say in return.

"I got into Princeton."

"That means you're leaving," he said, pulling a lollipop from his lips, his tongue stained cherry red.

"It *means* I'm going to Princeton."

He pointed out that going and leaving are one and the same, repeating something Grandpa Tuke had told Trajan and him once their father announced his plans to move to the other side of town.

"It just depends where you're standing in the end. One of us will be gone—that'd be you," he elaborated, using the lollipop as a pointer. "I'll be the one left standing." He looked like he missed her already, his whole face reacting to the news. Not just the eyes.

Why did he have to get deep just when she had come to expect less of him, had lumped him together with her brothers and seemingly every boy who carried on like her brothers did, the sum of their consciousness amassing slightly less considered thought than an overturned rock? Why did he have to show himself as layered now that she'd accepted him as ordinary, limited like her brothers, built along a single dimension?

"You could come and visit," she stuttered. "After I get settled."

"Maybe I could come visit," he stuttered back at her. "Once you're settled."

Her next words would have been *I love you, Langston.* She did in part love him, had since the first or second grade. Saw in him what every other girl saw, only she had seen it first. Knew he saw something in her too. More than anything, having reached the point most girls do, she needed somebody to be in love with—and who better than the boy she had known practically her whole life?

That's what she stood there wanting to say when a bunch of guys from the wrestling team came barging in. Kyle Fitzpatrick tugged at Langston's shoulder as the group thundered past. "C'mon, lover boy. A bunch of us are heading over to the casino. Gonna screw around in the arcade awhile. Maybe catch us a few skeezers down on their luck."

Langston motioned toward them, one hand pumping the air to say, *I won't be but a minute.* Then he turned his full attention back to Angelica.

"I'm *going* with them," he said. "But don't believe for a second I'm *leaving* you."

"You're such a goofball," she boasted, her eyes trained on him as though acting of their own free will.

"Yeah, but I'm your goofball," he replied, his eyes locked on hers.

He stepped to her before she could protest, before those eyes could question how it could be that he was still hers. He kissed the full pout of her lips, the tips of his warm, brown fingers on her skin adding to the blush of her cheeks.

He pulled her body close to him, his nose full with the fruit-fresh scent of her hair. He wrapped her inside his arms for the longest while. She understood in that hug what about him was so magnetic. He was clear and real and present, there any time she needed him. Deep anytime she worried he had lost dimension.

"I love you, Langston Hopkins," she whispered to his shadow as he disappeared down the hallway in a sea of shoulder bumps and jostling lettermen's jackets.

Every Shade of Green

Graduating together had a galvanizing effect. It didn't matter which corner of the valley you were from, you had made it through, together. Graduation night was spent celebrating at the base of Indian Leap Falls. Preston was there, Taftville was there, Yantic and Norwich were represented. Even Norwichtown showed up in small numbers.

Langston saw Yolanda a short distance ahead of him as he picked his way through the sea of familiar faces. Tasha couldn't be far away, unless she was off with her boyfriend celebrating his graduation from nearby New London High. Langston had heard there was a fireworks display planned at Ocean Beach. Nobody he knew was going, but Tasha would undoubtedly be there beside her man, the boy whose attention she'd captured at a track meet sophomore year.

Tasha's man was a big ol' dude. He nicknamed himself Incredible, as in the Hulk. One of those guys whose muscles have muscles. The kind of guy, back in his fighting days, Langston would have worked to convince that a physical altercation was beneath them. "Don't you see that's what the crowd is hoping for, to see us brain one another," he would have insisted, sliding an arm around a tree trunk of a neck.

Incredible's face appeared countless times in the local papers. He made all-state in football. Lettered in track, meaning he was fast, too, a runaway freight train, muscles on skates. Tasha said he was having trouble deciding between Hampton and Virginia Tech. Poor thing. Langston had Stop & Shop and Waldbaum's to choose from, his postgraduation prospects limited to the deli meat department or fresh produce. He had thoughts of making good on the lie he'd gotten in the habit of telling whenever Angelica asked about his plans beyond high school. He said he was leaning toward community college: Three Rivers or Connecticut College, the latter of which would at least get him out of Norwich. That way he'd be going away to college just like everybody else he knew.

He overheard his mother on the phone with their Aunt Sherry.

"I will be shocked but delighted if he gets himself together to do something of any worth." It had taken him the whole school year to do it, but he managed to fill out the applications his mother brought home, though he had yet to drop any of them in the mail.

Langston continued to scan the faces swirling around Yolanda for any sign of her cousin. Something about the day—graduating, the finality of it—made him want to see Tasha all the more, somebody he once knew. He didn't miss her as a consequence of the time they'd spent, their abbreviated history together, so much as he missed what could have been, who he might have become had he managed to connect with someone and have her close by his side. Last he'd heard she was going away to school, too, on a track scholarship to Norfolk State. Tasha and Incredible off to Virginia together.

She pushed her way over as soon as she caught sight of him. "Hey, stranger. What are you doing way out here?" she asked, believing he surely couldn't have walked all this way at night.

"I'm here looking for you," he said, mischief at work inside his smile.

"Boy, you need to quit playing," she laughed, searching his hand for a plastic cup of something, studying his eyes to determine whether he'd been drinking. "There's no way you could have known I would be here." He wouldn't have guessed it—a kegger down by the falls was definitely not TD (Tasha Davies) cool.

"Unbelievable around somewhere?" he ventured, looking for signs of a runaway freight train.

"*Incredible*," she corrected, teasing him with her eyes, testing her own resolve to see whether she was up to his level of play.

"Incredible. Right. He off someplace trying not to turn green?"

She gave his shoulder a playful shove—a love tap, he imagined. "Behave," she warned. "He went to his grandmother's house for a graduation dinner. We're supposed to meet up with him later tonight."

Isn't that sweet, Langston thought. He didn't realize superheroes had grandmothers.

She teased with her eyes again, interested to know why he was so curious all of a sudden to know about the comings and goings between her and Incredible.

"I'm the one who should be turning green," he joked. "Green with envy."

"See. That's why you and I were never going to work. Your game is weak, sweetie," she explained matter-of-fact, a moonlit smile on offer to ease the sting. She rested an arm across his shoulder—easy, comfortable, a part of her feeling the finality of the day as well, standing in the company of someone she once knew. She waited for his eyes to wander from hers like they did on the day they met, on the day they kissed for the first time, on the day she told him they no longer went together.

She was first to break their stare. "Speaking of jealous, isn't that your little girlfriend over there?" she asked, tugging at his elbow before he could turn to look. She gave him a *Heaven forgive me* squeeze, her ear pressed tight against his neck. She said good-bye to him with a single kiss to the cheek, a light frosting from the gloss of her lips just catching the corner of his mouth. "Take care of yourself, darling."

He watched as she walked over to rejoin her cousin, giggling with a gaggle of friends, tonight a night for everyone to show their teeth. He stood mesmerized by the sway of her fully grown curves, her appeal at last visible to the whole wide world. "Take care, sweetie," he said quietly.

He turned away, his hand at the back of his head making the stations change. His thoughts ran backward to the last thing she said—*darling*. He knew how she meant it: He didn't stand a chance with her, but she was sincere in her desire to see him continue to make a way for himself. He hoped to see her do well at Norfolk State. Wished them both the best in VA.

He sensed somebody waving at him, a small, little wave. *Green with envy*, he heard Tasha saying. Saw a single palm raised slowly from the hip. *Your little girlfriend*, Tasha continued. The station inside his head eventually found its focus, Angelica flickering into view. What was she doing out this way? The Falls were not typical A-Chu either.

"Who are you here with?" he asked, the ridge of his crinkled brow confirming his surprise to see her.

A subtle tilt of the head led his gaze in the direction of her big brother Albert. He locked eyes with Langston for a lingering half second, wrinkled the corner of his mouth, and then shrugged off the expression. Whatever was going on between Langston and Angelica was no longer his concern. He continued toward the exit from the Falls, Angelica trailing behind him, dutifully obeying the conditions she had agreed to in order to be let out on graduation night.

Langston looked around for anyone else he cared about, then started the long walk home, alone.

TWO

Trajan entered high school with two sets of friends: the group of boys he'd grown up around and those he had competed against in district-wide soccer tournaments since the dawn of time. Ezrah and Ephram Sessions had come with him from Preston. Ezrah asked that people call him E-Z; Ephram went by Bunny, a childhood nickname he'd not been able to shed, erasing any connection either boy had to his biblical name. Bunny Sessions was Trajan's best friend away from the soccer field. A year ahead of his brother, E-Z threatened each year to fail, joining Bunny and Trajan in their grade. His first year at NFA was no different. Bunny kept up with his grades but was otherwise full of mischief, the biblical name notwithstanding.

Dottie overheard Bunny telling Trajan about her when she last had them in class together. "Your mom can put the fear of God in you with a single stare."

"Bunny Sessions, you're not so big a devil that I need to pull anyone extra by my side. I can handle you just fine on my own. We'll leave God to more important matters," she quipped, disarming him with another of her stares. Halved the distance needed on their next encounter to put the fear in him again. She maintained her hold on him partway through middle school. That's when most errant seeds eventually topple off course. Some come back around. Some don't.

Mathieu Sessions entered the Thames River Valley with a temporary stay in mind. He wound up trapped in Preston, the town like flypaper attaching to his bare skin, draining the life from him. He met his wife while traveling throughout New England as part of the contingent sent from the Lesser Antilles to represent the Caribbees Baseball League in exhibition games against local double- and triple-A ball clubs. Merita was a free spirit. Mathieu was just as free. What began as a fling, a place to lay his head anytime the team visited the river valley, soon sprouted roots, E-Z planted inside Merita's belly.

Mathieu took delight in the prospect of welcoming his first child into the world. He had been his father's big guy, his first son. He was overjoyed to learn they were expecting a boy as well—first son to a first son. His mind swelled with thoughts of all the things he would teach his son to do: to stand firm in the batter's box waiting for a curve ball to break from its collision course with your head, prepared to swing the bat just as the ball veers across the plate; how to catch a fish with a simple hook and string; how to skip a rock across the skin of a restless surf.

Mathieu was proficient in the field, sure with his glove, a switch-hitter batting with equal on-base percentage from either side of the plate. He worked to remain just as industrious in the off season, helping build boats and construct boat docks back home in St. Martin. There was nothing he could not fix with his two hands, no adversity his mind could not overcome. He took odd jobs repairing diving rigs, wenches, small cranes, setting aside a few dollars each week to supplement the meager stipend he would earn come springtime as part of the traveling team.

Baseball season came to a close, leaving Mathieu for the first time on his own, his teammates having returned to their respective island existences as responsibility mounted across his shoulders. He landed a job at Electric Boat as the due date approached, vowing to return to baseball in time for spring training the following season, the smell of freshly cut grass and the residue from newly chalked lines lingering in the air, framing his love for the game.

He rushed to the hospital when the call came. He was ushered into a tiny recovery room surrounded by his wife's people—soon to be his people, his mother insistent on seeing him do right by the woman who bore him a son. Mathieu took the child in his arms, counted fingers and toes: ten of each.

He struggled the following season to muster sufficient time off to play ball, joining the team when he could during their brief time in the tri-state area, relinquishing his spot to someone with fewer worries away from the field as the team headed south to the Carolinas, Georgia, Florida.

He watched with dismay as his son grew. Ezrah's feeble hands competed against clumsy feet in an effort to disqualify him from even playing outfield. He talked incessantly as though fascinated by the clicking of his own tongue. He preferred to stay indoors, watching the ebb and flow of people in the street, listening for the slow trickling of cars moving past. By age four he could name the make and model of every American car brand, could identify a good number of Japanese and European makes as well, yet had no answer when asked to name one team from the National League and one team from the American, despite constant coaching from his father. Mets or Yankees—what could be simpler?

Mathieu blamed his son's poor conditioning on the climate in Connecticut, on the harsh winters, the abbreviated summers. Mathieu and his friends had spent their days on the beach climbing trees for fruit, searching mangrove roots for crabs and other small creatures, testing their worth against the will of the sea. Yet his adult steps in life became less sure, a man tasked with raising a son in a land foreign to him.

The following year another son came along stricken with a similar strain of physical ineptitude, a slow-footed playmate stuck behind the looking glass alongside his older brother, content to watch the world go by. Another spring training season came and went with Mathieu Sessions's feet planted in dry dock at Electric Boat. A couple seasons in and interaction inside the Sessions household became limited to basic coexistence among relative strangers: eating together, sleeping underneath the same roof, otherwise failing to relate. Flypaper was the only thing holding their family together.

Ton Oncle

The Sessions family took their sons to visit relatives in St. Martin over Easter break in Bunny's last year of grade school with Trajan. They stayed gone a week, arriving in time to celebrate Good Friday in the company of family. Bunny returned to school the following Wednesday, his skin flecked with sun and nearly as brown as Trajan's, his dark, curly locks turned light at the edges.

To hear Bunny tell it, their adventures spearfishing with his and E-Z's great-uncle were the highlight of the trip. "Only tourists consider free diving for sport," T'Onc admonished his nephews, disdainful of the tourists who viewed his means of living as a form of amusement. "Feeding your family is fair reason to risk death at the bottom of the ocean, not testing the width of your chest." (Bunny had misheard their grandmother's pronunciation. *"Cela est ton oncle—* This is your uncle," she said to him. Bunny leaped to respond, taxing the limits on the little bit of French he had mastered to this point. *"Salut, Ton Oncle,"* he announced—Hello, Your Uncle—casting T'Onc as everybody's uncle.)

T'Onc woke Bunny and his brother ahead of the sunrise, rowed away from the cove while the rooster sat on its hindquarters resting, still dreaming of the morning reveille that was his ritual to perform. T'Onc waited until they were well into the deep, a gentle sway jostling their narrow wooden skiff first this way then the other, before inquiring whether either boy knew how to swim. Bunny and E-Z swam well enough, but they eyed the coastline anxiously as details along the beachfront dissolved into one thin line.

T'Onc lectured them as he rowed, his spine bent to the task, his shoulder blades seeming to know the way blind. "Diving requires a different focus on breathing. Those who don't know test one another to see who can hold his breath the longest. A man for whom diving is a way of living learns to breathe underwater." The boys blinked at one another incredulously. Learning to breathe underwater became Bunny's new preoccupation.

T'Onc inhaled slowly as he steadied their craft against a rising swell. Slower still as he turned the boat in the direction of the beach in preparation for their return trip, he rested the oars securely in place. His eyes were a slit against the rising sun as he slipped his arms free of his shirt and got his fill of clean air, his chest rising in slow deliberation like a bicycle tire at the end of a hand pump.

He grabbed his spear in a large bronze mitt, angled his body over the side of the boat, and disappeared beneath the surface, his feet twisting behind him until he became lost in the depths. Bunny and E-Z crowded the side of the boat, waiting for their uncle to be brought back to them. They measured how long either brother could hold his breath. They became agitated once the wait eclipsed their best times nearly twice over. Slow bubbles eventually began to surface, a free hand guiding the way, T'Onc's watch catching a glint from the morning sun.

He released his last bit of air as his face broke the surface, filling up in long gulps, the tire having gone flat again. He produced a string of sparkling blackfins skewered on either side by the iron tip of his spear. He hoisted his body up the side of the boat and worked to get a leg over before plopping down beside them exhausted, the sun glistening on droplets of water dancing across his skin.

T'Onc lay winded inside the boat's shallow hull, his chest heaving in an effort to return to a normal pattern of breathing. He sat up slowly, fastening the few buttons on the front of his shirt. He took the oars in his hands and then bent his spine for the blind row back to shore. He and his nephews returned to a hero's welcome, grilled tuna and grits on the menu for breakfast, johnnycake baking in a nearby oven.

Bunny came in from the playground determined to have a go at a new personal best. Mr. Driscoll read to the class the first five minutes after recess. They had gotten midway through *To Kill a Mockingbird* a few stolen pages at a time, the ritual meant to quiet them in preparation for an afternoon spent on lessons in fractions and basic geometry. Bunny stood in line at the water fountain before filing into the classroom. He filled his lungs with air, pumping the tire, before letting his breath go in a string of evenly metered bursts, repeating the exercise every couple of minutes or so. His aim was set on dropping his head below the surface as Mr. Driscoll began reading and staying submerged the full five minutes.

Bunny took his seat on the far side of the room, breath held. He leaned back, the front legs of his chair lifted to give the sensation of floating. He thought about the breakfast on the beach that morning in St. Martin. He held a general dislike for tuna fish, didn't much care for grits. Yet he contemplated when he might have eaten anything so delectable, paired with one another or separate. He grinned bleary-eyed at Trajan as the last bit of air slipped from inside him. He listened above the slow beating of his heart to find Mr. Driscoll still reading. He plugged his airway with a flattened tongue against the roof of his mouth, postponing the need to breathe again, when the chair buckled beneath him. He came crashing down in a loud shuffling of desks. He lay there drooling as the school nurse strapped a plastic mask over his mouth and nose and began pumping with her hand to refill his lungs with air.

Bunny wasn't permitted outside for recess the remainder of the school year, the nurse failing to recognize that his shortness of breath was self-induced, not allergy related. He claimed he could have lasted had his chair not given way. Trajan realized that the chair collapsing was likely the only thing that saved his friend from blacking out cold, feared this was just the first in a string of escalating antics from his neighborhood best friend, Bunny Sessions.

Baby Brother Blues

Bunny spent the bus ride from NFA each afternoon collecting numbers from the backs of work trucks, panel vans, delivery vehicles, an open invitation—*How's my driving?*—posted along with a toll-free number to dial. The boys invariably wound up in Dottie's living room, Langston hanging back after school, screwing around with his friends, watching the girls go by. Bunny would grab the phone and place a half-dozen calls, reporting epic carnage to the operators on the other end of the line: driving on sidewalks, sideswiping parked cars, corners taken on two wheels.

Langston barged in on one of their prank calling sessions. He could hardly believe his ears. "You realize our father drives a truck for a living, delivering heating oil around town, doing AC repairs on the side? That sort of thing," he grilled Trajan after sending Bunny and E-Z on their way, the skill with his left foot still posing a credible threat. "What if it had been his number you called?"

"I think I'd recognize Dad's truck," Trajan argued. "Plus, Bunny only takes numbers on the Norwich side of the bridge, before we reach Preston."

"That's supposed to make it all right?" Langston groaned. "It doesn't count, seeing how the guy you manage to get fired lives on the other side of the valley?"

"We didn't get anybody fired," Trajan insisted. "They know it's just a bunch of kids messing around. They usually hang up on us partway through."

"You shouldn't be playing on the phone in the first place."

Trajan complained that he hadn't placed any of the calls.

"That's your excuse for everything," Langston complained. "*It wasn't me* is going to catch up with you soon enough, you and your idiot friends."

Bunny and E-Z kept their distance awhile to allow Langston time to cool off. He, in turn, agreed not to tell on them. Took them at their word that they wouldn't make any more calls. Upheld the obligation he felt to help his brother ease into high school, establish a few close ties to help sustain him, shedding any unneeded baggage along the way. *With any luck, he'll outgrow Bunny's influence. Will shake free of the hold E-Z has on both of them.*

A SECOND ODD PEA

Trajan wasn't nearly as spooked by the move to NFA as his brother had been just a few years prior. He had played in interleague tournaments throughout the valley. He'd even been to Norwichtown a couple of times leading drills on position play, on passing and ball-handling skills hosted at the recreation center on behalf of the Youth Soccer Association. He developed an instant rapport with anyone who shared his love for the sport.

On field, Trajan anchored a soccer triumvirate. They called themselves BLT: Ben Carlsson, Steve Lighty, and Trajan. (Steve went exclusively by Lighty.) Ben was the resident city boy of the crew, claiming Norwich as his home address. He had spent his middle school years at Saint Bernard, a private Catholic school in Uncas-ville, half a district away but still closer than Preston. Ben looked like a movie actor, wore a knit Oxford scarf coiled on his neck winter, summer, or fall. He held his blond head in a permanent upward gaze. Not that he was above anybody, especially having to return to public school after his father was laid off from Pfizer. Ben adopted an air of social oblivion, used it like Teflon to keep himself apart from the khaki slacks and plaid skirt sameness of parochial school. He used the same mask of indifference to ease his way into the frenetic pace of the social scene at NFA surrounded by kids who might have taken little interest in him if it weren't for his outlandish demeanor. He walked the halls of NFA like he was on a stroll, the world inside his head stuck on sunny day, his thoughts consumed by melodic bird twitter.

Lighty went home at the end of the day to Yantic, a second jug handle that hung opposite Preston on the other side of Norwich, another cow pasture stretch of two-lane roads paving the way to the bustle of NFA. Together, BLT were the perfect offensive threat. Loving to run, Trajan played midfield and left wing. Lighty, the most skilled ball handler of the three, played right wing opposite Trajan, trading off at center when needed. Ben was the designated striker. No opponent, regardless of size or speed or apparent skill, rattled Ben Carlsson, bird folly in his head and ice water in his veins.

Then there was Carmen Padilla. She and Trajan met in the lunch line. "Good game last night," she offered.

"Huh?" he asked, his mind fumbling to process her remark.

"Last night. You guys played a good game," she proceeded to explain. They'd lost by one measly goal to Montville but had played them tough. BLT made varsity for the first time that year. As sophomores, they didn't start but had been called on to spark a rally after trailing 2–0 midway through the second half. Trajan and Lighty kept up the pressure, turning the Montville midfielders on their heels. Ben was like silk, slipping in and out of their defense at will. He scored the team's only goal with a flick of his heel as he scampered across the box in the eighty-second minute, a plume of blond locks trailing the play. He netted a second goal a couple of minutes later, knotting the score according to the initial ruling by the referee. The linesman came rushing in a moment later to call Ben offside, a questionable reversal that caused those on the NFA side of the ball to question the official's allegiances.

Trajan started looking for Carmen in the stands. He found her at most home games, her almond-shaped eyes trained on him whenever BLT were on the field. One of her friends eventually asked him for his number.

The telephone rang a minute past the time Dottie permitted Trajan to receive calls from his friends. "Hopkins house!" Langston yelped, pizza-delivery style, into the handset that hung in the space above the kitchen counter. "How can I help you?"

"May I speak with Trajan?" Carmen asked from the other end of the line.

"Who, may I ask, is calling?" Langston inquired, attempting to seem polite in return.

She said her name: Carmen Padilla, sweet like Angelica might pronounce a name the first time she said it for you, but a different brand of sweet. Personality to rival Tasha's, though one all her own. Langston had once tried to decipher which he preferred. It was like trying to decide which was more glorious, sunrise or sunset. Each deserved equal time to shine.

"Butt-head," Langston yelled down the hallway loud enough for Carmen to overhear. (He had caught on a few years back which name was the less coveted of the two.) "Carmen Pad-iyy-yah on the phone for you," he crooned, pronouncing her name as though it were an amusement park ride, a roller coaster at work beneath his tongue.

Trajan snatched the phone from his brother's hand. "Carmen, I wasn't sure you'd call. Can you hold a minute? I'm going to take it in the other room."

He handed the phone back to his brother. "Hang it up," he said, his eyes trained on Langston in one of their mother's no-nonsense glares.

Langston gave his brother's neck a squeeze. "Okay, baby-bro," he said, then returned the receiver to his ear, listening for the loose rustling as his brother lifted the phone from its cradle in their mother's bedroom. It appeared Trajan had at last outgrown Langston's reach.

RING IT

Langston went everywhere on foot. He'd completed driver's education his junior year and had applied to get his learner's permit when his mother discovered he'd stopped taking his medication. She needed to count her pennies to keep up with his prescription, pride preventing her from leaning too regularly on Chester to make ends meet. Two months had gone by and Langston had yet to turn up saying he was running low. She wasn't allowing her son behind the wheel of anybody's car with the possibility looming of another seizure.

Langston had no choice but to accept the limitations his mother imposed regarding use of her car, but he argued successfully that, being of age, he should be free to come and go as he pleased. Insisting Langston earn his own keep, Dottie convinced Mr. Sabonis to take her eldest on part-time in the Lithuanian Bake Shop so that Mr. Sabonis could spend more time with his grandchildren, his years winding down toward retirement. She encouraged Langston to stay late a couple of nights a week to help with the baking, her aim set on ensuring that her son learned a profitable skill.

Mr. Sabonis had fat, soft hands acquired from years spent in constant contact with fresh dough. Langston couldn't speak to his fighting skills but could attest to Mr. Sabonis's ability to talk his opponent to death. "Your mother says you are a good boy," Mr. Sabonis offered the first time Langston joined him for an overnight baking session. "Even a bad boy is entitled to a good mother, deserving in his mother's eyes of her complete devotion."

Langston wasn't sure how to feel about Mr. Sabonis's presumed familiarity with how he might sit in his mother's eyes but answered with no undue animosity, wishing for his mother's sake to make a favorable impression. "I won't let you down, Mr. Sabonis. You can trust in that."

"Mr. Sabonis is a man content with his life," he replied, twisting dough to form a pecan braid. "It won't be me you disappoint."

Langston dusted another tray with flour and lined the pan with parchment paper, his mind at work digesting Mr. Sabonis's words. Everyone expected something from him, but no one had asked that he demand something of himself.

Langston was amazed by the variety of things that could be derived from the same basic mix: a little egg wash in one batter, skip the yolks in the next, a different filling all around followed by a sprinkling of confectioner's sugar, and the display case sprang to life. Workers streamed in early in the morning having completed the night shift at the casino, immigrants from throughout the former Soviet Bloc: Latvia, Poland, and on rare occasions, Mr. Sabonis's Lithuania. They came to refuel on potato pancakes and filled strips—almond, poppy seed, prune—mixed with strong coffee, hot and black.

It has been asserted that the emergence of Native American casinos forever changed the cultural landscape in southeastern Connecticut. The tribespeople regained command over their plot of dirt, the rest of the world swarming in, anxious to get a slice of the pie. The Thames River Valley reached a critical juncture at the height of the casinos' success, its quaint veneer replaced by the glitz of newfound wealth.

Those who came to work were always welcome in Mr. Sabonis's bakeshop. "The working man is the shopkeeper's mainstay," he boasted. "I offer him a familiar taste, a place to escape his worries. He affords me the means to stay in business another year." Others arrived, drawn by the lure of illicit activity that goes hand-in-hand with high stakes gambling: prostitution, drugs, extortion, racketeering. Tales of their exploits lined the papers, filling Mr. Sabonis with disgust.

"With the dog come his fleas," he would say, flapping the newspaper in front of his chest. "They would be beheaded in their home countries, and all the better for it—a despicable death befitting a despicable way of living, profiting from the pain of their fellow man, preying on his frailties."

Those were the ones Mr. Sabonis labeled hoodlums, gangsters. His chosen vernacular showed the limits of his familiarity with happenings outside the bakeshop. The influx of Jamaican and Haitian hoodlums was known around Norwichtown more simply as drug dealers. Those communities, too, have their proud working contingent, though few found the urge to venture across the river in search of Mr. Sabonis's filled strips or potato pancakes. They would have been welcome in his shop had they found their way to his door.

Mrs. Krantz arrived each Thursday like clockwork. "How are the kaiser rolls?" she asked, as if they were people instead of food whose health was somehow in question.

"The kaiser rolls are fine," Mr. Sabonis responded, anticipating her next question.

"And the cheese babka?"

"Baked fresh this morning."

"Henh!"

Langston didn't know whether she was begging pardon or clearing her throat to say something new. In the end, Mrs. Krantz ordered a half-dozen popovers and a couple of sticky buns, questions about the kaiser rolls and cheese babka evidently her way of keeping up with local affairs.

Langston busied himself boxing her goods while Mr. Sabonis counted out her change. Something about her told Langston she'd know how to handle herself if ever it came to that: She held her pocketbook in a steady grip, her wooden cane at the ready. He speculated from her stout calves and broad lower torso that she had remarkable floor skills, that she'd be capable of subduing her attacker in a punishing leg lock until the authorities arrived to haul him off to jail.

"Be sure to tie the string tight," she instructed him. "I don't want the outside air to creep in and ruin things before I get home."

Mrs. Krantz studied Langston as he handed over her parcel. Her mouth had the look of stewed prunes, her lips pursed like she hadn't tasted anything enjoyable in quite some years. "Is this the young man?" she asked.

Mr. Sabonis nodded. "This is Dottie Hopkins's eldest son. He will be helping me around the shop."

"Good," she said. "The place could use a fresh touch." She turned to address Langston again. "Fly straight and this one will take good care of you," she advised. "Say hello to your mother from Mrs. Krantz. That's *Krantz* with a *K*," she added, making Langston feel he should be taking notes. "And tell your grandfather that my rhododendrons are in need of some care should he make it out my way before July Fourth. It's been so dry that I'm afraid the things will burn up with the first spark."

"I will," Langston responded.

"See that you do." That was her final word to him, their transaction complete. "Mr. Sabonis," she said, bidding him good day.

"We'll see you next week, Mrs. Krantz."

"Henh!"

Mr. Sabonis turned to Langston as the shop door clanked shut. "Well, my friend, you have survived the worst of it."

"But you said to push the pound cake. I totally forgot," he said, his voice duly apologetic.

"Oh, no. You must never attempt the hard sell on Mrs. Krantz. She is a stickler for freshness. Anything offered too exuberantly is bound to draw her suspicion."

Raspberry Strudel

Trajan spent the summer dropping by the bakeshop, impressing his friends with the sway his brother had earned over the shop's owner, who allowed them a small drink and a pastry each time they stopped in.

Bunny acted creepy around any adult he didn't already know, drained himself of personality in hopes of deferring the opinion they were bound to form of him. "What can I get you, my friend?" Mr. Sabonis asked as Bunny blinked, starry-eyed, into the display case.

Bunny bragged that he was going to order one of everything as they approached the shop entrance, prompting Trajan to remind him they were allowed one item apiece. "I'll have one item this time, another item the next time we come, then something different when we come again," Bunny responded, modifying his plan.

Trajan had already developed a favorite from the samples Langston brought home at the end of the day: raspberry strudel. "One of the same," E-Z announced, sparing himself the embarrassment of standing beside his brother and trying to choose from the myriad possibilities staring back at him.

"And you, my friend. Have you made up your mind?" Mr. Sabonis asked, hoping to speed along a transaction destined to net no profit. "You'll have the same as your friends. Strudel all around," he announced, condemning Bunny to the same boring fare no matter how many visits they paid the bakeshop.

Bunny Sessions rubbed Mr. Sabonis in a way he did not like. "You can see trouble brewing inside his eyes," he confided in Langston as the boys exited the shop one afternoon. "He grins at things no one else finds amusing, returns a blank stare anytime you try to engage him. Your brother would do best to steer clear of that one."

Angelica visited midway through the summer, too early for their final good-bye before packing her bags for Princeton. Too many lurking eyes around the bakeshop, Mr. Sabonis's especially, to afford them a proper greeting. She ordered a tray of assorted cookies, said her grandmother was hosting a tea to send her off. "Girls only," she blurted out, wishing she could have invited him. Her nose crinkled with nervous energy that worked to shield her anxiety. Langston wished he could tag along, serve them sweets made with the aid of his earnest hands, working hard to adopt an honest trade. She reminded him of everyone he'd ever cared about. She was expectant, like his mother, easily hurt, a trait she and his brother shared. She was quick to withdraw from anything whose outcome she couldn't influence, like his father; like Grandpa Tuke, she wasn't easily overlooked, whether or not she was looking to gain favor.

"That is a delightful girl," Mr. Sabonis remarked as the door clamored shut behind her. *Delightful indeed*, Langston thought, reminiscing on his brief hold of a shooting star.

The Way Home

Angelica was well into the fall semester at Princeton, arguably settled though not yet counting down the days until her first scheduled visit home, the night Langston set out along Rte. 165 in search of a rave some girls who'd stopped in the bakeshop earlier that day had told him about. Langston and his brother hadn't spoken at all that day. The fall soccer season was in full swing. Meanwhile, Langston was hard at work to remain in Mr. Sabonis's good graces, so it wasn't unusual for him and Trajan to go a couple days straight where their schedules didn't intersect.

Langston supposed the girls were about his age, if not a tad older. Younger maybe; heavy eye makeup confounded his ability to faithfully gauge years. Dirty blonde hair looked like it had been poured from the same bottle, applied amateurishly in one or the other of their upstairs bathrooms. Multiple earrings adorned each lobe, meaning they were still working to find themselves, though at least one pair, studded with sparkling diamonds, suggested they hadn't been left to struggle in the world alone. Definitely younger: private schoolgirls let loose downtown to spend more of their parents' money. The girls hadn't invited him, exactly. He seemed to have invited himself.

"A rave!" he sparked. "Where at?" His eagerness spilled across the display case filled with éclairs, assorted strudels, and hot cross buns. "The rock quarry? The abandoned sewing machine factory?" he offered, guessing.

"The sewing machine factory," he'd heard an echo. "Nobody ever goes out that way. It's going to be trick."

"I suppose I'll see you there," he said, his best shy nerd act at play for added effect.

"We'll see you tonight," they said, the bell hanging above the doorway tingling farewell as they pushed their way out of the shop and back onto the sidewalk.

He arrived at the Singer factory to find the place deserted. He'd heard about these silent rave parties where no one is permitted to speak. You're handed a glow stick along with a pair of wireless headphones. You hang the glow stick around your neck, illuminating everyone's face in a soft neon haze. Raucous techno music pumps through the wireless headsets, while you remain invisible to the outside world. A hundred kids smashing under the same roof, only nobody knows they're there.

He slipped through a cut in the chain-link fence. Climbed the stairs leading to the stacked stone entryway and proceeded to peer through missing panes of glass for an amorphous glow, signs of people milling about. Then: *BWOOP, BWOOP!* An insistent beam of light was all over him, the flashers spinning on the roof of a police cruiser painting the night sky in alternating jags of blue and red light.

Langston sat handcuffed in the backseat of the patrol car as the officers ran his name for priors, checked for outstanding warrants. He fidgeted to shift the weight off his hands, the cuffs cutting into his wrists. He'd gone so far as to slip the girls another couple of linzer tortes for free, a Langston bonus on top of the standard baker's dozen. Agitation swelled inside his chest. Those girls had played him. It wouldn't be the first time. His spirit sagged as he slumped forward, banging his head against the Plexiglas partition meant to protect the armed peace officers from him, his hands cuffed tight beneath his narrow backside.

His chest tightened a second time. He reached to extend an arm to ease the twitch in his leg when the clucking started deep in the back of his throat. He unballed his fists, laboring to control the spray of saliva spewing between his clenched teeth. He curled his spine to form soft angles against the hard plastic surfaces inside the back of the patrol car. He watched as Angelica disappeared in search of help. She ought to be settled at Princeton by now. He should go see her, lie with her in her tiny dorm room, that thick lion's mane spread full across his chest, filling his nose with fruit scents. He tugged against the length of interlocked steel chaining his wrists together. What was keeping Trajan with that cake spatula?

Where was his mother, his father? Which is the way home?

EXASPERATION

The phone rang just before three in the morning. "Mrs. Hopkins?" a voice asked from the other end of the line, its anxiety hiding behind an authoritative sounding tone.

"This is she," she answered.

"Is Mr. Hopkins available?"

"Mr. Hopkins and I are no longer together," she replied, resenting the intrusion. "He lives on the other side of town, if you must know. Is there something I can help you with?"

"It's imperative that you come to the police station."

"In regard to what, might I ask?" she inquired, dreading his response.

"In regard to your son, Langston," the voice responded, cutting hard against the beam of her happiness.

Suspect

Details of the circumstances surrounding Trajan's brother's death were difficult to assemble. The police report disclosed that the deceased had been detained shortly after midnight. After initial questioning, the officers placed the young man in the back of their patrol car, at which time the subject became agitated, slamming himself repeatedly against the glass partition that separated the backseat from the driver's compartment. The officers removed the subject from the vehicle upon ascertaining that the source of his distress was involuntary, assuring he posed them no material threat.

Paramedics dispatched to the scene would later testify at a preliminary hearing called on behalf of the Hopkins family by the district attorney's office that they'd had to instruct the officers to remove the handcuffs as they attempted to render aid. Officers Dooling and Wendt testified at the hearing that there had been no struggle, that the prisoner had been compliant from the outset.

"Suspect," the assistant DA, Ms. Consalves, said to remind them of the correct terminology to use when referring to anyone in police custody, the person's guilt or innocence not theirs to determine. "You failed to mention in your report that the suspect had been handcuffed?" she continued, beginning her inquiry. The officers acknowledged having cuffed the suspect before placing him in the backseat of their patrol vehicle.

The police union rep appointed to accompany the officers to the hearing added matter-of-factly that the patrol officers weren't required to indicate whether or not they had cuffed the suspect before placing him in the backseat. "That is, after all, standard procedure. No point including every ancillary detail in the incident report." He sought the ADA's approval with raised eyebrows for having used the proper term, suspect, rather than convicted criminal.

Both officers answered a swift *"No"* when asked whether they'd struck Trajan's brother. In reference to the medical examiner's note of abrasions on the subject's forehead and chin, the older of the two offered that they had attempted to remove the suspect from the cruiser to keep him from vomiting up his own tongue when he'd tumbled beyond their grasp and fallen to the pavement.

"Face first?" Ms. Consalves questioned, her stare unyielding behind tortoise-rimmed reading glasses.

"Yes, face first, if I recall correctly," the officer replied, twisting a new dimple in the knot of his standard-issue police blue tie.

Officer Wendt, the less seasoned of the two officers, was far less mechanical with his account, his eagerness to unravel the string of events that resulted in Langston's death rivaling that of Trajan. Officer Wendt took care to call Langston by his proper name. "Mr. Hopkins seemed fine back there at first. He claimed to be looking for a party some kids had told him about when asked his reason for gaining entrance to the factory. It didn't appear that he had broken in, what with most of the doors and windows having been busted out already."

Officer Dooling shifted his weight restlessly, the legs of his chair squealing in loud disapproval against the hard linoleum floor at his partner's testimony.

"We pulled him from the cruiser once we noticed Mr. Hopkins was in a state of distress," Officer Wendt continued. "In our haste, we must have lost our grip, allowing him to fall." His eyeballs swelled in their sockets, a protruding Adam's apple rocking deep inside his throat to coax out the words. "Without warning, everything inside him seized up, then his body went still, like a swift wind had blown across a candle and put out the flame. Then he just lay there."

The ADA thanked him for his graphic account, but asked that he stick to the facts, hoping to spare Mrs. Hopkins any further theatrics. "You admit, then, to having dropped the subject?"

"Yes," the officer replied. "I mean, we were holding him when he fell."

"And then he seized?" she pressed.

"Yes, I suppose that's how it happened," he responded.

"You suppose it happened that way, or you clearly recollect it having happened that way?"

Officer Dooling stood in protest. "You gonna open your mouth a single time today?" he said to the top of the union rep's bald head.

"Say something," he urged, yanking the rep by the elbow to stand alongside him. Then he turned to address the ADA, his red face gleaming. "What difference does it make whether he fell first or seized then fell?" Dooling said. "A man was in trouble back there. We did our best to help him. It's a god-awful shame he didn't make it in the end. But my partner and I are not the cause of this man's death."

Backseat Kinship

Trajan sat in the backseat of his father's car as he drove them home from the preliminary hearing. He saw a woman seated in the back of a car adjacent to them in traffic. She had a piece of tape affixed to her nose, attaching either nostril to an oxygen tank by way of clear plastic tubing. She looked pitiful sitting back there alone. In her eyes, he must have looked pitiful, too, alone in the backseat of their car.

After staring for an uncomfortably long while, Trajan gave a shy little wave, a subtle side-to-side movement of his hand to ask whether she was okay back there.

I see you, he said with his wave. *Do you see me?*

The woman waved back, her thin brown hand barely visible above the door frame so as to be imperceptible to anyone riding in the car with her. She adjusted the tape stretched across her nose, pressed it flat to make sure the plastic tubing was secure in place, before looking away. He didn't know whether she was coming or going in this world, waxing or waning, how long those tubes would sustain her. She couldn't know that, in the backseat of his mind, he was mourning the loss of his only brother, his mother's firstborn son.

As the car pulled ahead of them in traffic, Trajan wondered about his brother's last words, his final moment of conscious thought, whether incessant chatter from the police radio was the last sound he was likely to have registered. The dispatcher would return with at most two things to report. His brother had been detained once for shoplifting. He claimed to have had a craving for donuts, but he didn't have enough cash on hand for donuts *and* milk.

"And milk?" Trajan had questioned. Dew from the sides of the milk carton, sweating through his brother's T-shirt, alerted the man who owns the AM-PM to the caper as he counted change for the donuts.

"How are you going to swallow a dozen powdered mini-donuts without a splash of milk to wash them down?" Langston replied, his tendency to trivialize life's most important matters doing little to quiet the storm brewing inside their mother's head, her eyes a genuine goblin's stare, the depth and color of ink spilled from the nib of a pen.

Langston had been charged with fighting in public as a result of his final bout with Albert Chu. One of the clearer-minded kids had flagged down a passing patrol car, which escorted the pair to the emergency room. After taking their statements, the officer, again acting in accordance with standard procedure, cited both boys as interested parties in an altercation.

"Do you think we can sue?" his father asked into the silence surrounding his mother's disposition.

"The weatherman predicts rain today," Dottie replied, never diverting her gaze from the passenger side window. "Should we sue the sun for failing to shine? Or, if in the end, rainclouds fail to gather overhead, can we sue 11 Alive for leading us to believe it would rain?"

Exasperation shaped the expression between his parents, exasperation and pain. The pain his father had caused. The pain he could no longer spare her. "You can't sue our son back into existence," Dottie said, looking at Chester for the first time. "I won't be party to it, if that's your aim. I want to be home. Want my son back where he belongs, home beside his mother. I won't stand by and let you tarnish his memory with anything that won't, at the end of the day, bring him home to me."

Chester dropped Trajan and his mother off in front of their duplex apartment. Trajan wondered when they might see him again as the glow from his taillights disappeared down the block. He helped his mother inside the house. When had he gotten so big, outgrown his mother to the point that he could reach an arm around her and have her fit inside his shoulder? He escorted her to her bedroom door, the weight of her leaning as much on him as on any part of the creaky wooden floor, his body listing unsteadily in an effort to keep them both upright. He left her alone inside the room, the lights turned low, though he knew she wouldn't sleep. Feared she might never rest again.

The district attorney's office found the officers guilty of no criminal negligence, though their summary report noted several deficiencies in the patrolmen's readiness as peace officers to administer to persons in distress. Ordered mandatory retraining for the whole department in lifesaving measures. Ms. Consalves made a personal visit to the Hopkins' residence later that week. She offered to arrange counseling for Mrs. Hopkins, left behind the card of a social worker with whom the ADA was familiar. Said the woman had experience dealing with cases like theirs.

Mrs. Hopkins thanked her for her concern. She asked Trajan to be so kind as to show the woman to the door. Dottie Hopkins was nobody's *case*, in need of social work. She was the social worker around these parts, had dedicated a lifetime to assisting people in need, real need behind a problem from which a person had a chance of recovering. She was not above accepting help. She simply recognized the need that rested its full weight against her, understood how resistant losing a child could be to any sort of fixing.

KICK, MOVE

Sunday, December 31. Trajan didn't know which was more depressing: that it was Sunday, or that the holiday season was behind them. Christmas had been his brother's favorite holiday. The way he had of making all heads turn his way, smiles smiling in response to the smallest gesture, something he had done to cause them to smile. Trajan and Dottie had skipped Christmas altogether. The shiny ornaments, the precious keepsakes, only served to compound his mother's despair, each a small reminder of past joys, drowned happiness gnawing a new hole in a spirit already ravaged by debilitating heartache.

Dottie had instituted a tradition that the boys exchange gifts with one another. Trajan's gift to his brother usually consisted of something their mother had picked out—earmuffs, a sweatshirt adorned with sports insignia or race cars or spaceships or some other thing boys are supposed to be universally fond of. Trajan watched glassy eyed as Dottie dangled countless choices before him, seeking his approval. He eventually conceded, nodding vigorously over whatever his mother had in hand in order to be set free in the toy aisle, browsing for last-minute items to add to his list of wants and wishes. Langston insisted on doing his own shopping for Trajan. He had been on the receiving end of far too many pairs of slippers, long underwear, and warm socks to leave the task of picking out the right gift for his little brother to their mother's unshakably pragmatic ways.

When he was eleven, the boys' last year in elementary school together, Langston had set his sights on a silver referee's whistle, seeding his brother's infatuation with soccer. Trajan blew that whistle all of Christmas Day, loudly at first, charging anyone in his sights with all sorts of made-up infractions, then more quietly, Chester having issued a warning of his own. Trajan went to sleep that night with the whistle still stuck between his lips, tiny bursts of air sending the pea rattling against the hollow core of its metal casing. Dottie sent Chester in to get it once the boys were asleep, fearing her son might choke on the thing, condemning him to spend the rest of eternity with a restless whistling lodged in the back of his throat.

Innocents

Trajan took up his brother's preoccupation with traveling anyplace he went by foot—by skateboard, in actuality. His father gave him a portable music player for Christmas that year. He would drop his board outside his mother's front door, slip the headphones over his ears, pump his foot, and disappear from existence. He had no influence on the space outside his headphones. The clack of his skateboard against measured breaks in the sidewalk registered no sound. The wind angling around his ears went by breathless as he made his way in the darkness. On a night when his head was clear, Trajan let the music play cover to cover, one song after another. On a stormy night, thoughts of his brother crowding his mind, he skipped between tracks, unable to maintain a single line of focus.

He spent the majority of his time on the roll. He had no bedtime, no curfew, no one checking to see whether or not he had gotten home. His mother only asked that he stay on top of his schoolwork, something done with relative ease. Older brothers set the bar for younger brothers. Trajan only need do marginally better than his brother to earn favor with the same teachers who had found Langston thoroughly infuriating; Langston had always seemed up to the task, yet lacked focus to make the grade beyond the bare minimum required of him. Trajan was teacher's pet by comparison.

He'd start out in the direction of Carmen Padilla's, the first half of the evening spent on her parents' living room sofa, trying to keep

119

the plastic slipcovers from squealing and giving away any move he was contemplating. From there, he'd cruise past the AM-PM, fill up on donuts and milk, both paid for. He generally preferred to take the long way out of town when heading toward home.

The bridge along Rte. 2 makes a long arc across the river, requiring a minimum of foot pumping to reach the apex followed by a long, slow cruise back down to the opposing riverbank. He'd rest awhile at the bridge's tallest point, watch the moon rising above the persistent ripple of the river's shimmering skin. From this vantage point, the bridge looked as though someone had left a stretch of road out overnight and the river had grown up around it. You could row a boat across and be nearly eye level with the passing car tires, the bridge's short stanchions barely visible above the chop of the water.

On an especially balmy night, the moon bright in the sky, Trajan spooked a raccoon that had returned from foraging along the base of the bridge. The thing stood on its hind legs, teeth bared, its front paws in the air, aiming to project more formidably than its meager stature would otherwise suggest. The beast's gimmickry proved effective. The raccoons Trajan had previously encountered eyed him from a safe distance outside his mother's kitchen window. The ones holding court on her back deck were of the cute, cuddly variety. He might otherwise have expected a two-dimensional cartoon bandit cut from the television screen, its eyes covered in a carefully drawn black burglar's mask that inspired fear for your wallet, not for your life. Trajan's mind raced to assess the threat, calculating potential angles of attack in the tradition his brother had inspired. Would the thing come in low, go for the ankles in an effort to chop its adversary down to size? Would it launch itself instead from its hind legs, attaching itself to Trajan's face with pointed claws to disorient its victim?

He eased backward, fumbling with the off switch on his music player. If he was going to do battle with a crazed raccoon, it wasn't going to be to the tune of a Beastie Boys soundtrack, a group Chester had exposed his sons to early in their music appreciation, aiming to present a well-rounded view of the hip-hop culture he'd grown up listening to.

Trajan prepared to retreat, to drop his board and take the long roll back toward Norwich, when a car horn leaped into the vacuous space that the bridge's solid structure cut into the moist night air. The sound projected off a leaden sky, sending the raccoon darting into the roadway. With a bit of odd luck, the bandit managed to dodge two lanes of traffic, frantically waving its ringed tail for balance, when *SMACK*—the raccoon was sent sprawling against the guardrail. Trajan stood horrified as instinct told the thing to get up, to continue to flee; the raccoon tried repeatedly to right its body atop legs still wriggling in an earnest attempt at flight. He understood the possum: play dead, feign surrender, in an effort to preserve hope. The raccoon lay there clinging to life, clutching at every breath.

Trajan began to cultivate the belief that he could see people on the verge of dying, any living thing. Not demons and ghouls, evil spinning from the horned tips of their pointy heads. Trajan's brother, Langston, wasn't evil. That old woman left alone in the backseat of her mind wasn't evil either. There lay a frightened raccoon, freshly run down, straining against the pull of bright light. Each of these had at one time been an innocent living, breathing thing, making its respective way in the world, unconcerned by the prospect that death might strike, easing the last thump from inside their still-beating hearts.

Trajan stopped paying close attention to anyone left for him to care about, interaction with his mother relegated to muffled conversations from the hallway outside her bedroom. Tuke said he wasn't afraid the time he choked on a water bottle in front of Trajan, water sent down the wrong pipe, sending Tuke spewing and sputtering, death calling to him.

"If a sip of water is going to kill me, then I deserve to die," he assured his grandson once he regained use of his windpipe. "I accept what fate brings me."

122

Mother's Nature

Tuke had gotten in the habit of letting the boys tag along with him whenever he went fishing. The void was palpable the first time he and Trajan found themselves at the lake's edge alone.

"Grandpa Tuke, is fishing your favorite thing to do?"

"Unh-hunh," Tuke responded, hoping his economy with words would discourage further conversation from his grandson.

"You come out here all the time. How come you never bring home any fish?"

"I don't come here to fish."

"Then why do you come?"

"To see nature," Tuke responded as the sun opened its eyes on the world, sending a soft glow along the horizon. "Fish I can buy at the grocery store. I come to commune with Mother Nature, to remind myself how small we are, how big the universe is around us."

"How do you know nature is a she?" Trajan continued with his questions, condemning Tuke to a long morning after all.

"Man is too concerned with himself to do all this," he explained, "to fill the world with the birds and trees and fish. Man is consumed with what he has in hand, what he is bound to get. He doesn't invest his time worrying about anything, the fruits of which he will never live to see. It takes a mother to understand that current ways of living take their toll on future living, to comprehend that life without something bigger than ourselves, something not easily attained, is not a life worth living."

"Where do people go when they die?" Trajan asked, finally getting around to the thing he most wanted to know.

His grandpa consulted the same wisdom he'd been given when he was Trajan's age, his Big Pa having been called on. "There is a wandering spirit god sent down from the heavens to carry a being home."

123

"He reaches down and snatches people?" Trajan asked, Tuke's account not serving to ease his anxieties.

"There is no single *He* doing the bidding. There is a spirit that moves among us, settles in the form of some living thing, then moves about the world making those final calls, rests his eyes on a person to indicate their time in this life is done."

"Did the spirit god snatch Langston?"

"Your brother is closer than you realize, looking down to guide this conversation. Don't be afraid for your brother. He is not afraid for you. He knows as only he can, nothing happens in this life before it's time."

Tuke fingered the part down the middle of his gray hair, remembered thinking as a boy, when he'd been given similar explanation, that *never* is a good time to die. "Your grandma is looking down on me, too, making sure I do right by your mother," he continued. "That your mother gathers her spirit in time to do by you again."

"Where'd she disappear to?"

"She hasn't gone anyplace she can't get back from." Tuke stood staring into a face that was more Dottie's than his, more Trajan's grandma than anybody's. "Trust that your mother will get back to you as soon as she's able. When you most need her, trust that she'll be there. She is your mother, after all."

124

WIDOWER'S FATE

E-Z was living in his parents' attic by the time his turn came to cross the river and head to NFA. Grand-mère had buried yet another husband. She and her brother, T'Onc, had had another falling out over the little plot of land their grandfather left the two of them. Life for T'Onc had not gone at all how he had dreamed. Catching a fish guaranteed him a single meal and nothing more, tasking him the next day with catching another fish and yet another the day after that as well. He had come to realize that there were more fish in the ocean than he had days left in him to fish. Many of his comrades had begun captaining water taxis and pleasure cruise ships, guiding tours around this tiny island gem of theirs, sacrificing their waters, their beaches, their home. They had given in to the tourists' way of thinking in an effort to shed their hand-to-mouth existence. Being his grandfather's surviving male heir, T'Onc believed he should be granted permission to do with the land as he pleased. He had a spearfishing resort in mind. If the tourist was content to dole out hard cash for the opportunity to risk death, why should he be the one who fails to profit, left holding onto tradition?

As the elder of the two, Grand-mère felt a sense of obligation to put the land to some use that might benefit those branches of the family tree who had yet to spread their leaves. She regarded a fishing resort as one man's fantasy, idle ramblings from her only remaining sibling, who sought to extract little from their father's land outside of sufficient means to fund his own retirement. *Impétueux* was the label she assigned to T'Onc—impetuous. He argued that, seeing how she had so much interest in family, she ought to be with them. He sent her to Preston, believing her desire to return home would, in time, inspire a new way of seeing things, irrepressible homesickness breeding a less combative attitude in her.

It was decided in advance of Grand-mère's arrival that E-Z would give up his room. Their new houseguest was far too frail to endure being carried up and down the stairs. E-Z's move to the attic was central to Mathieu's offensive to force some separation between his two sons, which was part of his larger, never-ending battle to curb their mother's tendency to baby the two of them—Bunny especially. Mathieu persisted in trying to provoke some backbone from his eldest son. His efforts instead exposed an irrepressible urge in E-Z to single out anyone of lesser stature, exercising all his might against that person for no greater purpose than to feel bigger by comparison. E-Z possessed his father's high-rail tendency toward manic swings in his personality, could in a split second go from back-slaps and belly laughs to wishing somebody who had crossed him, dismissed him, left him holding the bag, dead. Bunny's attention deficit seemed understated given the abundance of triggers present in his daily household routine.

Bunny wanted to change rooms too. "Why can't I move to the attic with E-Z?" he pleaded.

"I'm afraid the attic is a one-man operation," their father insisted. Bunny's mother passed Bunny a look that said, *we'll see,* meaning she would speak to their father after the boys went to bed.

"They need to do some growing up," Mathieu complained. "By the time I was their age, I had a boat of my own. Was well on my way to making my own way in the world." *He had a fine life before he became involved with her* is the thing he wanted to say, before the brown-eyed girl he met while playing semipro baseball in the river valley became brown eyes and a baby (two babies, once Bunny came into the world), saddling him with undue responsibility. But he bit his tongue on the words. *Know where to put the period,* Grand-mère had advised him over the years. She couldn't keep her son from breaking a woman's heart. She could, however, keep him from throwing his contempt in his woman's face. She subscribed to the old-school

127

belief in making do, keeping the peace at any cost. Love the one you're with, even if you don't truly love her.

In the end, Mathieu's wife convinced him to let Bunny take E-Z's room. That way he'd be moving too, farther down the hall away from his parents' bedroom. Besides, Bunny's room would afford Grand-mère easier access to the bathroom. It was settled: E-Z would get the attic to himself, brokering another day of harmony in the Sessions household.

Grand-mère would learn nothing of the commotion that preceded her arrival, though E-Z had to suspect she knew: another household turned upside down to make way for her landing, a son obeying his duty, a daughter-in-law forced to swallow her tongue.

E-Z chose to ignore the circumstance that had liberated him from his brother's incessant blathering, didn't stand around long looking that gift horse in the mouth. He slathered himself in new-found freedom, transferred his clothes to a collection of plastic milk crates pressed into duty, anchoring planks of wood that served as part desk, part bookshelf.

A narrow valley, boxed within the space below the roof's ridge-line, gave way on either side to steep angles. The milk crate contraption occupied one side of the room; his bed filled the other. The long rake of the ceiling left precious little vertical wall space, but he lined what space he had with posters, Bunny claiming that E-Z's taste in artwork was too much for his meager constitution. E-Z hung a photograph of a bullet, slowed by a high-speed shutter, tearing into the bark of a tree angled down at him on one wall, and, above his bed, a coiled tree snake slithering in and out of the eye sockets of a human skull. He lined the ceiling's flat spine with a time-lapse series animating a swarm of killer ants as they reduced a fallen wildebeest to a memory, rawhide strewn across loose bones.

E-Z lay down each night to images of death staring at him from every angle. He couldn't come and go as he pleased. But his parents no longer looked to impose the same strict bedtime on him as they did when he bunked next to his brother's room, given their belief that a rested Bunny was less likely to act out at school. Only E-Z seemed to recognize that Bunny's restlessness in the classroom had little to do with a break in his sleeping pattern.

E-Z stayed at the window late into the night surveying the sky, monitoring the rustle of wind in the trees. He eventually caught sight of Mr. Gurley busy behind the pane of glass in his front window. Having no close relations in town, no routine outside of retrieving the newspaper at the end of his driveway, his activities were no longer confined to daylight hours. He sat across the street each night reading his newspaper, dining on a prepackaged meal well past midnight.

Mr. Gurley had lived in the house alone since his wife passed. The boys had no recollection of the late Mrs. Gurley, making her widower seem a strange old coot whose family had drifted away, presumably for their own protection. Quite the opposite was true. Mr. and Mrs. Gurley had never had children of their own, but they maintained a hand in raising Mr. Gurley's niece, who became a permanent fixture around their dinner table, classmates in tow, during any school break that didn't afford a trip home to Chicago. Life in the Gurley household brimmed on hi-hat a few short days at a time, the girls' nonstop shrieking and giggling offering a welcome break from the low murmuring that passed for conversation between Mr. Gurley and his wife. The niece graduated from Brown University long before any of the neighborhood kids had enjoyed their first day in grade school, again confounding clear recall.

E-Z manned his post in the window night after night, watching Mr. Gurley, anticipating a breakdown. Widows seemed capable of lasting long after their men passed, decades even, depending how early life had claimed their husbands and how their men had lived. Widowers, on the other hand, tended to follow their spouses to the grave with alarming haste, the shattered bond calling them to lie down beside their beloved at the earliest opportunity. Mr. Gurley was well overdue. Plus, the holidays would soon be upon them, signaling a universal tipping point for the newly dejected.

E-Z continued monitoring the situation from across the street. The curve of Mr. Gurley's spine said that he was not long for this world, parts of him submitting voluntarily to their final resting place. The slow shuffle of his feet across low shag carpet suggested that he had begun employing ways to conserve his energy, intent on outlasting the widower's fate.

E-Z's mother informed him that Mrs. Gurley had suffered a heart attack while preparing the Easter holiday feast and passed a few short days after entering the hospital. Mrs. Sessions usually took Mr. Gurley a plate after the family had eaten its Easter supper. Once the holiday had come and gone without incident, E-Z began concocting all sorts of strange possibilities for Mr. Gurley. E-Z began suspecting Mr. Gurley of planning a one-sided suicide pact to be carried out on the anniversary of his wife's death to increase the likelihood that their souls would find one another in the afterlife. He spied stacks of newspapers lined along the living room walls, observed Mr. Gurley replacing a blown lightbulb. He imagined a glass shell filled partway with kerosene. One flick of the light switch and *BOOM!* He would once again be one with his dearly departed wife, the stacks of newspapers that lined his walls assuring a swift and total demise.

Another season passed to find Mr. Gurley still among the living, despite the curl of his spine relenting further beneath the will of unseen forces. E-Z soon realized he was rooting for the old goat, wanted to see him break a hundred if he hadn't already, to defy all odds. The two continued their nightly routine well into E-Z's junior year at NFA, Mr. Gurley oblivious to the horse race in which E-Z had him entered. He continued puttering about, stacking newspapers, staggering ever more slowly to and from his vinyl-clad recliner.

E-Z arrived at the attic window one night to find Mr. Gurley's favorite chair empty. No newspaper, no prepackaged dinner, no slow feet shuffling across the low shag-carpeted floor. A Range Rover pulled into the driveway the next day with Rhode Island tags—the niece from Brown University, as E-Z would later discover. Mr. Gurley had meals delivered three times a week. The volunteer delivery driver had noticed Mr. Gurley was unusually out of sorts—slurred speech, his hand trembling, one side of his body refusing to go how he needed it to go—obvious signs of a stroke. He pushed Mr. Gurley in the direction of his favorite chair and then used the kitchen phone to call for an ambulance.

A CT scan taken at the hospital confirmed a brain hemorrhage. By nightfall, Mr. Gurley had slipped into a coma while E-Z held vigil from his place at the attic window. The doctors asked his niece whether she wanted them to operate, advising her of the slim chance of recovery given her uncle's advanced age. She elected to leave him be, let him go be with his wife if those were his wishes. He was gone by week's end.

E-Z asked to attend the funeral. He wanted to go. Wanted to climb on top of the casket and demand an explanation. After all he and Mr. Gurley had been through together, why give up now? They were supposed to break a hundred, beat the odds. He began placing bets on Grand-mère instead. She had outlived three husbands. She could see a hundred easy.

THREE

In 1994, the federal government granted the Mohegan Tribe recognition as a sovereign state, paving the way for the tribe to build and operate a casino exempt from federal taxes on its reservation in Uncasville. (It should be noted that gaming tribes contribute 25 percent of all slot revenues to the state, balancing the toll exacted from those residents unable to resist venturing a roll against the house. Even a house built on tribal grounds is guaranteed to win.) The town surrounding the reservation was named in honor of Uncas, who, in the early 1600s, led the split from the Pequot to form the Mohegan Tribe—or Wolf People, as they were known—becoming the tribe's first Sachem, or Big Chief. The Mohegan Sun Casino and Resort has served as a source of recreation and economic growth in the region since 1996.

The Mashantucket Pequot opened Foxwoods Casino in 1992, just a stone's throw across the river in Ledyard. Initially feared to be an eyesore, Foxwoods blends remarkably well with its surroundings. Dogwood, cypress, and elm line the hillside, the landscape's half-moon shape cradling the casino grounds in lush green. Make no mistake: Foxwoods shows ample signs of newfound fortune, only its prosperity appears to have crept in, the resort disguising its wealth from the neighbors, blending as best it can into an otherwise dormant countryside.

The Mohegan Sun Casino and Resort showed up with trumpets blaring, a trove of riches put on full display. The newly erected off-ramp from I-395 circles the compound. An elevated driveway makes a long, sweeping arc that takes its sweet time high above the entranceway before descending into the parking structure, a journey that might take you from the heights of the tallest treetops to the depths of hell, depending on your luck.

The Bureau of Indian Affairs granted the Eastern Pequot federal recognition in early 2002. Dottie was elected to the inaugural tribal council, owing to her even temperament and her years of committed service. In the spring of 2005, the BIA reversed its position and revoked the Eastern Pequot's status, the state calling into question sufficient evidence of uninterrupted residency on the land over which the tribe laid claim before they could devise any means of deriving profit from it. The state sided against them in the end, just as Chester had predicted. It was the straw that broke Trajan's mother's back.

"If I was a spiteful woman," Dottie confided into the phone to the boys' Aunt Sherry one night, long after Trajan should have gone off to sleep, "I could find someone to hate, someone to blame. If I was a churchgoing person, I would know how to pray, could call on my God and bring an end to this ordeal."

Trajan would have heard her sobbing had she cried herself to sleep at night. Would have spotted the visible clues had his mother taken to squandering her days lost in a fit of angry tears. Never one to throw fits, Dottie Hopkins instead—ever so quietly, ever so calmly—withdrew.

Sunshine and Rain

"Ma," Trajan asked through his mother's closed bedroom door, taking the knob in his hand and hoping to be let in. "Can you hear me?"

"I hear you fine, Trajan," Dottie responded. "What is it you need?"

His mother had been sunshine and rain since the night his brother died. With any luck, today she would be sunshine. He thought he'd heard her showering that morning while the sky was still dark outside. He hoped that a stand-up shower might spell a departure from her lie around, tub-soaking ways.

"I came to remind you that today is your birthday."

"I know today is my birthday. You think your mother has gone soft in the head?"

"Is there something special you want to do today?"

"No," she replied. "Today is nothing special."

"But, Ma, it's your birthday. We need to celebrate."

"Celebrate what, Trajan? Another year on this earth? I celebrate warm baths, clean sheets to lie in afterward. These things I do on a regular basis. Why wait one day a year to celebrate?"

"Ma, I'm being serious."

"I'm being serious, too," she assured him, groans from the mattress, suddenly put-upon as his mother shifted position in bed, grumbling through the shut door. "Tell you what," she offered. "How about I give you my birthday on top of your own to do with as you please, seeing as how you have so much celebration in you. Wouldn't that be special?"

Trajan let go of the knob, defeated.

"Happy birthday, Trajan," his mother beamed from the other side of the locked bedroom door. "Be sure to have a slice of cake for me."

He rested an open palm on one of the door's raised panels, registered the empty feel of its hollow core. "Happy birthday, Ma," he whispered into the door frame before turning up the hallway. "Here's to another year."

She understood his plight. Witnessed boys his age left standing in the gap, consumed by the circumstance surrounding problems beyond their years to grasp. *I'll be back to you in time.* She made her silent plea while she could still bear to rest her eyes long on his skin, his profile a mixture of Chester and Langston, blended by his share of time spent inside the hem of her skirt. *Countless time. Someday just this side of forever, I'll get back to being your mother. This much I promise.*

Masquerade

She rose each day with every intention of getting over it, of slipping out from beneath the burden of grief that time had heaped on her, of setting aside her troubles and taking back her life. When Dottie was a girl, Tuke had taken her to see the movie about the boy in the plastic bubble. The boy in the movie longed for a taste of the outside world. She wanted just the opposite; she wished to bring the rest of the world inside the bubble with her, seal it tight on what she had before any more of it could slip away.

Tuke fixed her daily meals after Trajan left in the morning: cereal with coffee and toast for breakfast, a bagel or fresh pastry on special request. He left extra provisions for lunch on a tray next to her bed: peanut butter and crackers, bread and jam, nuts and dried fruit, things that could be trusted to keep without refrigeration. He enabled his daughter in that way, accommodated her weakness, her failing. Dottie ate her meals in strict order as the sole means of keeping her day right-side up. She slept when she was tired, sat up when she had the energy. She noted the time as Trajan slammed the door each morning. This part of the day was foreign to her, the rest of the world having gone off to work or school, not to return for another several hours.

Winter cuts the day in peculiar ways. The sun starts strong in the sky, causing icicles to melt along the windowsill. Before long the clouds set in, allowing the icicles to regain their shape, longer even, water dripping from the snow-covered rooftop increasing their potency. By three-thirty, four o'clock, the sun has begun its retreat, the sky heading toward the black of night. *It's no wonder birds choose to fly south for the winter,* she thought. *This is no way to live.*

She listened to the rain outside her window. Delighted in knowing she didn't have to go out in the wet, had no place to be. It didn't rain inside her bedroom. Neither snow, nor sleet, nor hail fell from the modest height of her popcorn ceiling. She took steps to contend with the hot and cold, light and dark in her day, worked to maintain a constant equilibrium in the world inside her bubble. She buried herself beneath another layer of blankets when the cold came knocking at her windowsill, donned long sleeves and warm socks. She switched the light on anytime the sun refused to shine. Lifted the window shade when the sun deigned to cooperate.

Sound proved wildly less obedient. Weather doesn't masquerade, hot pretending to be cold and vice versa. The sound of an empty house played havoc with the calendar. Trajan was a bundle inside her arms the last stretch of time she'd spent at home during the day, Langston a toddler running small errands back and forth to the kitchen for his mother. Any voice she heard belonged to a child of hers, sometimes both boys calling to her at once, babbling in sing-song unison. Their voices were school-age as the day came to a close, racing one another to her front door after the school bus dropped them off. By nightfall, she was alone again, resting in the place life had left her, sitting alone inside her bubble.

Grandpa Tuke bought Langston a collection of Smurf minia-tures one year for his birthday, a bubbling brood of big-eared blue gnomes cast in rubberized skin. The boys would spend entire days on the back deck, weather permitting, working to defeat the wiz-ard Gargamel, sworn enemy of the Smurfs, a tiny armful of which Langston carried everywhere he went before his brother came into the world: Papa Smurf, Brainy Smurf, Lazy Smurf, Smurfette. To his mind, Trajan may well have been the latest Smurf character cre-ation: Baby Brother Smurf.

Langston used to drag his brother around the house day and

night like a favorite pet. "C'mon, Trajan. Time to get up. Time to go outside. Time to play. Time to go back inside. Time to rest. Time to eat. Time to go to sleep." He spoke to Trajan so continuously that the little fellow abandoned interest temporarily in learning to talk. No need to ask what they were planning to do next. Just wait a few minutes and his older brother would tell him.

Once Trajan began talking, his brother's name refused to come off his tongue the way it needed to. "Wangston," he would say, "I'm going to tell Mom if you don't quit."

"Stop being such a baby," Langston complained.

"I'm not being a baby," Trajan insisted, even on occasions when he was being a baby.

Dottie wished she could keep them babies forever, hold them in the safe confines of the tiny space Chester had fenced in on one side of their duplex apartment where the worst either might suffer was a bump on the noggin from a tumble off the red and yellow plastic Playskool slide Dottie had purchased for the two of them to share. "Big boys know how to take turns," she advised from her place at the kitchen window, wanting them to learn to get along with the world in spite of how ill-prepared she was to see them grow up.

Chester marveled at how easily Dottie took to the responsibility of parenting a child. He admired the dedication as he labored to muster her level of commitment, struggled to comprehend his wife's newfound baby fixation. He couldn't wait to see the little men they would grow to be but was not inclined to descend into the same *goo-goo, gaga* type of smothering affection. But then, he hadn't carried them, hadn't been called on to provide sustenance from womb to bosom to the brightly colored tip of a rubber-coated eating utensil meant to hold their interest as she coaxed them to make their way to the bottom of the bowl tinted the same shade as the spoon—*all gone!*

Chester's strong parenting instincts kicked in as each boy hit five or six, ready to start T-ball. By seven or eight, the two were best buds, his little man accompanying him to the dojang to begin martial arts training. The age difference afforded Langston a three-year head start in learning to relate to their father, drawing Trajan and his mother that much closer. The balance promised to correct itself so long as Chester saw fit to stay, provided he and Dottie developed some means to hold it all together, affording Trajan a few years at the center of attention after Langston had flown the coop. None of them ever made it that far.

Both had been on hand to witness their sons' first steps, spread out across from one another, calling for baby boy to stumble back and forth between the two anchors in his world. But she had been there to see all the herky-jerky early attempts, the tumbling falls, the hard backward plops onto their padded bottoms. She celebrated the eventual triumph, witnessed the satisfaction on their shining faces as they clapped with flat, inarticulate baby hands upon realizing they could walk, their determined little wills poised like never before to decide the places they needed to go (in Trajan's case, generally opposite from where she might want him to be; Langston seemed content to toddle behind her, lost in a world conjured inside his imagination.) They were Chester's boys without question. But they were her babies first, justifying any compulsion she felt to lament their departure even before either boy had slipped beyond her grasp.

BROWN FLECKS

At the end of the school year following Langston's death, Rosalie Anne Quigley concluded a respectable twenty-year career teaching early American history. The vice principal had advised her of Langston's original injuries, the tendency for his focus to wander. He became one of her favorite pupils despite exhibiting lackluster performance in her classroom.

She sought his attention when she reached the point in her lecture where the Pilgrims had landed. She looked for him again when the support of freed slaves was enlisted to help fight the British during the Revolutionary War. It would have delighted her had he shown some interest, any interest in the knowledge she was trying to impart:

knowledge of his people and their struggles, of his proud heritage to help secure his rightful place in the world. She privately held onto fascinations that Langston might find interest in the woman administering the lecture, if not the subject matter itself. Laid out her clothes each morning wondering how he might find her in this outfit, whether he'd take notice, though he never did.

Mrs. Quigley was not without appeal. She was the kind of woman people might have considered handsome, fetching in her day. She wore her auburn hair loose about her shoulders whenever she was feeling in particular need of attention, left two whole buttons unfastened on her blouse, the freckles on her neck disappearing in a perilous chasm of brown-flecked cleavage. Ample hips did an adequate job of filling the pleats of her skirt, sensible pumps providing her backside added lift, though she was no match for the skintight jeans and tiny skirts raised *nearly up to there* that the girls in school had grown accustomed to wearing. Langston's attention, when focused, was spent elsewhere, leaving Mrs. Quigley to pine away in silence while the hopes she had for him, proper and otherwise, wafted ineffectually above disinterested eyes.

The Dutiful Second Seed

Trajan joining his brother at NFA during Langston's senior year filled Mrs. Quigley with renewed ambition. He was a delight unto himself despite lacking much of his brother's corporeal appeal. He was a tad taller, though even more slender, the length of him spread sparingly across a gangly frame. Where Langston's eyes were guarded, walled off to anything beyond his immediate reach, Trajan's gleamed with considerable capacity for comprehension, compassion for someone else's condition, the idle yearnings of Mrs. Quigley included. Trajan became her new favorite subject; his brother continuing to prove resistant, Trajan was fresh clay to mold.

"Can anyone tell me what the colonists most wished to share with the Indians?" Mrs. Quigley asked at the start of Trajan's second term in her class.

"Thanksgiving?" Ina Murdoch asked with a tentative raise of her arm, unsure of her answer.

"Interesting, Miss Murdoch, but Thanksgiving was originally intended to celebrate good harvest, a tribute to the heavens for plentiful bounty. That the Native Americans had a similar tradition is an unfortunate coincidence that resulted in the holiday as it is celebrated today."

Trajan liked that Mrs. Quigley passed judgment in her classroom, related facts as she saw them, though he suspected the school board frowned upon this practice. *Administer the approved curriculum as prescribed; don't preach to our kids.* His mother had suffered most of her tenure under similar restrictions, wishing to send strong-minded individuals into the world. The school board seemed to prefer spoon-fed, cookie-cutter thinking.

"Anyone else?" Mrs. Quigley soldiered on.

"A percentage of the slot earnings," Bunny Sessions joked, stirring a tiny roar of laughter among his classmates.

"Thank you, Mr. Sessions, but I would venture a guess that the term 'one-armed bandit' had a different connotation at the time of colonization."

Trajan pushed his hand in the air. "Religion?"

"Mr. Hopkins! Yes, the early American settlers felt it imperative to share Christianity with the Indian," she beamed, locking eyes with Trajan before averting her stare.

"Every pagan needs saving. Isn't that right, Mrs. Quigley?" Deshawn Hadley questioned. The Hadleys were Mashantucket Pequot. He attended classes every weekend on tribal cultural enrichment. His tribal lessons had begun conflicting with the school board–approved curriculum, causing him to act out more than he would have otherwise.

Mrs. Quigley had just asked him to elaborate on his perspective when the bell rang, signaling time to shift to sixth period—algebra II—followed by PE to end the school day, allowing them to dress early for soccer practice.

Trajan followed the trickle of kids into the hallway. Bunny had a whole theory going about the crush of people spilling into the hallways each time the bell rang. He likened the bustle in between class periods to the main concourse of a shopping mall the weekend after a major holiday, Thanksgiving for example. Some kids were there for the social outlet, wanting to be seen. Others came to school for lack of anything better to do. A handful came looking to get something out of the deal, to learn something after all. Those were the serious shoppers.

"What about the teachers?" Trajan asked. "Why are they here?"

"Store clerks," Bunny responded. "Some are enthusiastic about the wares they're peddling. Others are merely here taking up time between coffee breaks, making sure nobody shoplifts."

"And Principal Adams?" Trajan wanted to know.

"Head of mall security."

"How do you explain the empty halls during class periods?"

"Weekdays, mid-afternoon—slow shopping days," Bunny explained, flicking his eyebrows at them, hoping to recruit a few converts to his way of thinking. They threw their hands up at him. Bunny continued to plead his case. "Seven class periods; seven days in a week. You think that's a coincidence?" Trajan began to worry his friend was starting to believe his own foolishness, the connection to Crystal Mall real in his mind.

"You sure put a lot of thought into this," Lighty conceded. Bunny beamed, having missed the jab inside Lighty's remark. Lighty considered Bunny idiotic, his incessant babbling the aimless meandering of a feeble mind, a bent sail flapping in the wind. The same kid who barely managed to tread water in the classroom, just like his brother, had conjured a whole world to relate the movement in between classes.

Trajan considered ants in an ant farm a more fitting comparison, all of them moving in like directions, each with his own bundle of responsibility to carry. "We need to find you a girlfriend," he joked. He liked seeing his friend apply himself. He appreciated the accomplishment but couldn't resist a jab of his own. Plus, he never missed an opportunity to remind everyone he was the only one among them who had somebody, his relationship with Carmen Padilla still simmering on slow burn.

Trajan tried to catch up as Deshawn accelerated through the crowd of holiday shoppers in the main hallway.

"You should give Mrs. Quigley a chance," Trajan said. "You'll see. She's one of the determined ones."

"You need to have more pride," Deshawn spat at him once they reached the doorway to algebra II. "You can't bring religion to a people who have religion already, can't impose a new system of beliefs and expect to erase theirs entirely. Who thinks like that?"

"Any day, ladies," the math teacher advised, herding them into the classroom. Mr. Grimes ate, slept, and drank algebra, bled blue for the wares he was peddling, yet he seemed to despise the patrons of his store, pondering at the start of each school year how a new group of kids could turn up seeming more dimwitted than last year's bunch.

Trajan sat staring at the back of Deshawn Hadley's round head. Who was Deshawn to accuse him of denying his heritage? Sure, Trajan would keel over from sheer boredom if made to sit through one of his mother's tribal meetings, but he respected the connection their people shared.

He tried on occasion to get Grandpa Tuke talking. But Tuke generally sidestepped any specifics until the subject of their tribal roots became unavoidable. Tuke stopped regularly at the full-service gas station on his way from the casino. He preferred full service when he could get it. Said it reminded him of simpler times. For himself or for all of mankind, Trajan was never certain.

"You're all set, Chief," the attendant bellowed after them as Tuke eased away from the pump.

"Why does he always call you Chief?" Trajan wanted to know.

The man surely meant no harm. It was just an expression—buddy, pal, chief. Use of the term had a separate connotation for Grandpa Tuke. Fort Shantok for him was sacred, Indian Leap lauded, celebrating the triumph of one warrior chief over warriors led by another chief. He stewed on the word awhile, let the thought catch fire behind his gray eyes.

"This man wants to lump us all in one great big ball," Tuke finally muttered in response to his grandson's question. "Wrap us in feathers and headdress and then dismiss us like some cartoon impersonation of our proud ancestry. If we were buddies, he would understand how much I detest being called Chief."

DUCK, DUCK, GOOSE

Trajan duck, duck, goosed his way through the subtle onset of interest from Mrs. Quigley. She was easily his mother's age—*duck*. She
taught in his school, plus she was married—*duck* and *duck*. Then he'd
catch another glimpse at the speckled plunge of her neckline, the
pull of her skirt against the gentle swaying of hips as she erased the
whiteboard—*GOOSE,* sending his hormones raging with unrelent-
ing verve.

She entered the classroom one afternoon with a third button
slipped open, presumably by accident. Nearly an entire class period
passed and no one thought to step forward to let her know her top
was hanging loose. Even the collection of girls in the class failed to

come to her rescue. So long as her embarrassment didn't draw attention to any of them, they were content to sit with their mouths shut
and let the boys gawk, shy awkwardness masking their connection.
Mrs. Quigley's eyes eventually trailed the aim of somebody's hungry
gaze to the cup of her lace bra, visible nearly to the ridgeline formed
across her nipple, which also might have been seen had she only
leaned far enough forward. She scurried out the doorway, stepping
into the relative privacy of a vacant hallway to fix her blouse. She
returned wearing a new shade of red, the freckles along her cheek-
bones nearly lost against the blush of her skin.

Torment

Mrs. Quigley attended Langston's memorial service. Trajan found
encountering one of his teachers outside the classroom disquiet-
ing. He imagined them eating all their meals in the school cafeteria, watching TV in the teachers' lounge until bedtime. As far as he
knew, they slept like vampires, hanging upside down in empty gym
lockers, showing up the next day armed with mugs of stale coffee,
their eyes peering over heavy reading glasses, dull wooden pointing
sticks in hand, prepared for another day of kid prodding.

152

Yet a number of his former teachers came to pay their respects.
Mr. Day, their elementary school principal, stopped on his way out.
"May you find comfort in the Lord" were the words he used to fill
the space between them. It's something people say when nothing
else seems to fit. Trajan thanked him for his kindness. He extended

a hand, keeping a steady grip around his mother's waist with the other.

Mrs. Quigley also passed them on her way out. She told Trajan to call on her if he needed a friend, to come see her whenever he had a free period. She turned to Mrs. Hopkins. "I am sorry for your loss," she managed before her shoulders heaved and the tears began to fall. She was a sniveling mess as she left the sanctuary. Trajan thought to offer to see her to her car, but he had his hands full already, Mrs. Quigley's sniveling nothing in comparison to the river of tears his mother had left to shed.

Mrs. Quigley kept a silent watch over Trajan once he returned to school, channeling her concern for him through the vague hopes teachers tend to have for their pupils, especially those whose situation seems beyond their mettle to handle on their own. She went to find Trajan the day Paulo Ramirez was caught smoking reefer in the boys' bathroom. Trajan and Paulo knew one another by association alone, by consequence of Trajan's father having taken up residence with Paulo's mother.

Chester hung his coat on the same hook each night, dropped his keys in a dish on the kitchen counter, yet continued to question where he belonged. He'd purchased a fresh doormat from the Kiwanis Club the year he and Dottie split up, its fabric the color of a paper grocery bag, embossed with a crimson *H* for *Hopkins*, one of four fall colors he was asked to choose from: crimson, amber, pumpkin, evergreen. It sat resting outside his ex-wife's front door. She was Hopkins. Trajan and Langston were Hopkins too. The mat had no place outside his current residence.

Chester had been the one to answer when the school called to inform Mrs. Ramirez of her son's suspension. Coincidence placed him next to the phone, a string of nearby deliveries permitting him to break for lunch in the relative comfort of home rather than the front seat of his truck. The hairs on his forearm said to let the phone ring. No one would be calling to speak with him this time of day.

He ignored his original instincts and picked up the receiver, which landed him in the principal's office to cause quite a commotion, by all indications. The walls shook with the sound of his thunder, the waiting area outside the principal's office awash with frenetic energy, loud foreboding sent to terrorize the sprinkling of kids lined up outside the office door who'd been undoubtedly called to answer to lesser charges.

"You must be out of your goddamned mind if you think I'm going to run up here every time you decide to act a fool," Chester bellowed for the whole school to hear. "Norwich Police can come get you for all I care. It'll piss your mother off something awful, but I'd rather deal with her than stand here to account for your good-for-nothing ass."

Mrs. Quigley pushed the door open and poked her head in to tell them Trajan was outside wishing to speak with his father. Chester proceeded to pace the carpeted floor, hurling insults in the direction of Paulo's bowed head. He looked haggard, beat, from half a day's work, his recent handful of troubles, a lifetime of buried regrets.

Trajan hadn't spoken to his father since the holidays, a quick exchange of gifts outside his mother's house before Chester headed home to his second family, a second set of makeshift joys to celebrate. Had the two been in closer contact, Trajan might not have noticed the subtle shift in his father's demeanor: the long slope of his forehead gone slack, smooth skin replacing the hard crinkles on his brow; dull eyes narrowed from endless worry that looked past anything that wasn't immediately in his way; his feet wearing a groove into a path along which he wouldn't wish his worst enemy.

"What's happening, Pops?" Trajan asked, imitating his brother, his tone intentionally aloof in an attempt to defuse their father's anger.

"Now is not a good time, son." Chester had taken to referring to Trajan exclusively as son, looking to reinforce the bond. Langston he called by name, like saying Tuesday instead of yesterday when the day amounts to the same. Let enough time pass and yesterday slips into the day before yesterday and then the day before that, becoming quickly forgotten as the balance of the week piles on. The name, Tuesday, remains unambiguous, not easily misplaced.

"When is it going to be a good time?" Trajan asked. "We eventually have to talk about it."

Mrs. Quigley excused herself, motioning for the vice principal to follow suit. Principal Adams remained out of obligation to oversee any family conference held on school grounds. Even a discussion between a father and his son about the death of the other son required him to remain in attendance. Paulo stood by like an innocent bystander despite having stirred the commotion in the first place. He needed to hear this too. He needed to understand what had Chester so boxed in, seeing how the two shared a roof.

"Why is it you always seem angry?" Trajan asked, sensing the temperature in the room rising, his father threatening to boil over again.

Chester puzzled on Trajan's face a good long while before answering, trying to determine the full intent behind his son's question. "I'm not living the life I hoped to lead."

"Which life did you hope to lead?" Trajan asked him.

Confessional

What Trajan didn't know is that his father, too, had stood in the hallway outside his mother's bedroom door and confessed all his sins, begged her forgiveness for any way he had let her down. He dropped in on her whenever he had a job close by delivering heating fuel to one of her neighbors. She'd had to let him in the first couple of times, had to flee her sanctuary to put an end to his nonstop pleading. "Dorothy, please," he begged, threatening to cause a scene outside her front door. "I don't want anything more than to look at you, to see that you're okay."

The door opened a crack and then hung silent, amplifying the space that had grown between them. Dottie's voice lingered at the entrance to the hallway. She insisted he come inside before the neighbors started gawking. Chester gave the door an apprehensive shove, nudging his way farther into the place he had once called home. Dottie looked placid, unmarred. An unwavering stare stood in place of bleary eyes, the bloodshot expression of a person racked with pain that Chester had been anticipating replaced by the most serene expression of acceptance.

Trajan had been startled by the same contradiction. He'd come home on occasion to find his mother's bedroom door propped open, dwindling sunlight extending down the hallway, begging a visit. She appeared calm, refreshed, composed beyond anything the present circumstances might have deemed possible. The only physical sign of turmoil brimming inside his mother was her complexion start-ing to fade, turning lighter from the lack of sun and outside air, her Native American roots peering slowly through the Georgia-baked brown of her skin, her father's deep-set eyes taking command over her mother's doting smile.

Chester followed her to the bedroom. He took a seat on the bed opposite her, his posture not overly assured, not overly timid either. He hadn't realized how badly he missed seeing her, missed being in her company. She seemed content having him there, sitting beside her, breathing the same air with her again.

She told him she had no problem with him stopping by, on two conditions: (1) he use the key she kept inside the rain gutter the next time he wanted to see her; she was in no position to leave her bedroom for anybody, least of all her ex-husband, and (2) he could visit anytime he liked, as long as he went home afterward to say where he'd been. She wasn't going to have him treat anyone as badly as he'd treated her. "Not even that low-down hussy deserves anyone so trifling." She turned to face him, locked on him with one of her stares to let him know she still had plenty resolve should he be there looking to start any sort of foolishness. That's the first inclination Chester got that Dottie was getting her wits about her. That he was again *trifling*, that Callie Ramirez was *low-down*, meant she was on the mend.

He committed to playing by her rules. Hoped, through close association with the mother of his children, to get himself on the mend too. The first part he gladly obliged. He didn't need to give the neighbors reason to gawk any more than she did. The second part he managed clumsily, the way he tended to do. He told Callie anytime he'd been there but fumbled with some made-up excuse: something at the house needed fixing; they had tax information to go over or custody papers to review. The lies he told sounded more contrived than the actual truth of the matter: He and his ex-wife needed one another. Not in any physical sense. Not tending chores around the house either. They'd lost something, that thing that was part her and part him. Even during the most tumultuous stretch of time, when she could hardly bear to look at him, they shared those two knotty-headed boys. When Langston died, they shared that too.

TOMORROW SUN

Trajan waited his whole life for whiskers to grow and hide his pock-marked skin. But whiskers had only ever made it as far as the end of his pointy chin, a few lonely strands dangling from the narrow expanse of his cratered face, their posture alone echoing a desperate need for change, sentiments mirroring his own condition. If only the rest of the world had cooperated, stood still a minute, a full day, if that could be arranged. Allowed Trajan time to regain his footing, figure what it might mean to start a day without his brother to lean on.

Aside from his green shorts and soccer jersey, everything Trajan wore was gray: light gray, medium gray, midnight gray, charcoal;

the uniform of teen angst, one Trajan had begun to wear with regimented consistency. It's as though he fell each night in a crumpled heap beside his bed, his jeans, T-shirt, and hooded sweatshirt resting until morning when he would reemerge wrapped in an equally dismal display of overlapping shades.

At fifteen, he was man of the house, a house that scarcely made a sound unless he initiated it. He'd gone from finding his brother's fascination with girls peculiar to being hardly able to contain his own budding interests. Friends he'd once considered close were wearing on him. New friends he'd made didn't fit entirely well. He wasn't left on the outside, sidelined the way his brother had been. But his brother had always been his in, had shown the way forward, sometimes by demonstrating what to do, other times by providing a painful example of what not to do.

He found himself hemmed inside a stifling quadrangle of confounding choices; he was to be a man, just not like any man he had ever known.

Don't be Mr. Day, in whose employment Trajan's mother remained even years after she found venturing outside her bedroom a task she was no longer up to doing. Appreciate the things Mr. Day continues to do for your mother, but don't be like him: too stiff an old man for her son to aspire to be.

Don't be Grandpa Tuke: too wild an old man to want to be.

Don't disrespect your father, but work not to be him either.

Be a good son, just not so good a son you eclipse your brother's legacy. Honor his memory, but don't be so much like him your mother sees nothing in your likeness outside of what she's lost. No, don't be him either.

As soon as he reached sufficient age, Trajan took a part-time job. Bunny's uncle owned a private cleaning service. Bunny followed in his brother's footsteps, helping clean after hours at the public library. Bunny invited Ben and Lighty to help as well, trading off nights with Trajan. On top of school and the many obligations the team already placed on them, Ben was averse to the notion of needing to be someplace. And Lighty couldn't imagine purposely electing to spend added time with Bunny Sessions, which left four nights a week plus weekends entirely to Trajan.

Their greatest dilemma was deciding how to subdivide the work each night. Bunny had the benefit of past experience, having worked under the table for his uncle since the age of twelve or fourteen. He and E-Z had, in the past, broken things out according to top floor/ground floor, with shared responsibility along the staircase, which seemed to Trajan more than fair. Naturally, Bunny objected, reinforcing his apparent need to remain contrary. He suggested they settle instead on a wet work/dry work division of labor, leaving him to clean the restrooms plus a windowless kitchenette where the library staff ate their lunches. Trajan had the rest of the space to work unaccompanied.

Trajan took command of a heavy plastic trash bin that he pushed around on wheels, emptying wastepaper baskets positioned at odd ends throughout the rows of metal bookshelves. He dusted the computer terminals that sat blinking in eerie unison, prompting patrons to enter their library card numbers followed by a password. He tidied the area behind the information desk. Who knew a flock of mild-mannered librarians would leave their workspace at the end of the day in such disarray? He rounded out the night by vacuuming the entire space before emptying the trash in the dumpster out back. By square footage alone, Trajan had ten times the work Bunny had to do. If you took the degree of difficulty into account, however—what with the brightwork of the sink fixtures to polish, plus the potential for various grades of accumulated filth in the toilets, not to mention the stainless steel receptacles for used feminine hygiene products—Trajan's share of responsibility was only twice as big as Bunny's.

Trajan didn't mind the work. It gave him something to do with his spare time. He especially liked the vacuuming. The vacuum was like a bloodhound, head down, sniffing out hidden grime. The low-pile textured carpet was chosen to hide visible signs of dirt. But direct the vacuum along the right path, and you were rewarded by the sound of a million loose particles finding a home deep inside the vacuum cleaner bag. The thick, push-broom fiber mat lining the entryway told a buried tale of all that had transpired in the library on any given day: who had paid a visit and in what numbers, what the weather had done outside. On sunny days, the vacuum cleaner unearthed little more than light dust picked up on the walk from the gravel parking lot. Come wintertime, Bloodhound got his fill on the sand and coarse salt left over after each snowstorm. It took two whole weeks of vacuuming the same spot before the rush of loose granules subsided. A tough stretch of winter barely left two days in between storms, keeping Trajan and his trusted sidekick on heavy patrol for months on end.

Independent Study

Retirement wasn't freeing in the way Mrs. Quigley had hoped. She missed her students, missed the daily interaction, the small surprises: witnessing some kid get it that everyone feared never would; seeing a group of disenchanted adolescents relate to the material in a way no one thought possible.

She missed Trajan. Seeing his face in the morning had once been reason alone to have a good day. She agonized over what had happened to his brother. Couldn't take another year of standing in the classroom where the possibility loomed to again suffer such miserable heartache. It alarmed her to think she had taken such interest in either of them. Unnerved her knowing the two were brothers, the blood in their veins pumping in a way that kept her heart racing. She'd met their father a couple of times: once at Langston's memorial service, and again in the principal's office standing beside the Ramirez boy. Neither encounter had presented him in the best light, though she was quite confident he could not move her the way either son had, his share of blood in their veins notwithstanding.

163

Rosalie had attempted, on the night before her wedding, the first adult conversation she'd ever had with her mother. "Mother," Rosalie had asked to the top of her mother's head as she knelt, busily re-smoothing the train of her daughter's dress to vacate her mind of bubbling nerves. "At what point should a bride get the feeling of being swept off her feet?"

"Oh, poppycock!" her mother exclaimed through the tiny collection of straight pins lodged between her teeth. "One of you is sweeping, the other is swooning. It sounds like a whole lot of fuss about nothing," she added pushing the straight pins aside with her tongue. She turned her attention to another fold in the train of her daughter's dress.

"Don't you want to see your daughter happy?" She wished to say giddy, ecstatic, over the moon, but had learned to stick to only the simplest terms when speaking with her mother about feelings of love and joy and happiness. Anything more was bound to be met with loud utterances of poppycock and other assorted complaints.

"Happy isn't all it's cracked up to be," Rosalie's mother assured her. "Put aside that fairy-tale nonsense, my love. What looks good from the outside may not be all it seems. Go for what's steady: a quiet life, a stable household, a man who will stand by you."

Gilbert Quigley was nothing if not rock steady. He had gotten on with Pratt and Whitney long before he and Rosalie were introduced, a coworker of his having dated one of her fellow teachers. He had been a dues-paying member of the Machinists Union for much of that time. He lived within miles of the house where he grew up. Still went over to cut the grass and trim the hedges once his mother became too feeble to tend the yard alone.

Gilbert and Rosalie wed as planned in a tiny chapel close to her parents' home in Willimantic, her mother seated in the first pew, Rosalie adorned head-to-toe in whatever happiness is cracked up to be. The two proceeded to build a stable life together, steady, uncomplicated. Rosalie chalked her apprehensions from the night before up to pre-wedding jitters. She'd made the right choice, the one her mother wholeheartedly approved of.

The Quigleys kept regular company over the years with like-minded couples, steady and stable in their respective set of uncomplicated concerns, giving Rosalie little cause, if any, to stray. Gilbert was a good man, a good provider, and a spirited lover when sufficiently stirred. He was handy around the house, fixing things before they broke, preferring preventative maintenance to unscheduled repair. But no amount of maintenance could heal a ravenous soul, a soul grown weary of a steady diet of incontrovertible contentment. Rosalie's mother failed to comprehend that lack of discord in a marriage doesn't necessarily equate with happiness. Romance, intrigue, a bit of the unknown—those things are the spice of life.

Mrs. Quigley stopped by the library at the start of the fall semester, told Gilbert she had research to do. Trajan had shown up early to get a head start on his homework in case the urge struck to venture out after Bunny's uncle would drop them home.

"Mr. Hopkins," Mrs. Quigley announced, appearing above the cubicle wall where he had tucked himself in, again out of context. "I must say, I'm impressed to find you at the library barely two weeks into the semester. I don't recall you being so studious."

"Just trying to stay on top of things, killing time before I have to start work."

"Work?" she asked, pretending she hadn't inquired about him, that the school secretary hadn't filled her in on his whereabouts after school when she'd stopped by the office to drop off paperwork. *The Hopkins boy,* the secretary had said. *He's managing as well as can be expected.*

Trajan mentioned that Bunny would be along any minute, waited for her to ask about him, one of her more colorful class characters. "How are you, Trajan?" she asked instead.

"I'm doing okay, Mrs. Quigley."

"And your mother, how is she getting along?" She didn't know what compelled her to ask about his mother, especially knowing, again by way of office gossip, that she was still having a tough go of it.

Trajan told her his mother was doing okay as well. It's all he knew to say. She studied his face, hoping to read something more in those shy eyes.

"Do take care of yourself," she said, anxious to get on her way.

Mischief has a way of recognizing mischief, even in its formative stages. Bunny was bound to question what she was up to, Mrs. Quigley not yet sure what had led her there in the first place.

Trajan became ever more studious in the coming weeks, heading straight to the library after practice. Mrs. Quigley found more things she needed to research.

"What hours do you work?" she asked the next time she managed to catch him alone in the stacks.

"Eight to ten after the library closes, then a couple hours on Saturday, longer if there's something special to do—shampooing the carpets, that sort of thing."

"Hmm," she replied, taking note. "And I trust you head straight home afterward, prepare for school the next day."

Most nights he went straight home. The library closed early later in the week. He went to see Carmen any night they finished before nine. Her parents sent him away otherwise. But something wouldn't permit him to tell Mrs. Quigley about Carmen just yet. "Some nights I head straight home. Other nights I hang back and mess around in town."

"Hmm," was again her answer.

She made a lucky guess on the Wednesday leading into Thanksgiving. School let out early. She supposed that the library would follow suit and close early as well. She approached the main entrance just before five o'clock. The sky had turned dark already, a crimson glow burning in the distance, the sun making its final bow for the night.

As she suspected, the sliding glass doors refused to budge. She returned to her car and took a ride around back, hoping to catch a glimpse of someone without anybody spying her. She heard a commotion as the back door sprung open. She watched Trajan wheel a garbage bin toward a huge metal dumpster. He lifted a thick plastic liner from the can, bulging on all sides with trash, and he heaved it WWF style into the dumpster before slamming the lid shut. The noise gave Mrs. Quigley a start, causing her arm to brush against the lever to her high beams, a momentary splash of light drawing Trajan's attention. He spun the can around slowly on its wheels, recognizing her but not knowing what to make of it, her car sitting alone at the back of the lot.

She cut the engine, walked toward him, stood in the light of the street lamp, preparing to plead her case. "The place shut early," she said, waving her hand in the direction of the main entrance.

"Thanksgiving," he explained. "Is there something you need?"

"Nothing that can't wait." She fell silent, surprised how far she'd come on the ridiculous notion germinated inside her head that he might share her level of interest.

Trajan had developed a knack at reading the churn of nervous energy bubbling inside a person, turmoil stirring inside silent eyes. "Give me ten minutes," he said, pointing to the far corner of the lot.

"I'll meet you over by the fence."

She returned to her car, backed into the farthest available space, and waited as instructed. He'd cut to the core of her anxieties and eased one worry but had given rise to new concerns.

Bunny exited the building first. "This was a mistake," Rosalie whispered to herself, holding her breath against the flight of butterflies fluttering inside her chest. She feared she'd been too coy, that Trajan had misunderstood her intentions, had come away with the misguided belief that the teacher in her was simply going around catching up with former pupils. Rosalie reached for the ignition. There's no way she would let Bunny Sessions catch her back here. Then, just that quick, a yellow van pulled up, Service Master written in sea-foam green on the side panel. Trajan crossed in front of the van and said something to the driver. He waited for Bunny to climb in and the van to disappear around the corner, and then he headed in the direction of Mrs. Quigley's parked car. She got out of the car when she saw him crossing the lot to join her.

"I'm glad you waited."

"I'm glad you asked me to wait," she answered, breathless, feeling like the most ridiculous teenager.

The moon was just poking its head above the treetops. "Nice night," Trajan offered.

"The sky is so clear this time of year," she said. "We'll be buried in snow in another month." Was she for real—the weather? Could she have been lamer?

He asked whether she was cold, unzipped his hooded sweatshirt, preparing to lend it to her. "Don't be silly," she said, dipping back inside her car to grab her wrap. She worried when she replayed this bit of conversation inside her head that the remark had come off as condescending. He wasn't being silly. The gesture was indeed quite sweet.

He pretended not to care, proceeding to talk about his schoolwork, the soccer season. She said she'd taken up gardening, was working to stay busy. Now she felt like a ridiculous old lady.

"This was nice," he said.

"This was nice, Trajan." She was teenaged again, not knowing what to do with her hands, where to rest her eyes to keep from staring.

He sat leaning against the hood of her car, his hands buried in his sweatshirt pockets, his gaze resting on the stars overhead. Trajan had begun to take comfort in seeing Mrs. Quigley's face around school as well. He felt a void after she retired, sought comfort in other things to ease the dread of going to school each day, knowing she wouldn't be there smiling to him in the hallway. Soccer quickly proved to be his only outlet. However, seeing her again this way, standing next to her in the darkness, seemed about more than comfort. He sensed her nervousness to be there. He had found the extra attention she paid him in the classroom embarrassing at times, carried out in front of all the other kids. Though, sitting alone with her in the parking lot that evening, the realization taking hold that she had gone out of her way to see him tugged at him in new ways.

Within minutes she was back inside her car. He told her he was okay when she offered to give him a ride someplace. He suggested she come see him again sometime. "We're here till ten, Monday through Wednesday; seven or eight the rest of the week."

She indicated she just might. He hoped that she would.

Lessons on Flying

She showed up the next week on a Thursday. She waited for him to wheel the garbage to the dumpster, flashed her lights at him as he maneuvered the can toward the back entrance. She showed up the Thursday after that as well, convincing herself each time that she was there to look in on him, to make certain he was doing okay. They sat studying the night sky, watching their breath float away in a stream of frosted air. She speculated on the possibility of an especially long winter. He hoped her internal almanac was off. He was not looking forward to sliding across frozen turf in soccer shorts once practice resumed.

171

A cold December quelled their impromptu parking lot visits. Trajan continued showing up on Carmen's doorstep, being let in more often than not, provided he was mindful of the hour. Mrs. Quigley kept to her side of town, waiting for crocuses to bloom, for her tulip buds to push their way through a covering of moist earth, for her garden to thaw from its long winter depression. Gilbert had begun the slow march into retirement as well. He spent his days tinkering in the garage. He lazed the weekends away, watching football through half-closed eyelids. She would peek in on him from time to time. "Is there anything I can get you, my love?" she'd ask from the passageway leading back into the kitchen. "Thank you, dear. I'm fine." She'd give him a little smile, letting him get back to the game on TV—steady.

She showed up at the library again in early spring, her prolonged separation from Trajan having sharpened her interest in him. She signaled to him from the back of the lot, her headlights blinking vague intentions of what she hoped would develop between them. They adopted a familiar posture, resting against the hood of her car. Her hand brushed against his hand, then his brushed hers. With time, they let their hands linger, one resting on top of the other. She found that leaning next to him against the car hood and looking into the darkness suppressed her tendency to stare, quieted the urge to fill the silence with awkward conversation. She eventually slid her fingers in between his, figuring it would be all right for the two of them to hold hands.

She wanted to know what he was planning to do once he

graduated, the educator in her recognizing that preparation for college starts well before a student reaches senior year. Trajan hadn't given it any thought. Graduation seemed for him too far away, life after high school a fantasy that he might never get to see. His brother, for all practical purposes, never made it beyond his school years. Rosalie was careful not to push. Offered to help him weigh his options once he reached the point of thinking about it. He admired her determination, the care she continued to show for him from the quiet confines of retirement. Inside his head he defended their time together, trivialized their dilemma, electing consciously to set aside what they appeared to have been conspiring to do. She became his confidante, his guidance counselor, his best friend. If only she played soccer.

He thought to teach her to skateboard. She was fairly certain, having with her last couple of birthdays rounded the bend toward fifty, that now was not the time to take up skateboarding. She submitted in the end, appreciating his attempt to make her part of his world. She wrapped her arms around his as he rolled her in slow circles across the parking lot. The wheels beneath her feet made her feel light and graceful with him in a way she had never felt with any man. She imagined them dancing, twinkling starlight decorating the ceiling of an impromptu ballroom setup, shimmering accents winking their approval from the far end of the galaxy.

Standing atop Trajan's skateboard, she was nearly as tall as him. Her backside pressed into his midsection each time they made a turn; her full weight leaned against him, looking for balance. Their final pass took a precarious downhill slope along the back fence to the place where she'd parked her car. She shrieked as the wind set her hair loose, untamed locks spinning away from her in a blaze of spiraling curls. She let him kiss her cheek as he brought the board to a halt, her feet once again planted against the consistent sway of solid ground.

He leaned her against the car hood again as they prepared to say their good-byes, pressed his body into hers. She thought about making love to him. Let the thought for the first time creep to its fully articulated form, lavish fantasy building inside her head. Oh, she just couldn't. Knew that if she started, she would never be able to will herself to stop.

In the end, she let her calmer self prevail. Lifted a thousand reasons not to into the sky and examined them against the pattern of twinkling starlight. She placed a hand against his chest, pried herself apart from him. She assured him they would find a way in time to explore their feelings toward one another, but this was not the place. She drove home, as tormented by the things she hadn't done as she was by all she had already compromised: her marriage, her principles, her professional integrity. Still, she felt like flying, rolled down all the windows in her car to feel the rush of wind in her hair, to test the feel of what might have been before pushing those thoughts back inside her head.

She returned to an empty house. Gilbert would be gone another hour or more. She was torn—grateful for the time alone to compose herself, to get her head out of the wind, but all the more troubled by what had compelled her to stray in the first place. She sensed those feelings had grown, that resisting the urges she felt would require a level of restraint she no longer possessed.

On the Differences Between Women and Men

Tuke had spent enough years living that it took someone he had come to trust without condition to outwit him, to get him to speak to them about something bordering on their genuine concern. Trajan had known his grandpa long enough to recognize that the conversation needed to start out sidelong in order to get Tuke talking in the first place.

"Tell me about women," Trajan asked, working to keep his pole still above the water the next time he found himself lakeside with Grandpa Tuke. He meant to say *girls*.

"They're the opposite of men—talk different, think different, act different. They look and smell different, too, provided you're reasonably choosy about the kind of women you elect to spend your time with." He turned his attention from his appointed spot along the horizon. "We talkin' hypotheticals or an actual situation you're dealing with?"

"What difference does it make?" Trajan asked, puzzled, his teenage understanding small in comparison to the grown-up predicament on his hands.

"If we're talking hypotheticals, then I'll advise you not to get pregnant and to come back when you have an actual situation on your hands."

"I know how not to get pregnant—how to keep from getting a girl pregnant," he assured his grandpa.

"Used to be that's all there was to it. There's stuff out there nowadays that'll kill you," Tuke offered. "Getting the wrong girl pregnant still might get you killed, depending on her daddy's temperament. Don't get pregnant, and don't get yourself killed either," he told his grandson. "So tell me again. Are we talking real or hypothetical?"

Trajan knew better than to stray too widely from the truth. He had inherited his ability to read people directly from Grandpa Tuke, the line between them passing through Dottie as well. "Hypothetical with potential to turn real."

"Okay," Tuke responded, mugging in cautious disbelief. Many a young man has thought the situation was in the bag, only to find quite the opposite in play from his partner's perspective. He asked Trajan what he wanted to know.

"Everything," Trajan beamed.

"That could take awhile. Your grandpa talks slow, plus there's so much to tell."

"How do you know when the time is right?"

"Seldom does a man have to guess when a woman is ready. They have a way of making their desires known, but you have to pay particular attention to know what a woman wants from you." Tuke shared Dottie's interest in molding Trajan into a certain kind of man, respect for the people in his life paramount. "And don't go in there misinformed," Tuke proceeded to explain, making certain his grandson grasped the delicacy of the matter at hand. "If you're not sure, ask. Don't go bullying anybody. There's plenty of time ahead for you to feel the need to press the situation."

Tuke tried to recall when last he'd been in the company of a woman he truly enjoyed, when last he'd seen Dottie's mother smile, when last he'd made her feel like smiling. Plenty of widows around Preston had their sights set on him; they pictured the handiwork he might do behind closed doors to rival the wonders he'd done trimming their hedges, clearing dead branches from their backyards. Mrs. Krantz believed she had a grandniece who would be perfect for him. Tuke was content to continue missing his dead wife, Estelle. His eyes went soft with the thought of her. He thanked Mrs. Krantz for thinking of him. But no, he didn't wish to meet her grandniece. She told him to suit himself. *Henh!*

Trajan needn't look further than Dottie and Chester to comprehend the differences between the sexes. Both had stayed to a point, coped with their struggles, made do. Each gave way, in the end, to shared pain. Perpetually perturbed, Trajan's father let his internal demons boil over, erupt to the surface every so often. His mother went invisible, battled her demons from the safety of her plastic bubble, her struggles on display for the whole world to see.

Trajan should have asked Tuke about the difference between women and girls: the first pulling at him—Rosalie willing something to occur between the two of them—the other raising her defenses anytime he came close to her, Carmen's Catholic upbringing escalating the dilemma crowding his mind. He decided to heed Tuke's advice to take his time, stop pressing either situation.

The first boy Angelica slept with reminded her of Langston: same height and build, similar coloration, though his brown skin was patchy in spots, as if he'd gone out in the sun thinking he wouldn't burn, then rushed back inside fearing he might. Now his skin refused to flake off the way it would had he allowed it a full, proper burn. The vague resemblance was largely the reason she'd gone through with it, patchy skin and all. That, plus her roommate, Susie, had been pushing her to get out there, to enjoy her college years. To live a little.

Gargoyles

Princeton could have been handpicked for Angelica; its lush expanse of green centered in the New Jersey countryside provided subtle reminders of Preston, her thoughts never far from home. Her welcome package told her to bring extra socks; the clothes dryers supplied free of charge in every dormitory ate socks. She was to leave the rest of her worries at home; she'd made the best possible decision she was ever going to make. These, after all, promised to be the best days of her life.

The Princeton campus is cut from another place and time; every quadrangle, every lecture hall, every dormitory is erected in rock and hard stone, from its stout foundation to the variegated coloration of its ancient slate roof, as if the founders had envisioned the university standing to serve mankind for all eternity. Humongous gargoyles protect the campus, perched at every angle along heavy buttresses. They are said to feed on the socks that go missing in the clothes dryers.

Angelica had visited Yale, Amherst, and Cambridge. Each had that Old World feel—the way a college campus ought to feel, according to Angelica—hallowed halls appropriate in scale to the vast knowledge that institutions of higher learning are meant to impart. But she found each lacking for one reason or another: most notably, that none of those schools was Princeton. There was no waffling once Angelica made up her mind about something.

She had been to New Haven countless times. Yale was woven into the fabric of the city the way noodles mixed with the sauce in her grandfather's lo mein. Angelica was many things; a city girl she was not. Amherst was never a serious consideration, the trip a concession to appease her grandma who had seen a TV ad: *Amherst—where life begins*. One college was like any other as far as Gam was concerned. Why not pick one closer to home?

Angelica's father drove her to visit Cambridge, home to half a dozen colleges and universities all crammed together. It was as though someone had taken cardboard cutouts of each school's campus map and stapled them on top of one another, never bothering to consider that a single mashed-together place had no chance of appealing simultaneously to the diverse interests of prospective students looking to get into Harvard, MIT, and Boston University. Plus she'd never master that accent—*paark yer caar in the garaage*.

Buttercup

Susie's family operated an agrarian food co-op in Burlington, Vermont. *Food from Here* was their motto. She and Angelica became roommates the year after Langston died. All Susie knew is that Angelica had suffered some tragedy. That somebody close to her back home had passed away; a grandparent, she figured, having reached the season in life when grandparents died. She committed herself to helping Angelica get past the loss, to move on.

Susie Lindstrom was a wild child. She claimed to have come to Princeton for two things: to earn a degree and to lose any virtue she still held in the process. Susie must have arrived with lots of virtue to spare at the rate she was using it up, though she remained on track to graduate in another three semesters.

181

"How are we going to celebrate your birthday, Begonia?" Susie asked. Angelica generally became some kind of flower whenever Susie was feeling chummy—daisy, daffodil, honeysuckle. Must be a Vermont thing.

"I tend not to make a big deal out of my birthday," Angelica replied. "Usually a family dinner before it gets busy in the restaurant, then cake and ice cream to cap off the night."

"I'm your family at Princeton, Buttercup," Susie exclaimed, plopping her gangly frame down on the bed beside Angelica. "The big two-oh. Still no drinky for you, but we at least have to get you laid."

Angelica's face went funny. She wasn't accustomed to such open familiarity between girlfriends, especially concerning the prospect of sex with a boy, something to which she'd given ample thought over the years but that she had never had occasion to see all the way through. "No thanks," she responded, hoping to push her roommate onto other topics.

"I offer you sex and you tell me no thanks," Susie replied, pretending to be offended.

Angelica's cheeks reddened. "Hold on a hot second," Susie probed. "You don't mean to tell me you're a virgi-gi-gahhh . . ." She convulsed on the word. She leaned back on her pointy elbows and stared at Angelica quizzically, as if she'd never before considered the possibility that a twenty-year-old virgin might still exist. To her, virginity was something everybody suffered through, like chicken pox, an affliction that Angelica would have done best to rid herself

182

of before coming to college. "We're going to have to do something about that quick, fast, in a hurry," Susie proclaimed, a declaration of war on Angelica's virginity.

Drop Day

A year into her college experience, the glitz of Princeton had begun to lose its appeal. Everyone there was largely the same, a hundred Angelica Chus any place you looked: impeccable high school records, stellar test scores, their entire lives spent working to remain at the top of every endeavor. The student population belonged to the same one or two upper rungs of the socioeconomic ladder, diverse only in the means by which their families had gained privilege. Angelica found Susie more or less normal, the product, like her, of a working family business. Now in her sophomore year, perhaps it was time for Angelica to give up some of her virtue, to shed her innocence.

Susie began scheming, targeting the drop day party on the Friday after next to set her plan into motion. Drop day was the last day in the semester to withdraw from any classes in which you were struggling or that you otherwise didn't wish to keep without impacting your GPA. It was a day celebrated each semester with wild cavorting and binge drinking, though not necessarily in that order.

Against her better judgment, Angelica agreed to let Susie fix her up, which in Susie's mind meant that she needed to dress Angelica as well. According to her, only a small handful of styles are deemed suitable for an on-campus affair. Goth seemed a bit cliché, given the surroundings rife with medieval architecture. Besides, Angelica didn't understand kids who pretended to be perpetually depressed—surrounded by people who, like her, had experienced genuine distress yet still managed to come off unaffected. The preppy look had enjoyed a revival of sorts, regaining a foothold among a small segment of the student population. Then there were the dweebs. Every movement, fashion or otherwise, needs an active counterculture to legitimize its purpose. The dweebs had perfected an ornately colorful nerd look in rebellion against the host of campus clichés. Langston, with his simple twill jeans and close-fitting short-sleeve T-shirts, would have found the lot of them ridiculous. He urged Angelica to remain true to herself, no matter how far she went in the world.

Susie opted for the glam look: old Hollywood, not blood-sucking, playing up her long legs and plentiful bosom. She and Angelica left their dorm room made over like a pair of proper tarts. The tight black dress borrowed from Susie's side of the room was a bit too snug for Angelica's taste, revealing parts of her she didn't necessarily wish to have show, putting her virtue on full display. Albert would be mortified. Susie wore something equally daring in red, a pair of formed cups sewn into the bodice to draw extra attention to the bouncy bits up top.

Susie entered the party as though launched by a plunger inside a pinball machine, planting her hiked up little booty on any lap that would have her, the business end of her skirt aimed—for added points, it would seem—in the direction of anyone willing to venture a gander. *Please tell me you have on underwear, Suze.*

Angelica struggled to match her roommate's enthusiasm. The music was awful, the sound of scared cats being pushed from high places. The crowd seemed reckless, celebrating the end of the world as opposed to the start of a period of accountability as the semester crested its critical midway point, a line across which there was no turning back.

Susie soon vanished, tiny bursts of merrymaking bubbling over the crowd as she made her way, like baskets of clean clothes flying sporadically above a mountain of dirty laundry. She eventually turned up again with a couple of above-average-looking somebodies in tow. The first Angelica recognized as Susie's latest conquest. The other bugged her eyes, her startled breathing limiting her capacity for clear thought: chestnut skin, nicely contoured chest and arms, deep-set eyes. Susie had gone fishing in the pool of lost possibilities and unearthed Angelica's one true love, a cartoon crayon cutout of Langston, reanimated from Suzie's apparent careful account of the one non-family photo Angelica had hung on the bulletin board above her desk. Susie evidently had so many men to spare that she could conjure one, lifted from the darkest vagaries. *You conniving little tramp.*

Who was Angelica to throw stones? After a few minutes of talking and a quick turn dancing to an endless frightened cat medley,

185

surrounded by hordes of her fellow honor students dressed as preps and goths and dweebs, she left the party with the one Susie called Todd, a boy she had only just met. Invited him into her bed for no better reason than that he sort of reminded her of the boy she used to know back home. Plus, it was her birthday, and she needed him, wanted him there.

She insisted they leave the lights off, pretending to be shy. That night, while Susie continued her exploits across campus, Angelica lay in the darkness and made love to Langston for the first time. Pressed herself inside his arms as he maneuvered along the tender flesh of her thighs, her body pulling to have him full inside her. Todd squeezed his eyes shut like he was embarking on a death ride as he pushed past the remaining bit of Angelica's virtue, releasing a primordial moan from the depths of her fourteen-year-old self who'd been left alone on the living room sofa with Langston, his hands wandering unchecked beneath loose-fitting summer clothing.

Just as things started to heat up, Todd began moving with all the finesse of a startled Chihuahua yapping in the face of danger from the safety of a closed screen door. He couldn't begin to comprehend the wealth of the kingdom to which he'd just been handed keys, the expectations she had heaped on him by coincidence of his lookalike status. He leaned in, seeming to find his rhythm, pushing, writhing, his face screwed in a concentrated little knot. He maintained an even pace for a full half second before the whole of his body tensed and the death ride was over. She imagined the first time was like that for most people: not at all how she'd imagined.

Then there was the aftermath to contend with. Susie had helped outfit her bed with fresh linen. Stocked her desk drawer with a three-pack of condoms, giving her that *seriously, you'd better use them* look as she slid the drawer closed. But Susie hadn't told her what to do with the boy afterward. How to get him to leave?

He'd barely said two words when they were introduced. *Hey, my name is Todd. I believe a frat brother of mine is screwing your roommate, Susie.* He didn't say the last bit out loud, of course. Had he said it, Angelica would have been obliged to inform him that his frat brother was but one of many her roommate was screwing.

Now the guy wouldn't quit talking. "What part of Connecticut are you from? Preston, you said?" He didn't think he had been there. She was happy to think he hadn't. What did her parents do? Why were her cheeks so flushed? She needn't be embarrassed.

"They just get that way," she said, assuring him she wasn't the least embarrassed.

So why'd she dye her hair that way, with those blonde streaks sprinkled in? "It's not off-putting, just a touch unusual." It's not hair dye, numbskull. That was his exit sign. *Time for you to go, buddy.*

She headed straight for the shower. Wanted to rinse herself of his smell. Not a bad smell. Just not the smell she'd been longing for, the air of youth and trust and shared familiarity. The smell she'd known

187

her whole life. She turned her attention to changing the sheets, turning her room back in time to the point before she'd let him in. She nicknamed him Nangston as she made a crease in the bedspread with the palm of her hand. *Not Langston. Never could be Langston.* She should have insisted he come visit. Ride the train with her that first day to Princeton, help her get settled.

Angelica was a blubbering mess against her pillow by the time her roommate returned. "Oh, Petunia!" Susie wailed. "Your first time can stir all sorts of odd feelings. Everything's gonna be okay." She rubbed Angelica's back with one hand, her other hand lost in the blonde-flecked mane of her hair. Susie could name every wildflower to bloom along the eastern seaboard, but she couldn't comprehend the chain of emotions that left Angelica lying in a crumpled heap across her bed, thoughts of making love to Langston spoiled by the chirping shrill of a Chihuahua yapping. Susie was Nangston too.

Human Endeavor

It was tragic irony that Angelica would also have been Langston's first had he been there, had he taken the ride to Princeton. Stepped onto the train platform to greet her, the burden of any baggage from home resting miles away: the rift between families, limitations placed on their time together, the final breakup that at the time had seemed so inevitable.

Langston had kept the same dark little secret: that he too was a virgi-gi-gahhh. That he'd never been with a girl. Tasha Davies had taught him to kiss properly, their lips returning to a full close periodically to keep their mutual slobbering under control. She pressed him against the cool metal surface of his locker door on her way to track practice one afternoon. Leaned into him, her hips leading the way until their thighs interlocked—one of hers between his, one of his between hers—to enhance the sensation of lying together, her tiny track shorts requiring little imagination on his part to picture her naked against him. The next week the Fugees broke up. By the same time the following spring, she and Incredible were an item, the muscle on skates enjoying his share of time spent pressed between Tasha's bare thighs.

Angelica had lifted her shirt for him one time. She bet him that the color of her nipples was the same as the back of his hand, their skin tone designer matched. She slipped a shoulder free from its strap, let the cup of her white padded bra fall forward. Langston pressed an anxious palm against the bright mound of her flesh, confirmed the color match with gleaming eyes. He wanted to take her nipple in his mouth as it grew hard with swelling interest, but he eased the idea back inside his head, conscious the whole while of his brother a short distance down the hallway, the muffled sounds of Super Mario attempting repeated leaps and bounds filtering in from their bedroom.

Angelica returned her breast to its cup, slipped the strap over her shoulder again. Pulled her shirt down before Trajan could come barging in, wondering what they had gotten up to. The next time they found enough time alone to attempt the move, his tongue poised to take her inside his mouth, Langston's eyes went wild and the clucking started, signaling the beginning of the first seizure he suffered in front of her.

Langston continued with the same hit-then-miss pattern of success with the fairer sex straight through to the end. When the timing was right—a girl with access to her mother's car or a living room sofa free from his little brother's prying eyes, if not enraged threats from her bigger brother—the fear of another attack would put him off the idea. The one time he'd attempted to go through with it, his equipment wouldn't cooperate. It stared limply at him like it wanted no part in the affair. The doctor warned that the medication he prescribed would diminish hormonal activity. He asked Langston's mother whether he was sexually active. "Lord, I hope not," she replied, dooming a normal sex life for her son before it got under way.

He began pocketing the pills his mother set out on the kitchen counter, stashed his alert bracelet in the top dresser drawer he shared with Trajan. Those things made him different, gave kids reason to label him strange. Gave girls reason to want to give him the slip, to play him, to send him in search of an invisible rave party that never would materialize. If he had his life to live over again, had he known that this would be his last endeavor, he wouldn't have tried so hard, reaching for something he didn't especially covet. He would have gone off in search of Angelica instead. He would have found her, would have spent his last moments on earth wondering how he had coped this long without her, why he had let her go in the first place.

SURROGATES

It is said man's survival is predicated on his ability to adapt to his environment. A group of boys with loose affiliation to their fathers augment one another's means to adapt. They share with one another all that they know. The lesser their collective experience, the more bound they are to heed one another's advice.

Infighting

"Hey, Trajan," Ben asked, "you and Carmen done the dirty deed yet?" Similar conversations had begun sprouting inside Carmen's circle of friends, kids in their middle teens anxious to see something happen in their lives, by vicarious association, if that's all they could muster.

"Carmen's a good Catholic girl," Trajan explained. "She says it's best we wait."

His fascination with Carmen Padilla was starting to fade, the time spent on her parents' sofa amounting to an endless procession in the same misguided two-step. He liked her, but not how Langston had liked Angelica—longed for her. He also gathered that Carmen didn't long for him the way Angelica had longed for his brother. But his need of a reason to leave the house, to cross the bridge each night and get away from Preston, kept him coming back.

"Those Catholic girls are the ones to have," Bunny said, adding his two cents. "They're taught the price of sin and forbidden fruit from their first days of catechism. They can't wait to put all that knowledge to practical use."

"What you boys need is an older woman," Ben added authoritatively. Kelly Bergen, a senior cheerleader, had waved her pom-poms at him a few times. Began using him to make her boyfriend jealous. Luke Farrow lettered in three sports, jock sports—football, baseball, basketball—leaving soccer to fruits like Ben Carlsson. Fruit or not, girls dug the hair, the cocky attitude, the air he projected that he could take or leave them. Truth be told, Kelly Bergen could take or leave him, too, her primary interest to jolt Luke's attention back in line before their high school years ran out, the threat of separate colleges already placing a strain on their relationship. That didn't diminish Ben's claim to knowledge regarding an older woman, a senior cheerleader of all things.

"I'm with you," Bunny said. "The new math teacher, Ms. Jenkins—she could get it all night." He closed his eyes on the thought and made small motions with his hands, fondling something inside his mind.

Trajan's throat tightened, choked on the loose prospect of what Bunny might know, might have gathered from some tiny shift in his behavior, the most subtle misstep.

"Earth to Bunny," Ben said, calling him back from his daydream. "Nobody said anything about a teacher. You need to think more practically. Someone within reach."

"Like an older cousin or something?" Bunny asked.

Lighty flew into him. "You're the only sick bastard who would stoop so low as to mess with his own cousin. Your kids are going to come out even more retarded than you, the whole family riding the short bus like a minivan." Lighty had little use for Bunny, didn't understand why he was around all the time, seeing how he didn't play soccer, wasn't part of the team.

Trajan felt a sense of obligation to Bunny. Bunny had brought Trajan his lunch to him the first week he was back at school after his brother died, wanted to spare him the spectacle of crossing the cafeteria and standing in the serving line, the whole school waiting for him to come apart. The gesture instead left Trajan to sit alone, the whole school wondering when he was going to come out of his corner.

Trajan came to Bunny's rescue. "He's got a point, Bunny. Your cousin isn't bad, but she's no Brenda Lighty." Trajan smacked his lips and rubbed his hands together, preparing to feast. "Now that's a tasty little morsel."

"Get off my sister, Trajan," Lighty warned.

"You're right," Trajan said. "It's time to get off your sister and give your mother a turn." He gyrated in Lighty's direction, taunting him further with an exaggerated twirl of his hips.

"Trajan, I'm warning you."

"Warning me what?" Trajan asked. "If I'm not careful, you're gonna sit your punk ass over there and not do a damn thing." He poked further. "What time is your moms picking us up? We have a game in the morning, and I can't afford to have her keep me up all night."

Lighty was on Trajan before he could finish getting the words out of his mouth. Trajan was up to the task, catching Lighty by the waist as he barreled into him, the two of them sent sprawling bowling-ball style onto the practice field. They each landed a couple clean blows before Ben and Bunny managed to separate them.

Lighty's sister had begun her freshman year at NFA that fall, two years behind BLT. Brenda was a cute kid, her pudgy cheeks still full with middle school freshness. She had a little crush on Trajan, which irked Lighty to no end. She'd picked up the notion that prox-imity to her brother somehow spelled proximity to her too. Brenda was flour and water, papier-mâché, fresh clay. She liked the little whiskers sprouting from Trajan's chin, the tangle of coarse hairs resting above his top lip. Hair on his face made him a man in her eyes. Trajan could have had his way with her, had that been his aim, but after two years playing together, Lighty had to recognize that Trajan would never do anything to harm his little sister. Bunny was a different story.

But something more was fueling their animosity toward one another. Trajan had invited Lighty to accompany him to Carmen's best friend's birthday party. Maria Santos and Carmen had grown up in one another's company like Bunny and Trajan. Carmen had other friends around school, other activities, other interests, but Maria was her mainstay, her *amiguita*—her neighborhood best friend. Neither Maria nor Carmen had any use for Bunny. He could be crude when he wanted, infantile any other time. But Trajan needed a wingman, someone to take the heat off of him under the full weight of Carmen's parents' scrutiny. (He should have invited Grandpa Tuke, had he taken the legend of his courtship of their grandmother into account.)

Maria suggested he bring Lighty. *Really—freckle-faced, russet-headed, Huck Finn Lighty?* Trajan wouldn't have thought it.

Lighty balked at the invitation. Trajan understood his apprehension. Their parties could be loud, tons of people he didn't know jabbering past him in Spanish like he was part of the wall. Music, dancing, food he didn't recognize. Trajan would help him through it. He had been there himself.

"I'm telling you, man. I think she likes you," Trajan said, leaning a shoulder into him.

"Sorry, Trajan. You need to ask somebody else."

"What's the problem, bro?"

"There's no problem. I just don't think she's right for me."

"What's to think about?" Trajan continued to probe. "A brown-eyed bombshell is down for you. All you need to do is show up."

"It's just that, you know, her family's from Puerto Rico."

The words struck Trajan high in his chest, knocked the wind out of him.

"Meaning she's not snow white. I get it," Trajan confirmed, shrugging off the insult as a stubborn chill settled in between them.

"I didn't mean it like that," Lighty argued.

"I understand how you meant it," Trajan replied, ending the conversation between them.

Moo Duk-Chung-Soo

Langston would have asked what technique his brother had used against Lighty—Moo Duk Kwan, Chung Do Kwan, Tang Soo Do? Trajan didn't speak that, had never paid attention to the mumbo jumbo Langston and his father used to spout. He used the tried-and-true style of swinging like a wild man, trying to hit him more than he's hitting you.

Look at your eye, his brother would have remarked, shaking his head. *How many times do I have to tell you? Keep your left up. Guard your chin.*

Mrs. Quigley wanted to know what business he had fighting. "I thought you boys were friends. I don't want to hear any more about you fighting, ruining that beautiful smile."

She usually refrained from being so direct. She'd compliment the shirt he was wearing, the belt buckle he'd inherited from his brother's dresser drawer, a buffalo nickel hammered to the size of a fist. It had been an early birthday gift Angelica had stopped by the bakeshop to deliver to Langston before leaving for Princeton. Trajan had begun wearing it in his brother's place to make himself feel less alone, less disconnected in the world.

Pops

Trajan and his friends' reach as surrogate fathers to one another had definitive limits. Each had his finite pool of knowledge to pull from, his set of family circumstances. Each had his father alone to emulate. Trajan and Langston's father had left; Ben's had stayed. Lighty's father may as well have been gone. The same might have been said of Mathieu Sessions. Trajan's father attended one match midway into their junior year, BLT having been named starters. Callie Ramirez had pushed Chester to go in an effort to fill the void in his life, to close the gap between him and the son he had left. Lighty's father worked as a house painter. He remarked at every turn how he *earned* his living, seeming to suggest the rest of the world had in one way or another been granted a pass.

Bill Lighty was the kind of dad who put food on the table, a roof over his wife and kids' heads, clothes on their backs, then spent the rest of the evening draped across his favorite lounge chair, the TV remote glued to the palm of his paint-stained hand. He would have paid attention to his son's soccer games had they been broadcast during commercial breaks of the televised games of his beloved Celtics or Red Sox or Bruins. Happiness in the Lighty household revolved around who had raised a banner that year, clinched a series, or lifted the Stanley Cup over their heads.

Mathieu Sessions—fisherman, father, full-time welder, minor league ball player. He left the house for a few months around the time Bunny and E-Z might have begun playing sports: peewee football, youth soccer, Little League. He sat at the helm, raising a family of disenchanted youth stomping the dream dead inside him that either boy would follow in his footsteps. He exhibited what Dottie described as a yo-yo mentality given the tendency around the neighborhood for his temperament to shift rail-to-rail. When he was up, there was a good time to be had anywhere within reach of the sound of his voice. When he was down, the boys did their best to remain out of earshot.

He'd venture out to the kitchen shortly after the boys returned from school, preparing to make the second shift at Electric Boat. When in the mood, his yo-yo at the top of its string, he'd bet them in silly trivia games: How many steps to the top of the Empire State Building? What is the longest suspension bridge ever erected in the US? He dazzled them with the knowledge he'd gained building submarines, lives depending on every weld he made.

"Do you boys know how a submarine dives?" he asked, pantomiming the move with a forearm trailing the path of his clenched fist. They shook their heads, waiting to be handed the secret he alone held, dangling it like bait in front of them. "It opens a hole on either side of its hull and sinks itself on purpose, taking on water a tiny bit at a time."

They had each been on a field trip to the sub base in Groton to watch a newly commissioned submarine heading out to sea, the crew assembled along the deck, saluting to them as they slipped past heading for deep water. The boys swooned at the prospect of filling the hull with water from the ocean. A break in either ballast tank and the sub was sure to sink, drowning everyone on board. If a seal were to stick, failing to release the full measure of water it had swallowed, the sub would never resurface, the entire crew left to perish at the bottom of the sea.

Tuke had played pops to Chester for ten-plus years, longer if you consider that Tuke hadn't taken Chester and Dottie's breakup personally. Chester ran across his father in-law every now and again walking a pattern of straight lines in someone's side yard, his push mower stretched out ahead of him, his silver ponytail dangling from the back of a large straw hat he wore to keep the sun off his face. The thought occurred to stop and help the old man, abandon his route for the day and volunteer his services as assistant yardman. But Tuke was a proud old man, bound to take any offer of help as insulting. Chester had learned above all else to respect Tuke's physical abilities.

He eventually passed one day just in time to catch Tuke packing up his gear, the Willis's lawn resting in his wake, perfectly manicured. Chester was out of his truck crouching, helping lift the mower into the back of Tuke's station wagon before either man could take time to reflect on the gesture, to determine whether its intent had been overly gratuitous.

"You do nice work," Chester offered, eyeing the lawn from the curbside as Tuke latched the tailgate. "I should have you out to my place sometime."

"I would think a man like you was capable of cutting his own grass," Tuke responded, indicating the unsolicited help had been gratuitous.

"Look, you want to go someplace and get a drink?" Chester asked. The two hadn't sat and talked about anything of any consequence since Chester moved out of Tuke's daughter's house. Tuke said he wasn't accustomed to drinking midday, especially seeing how he had two more yards to hit. But he knew another place.

Charlene's diner sits just a bit up the road in Jewett City. Tucked in among a stretch of former private residences, the dining hall still has the look of someone's living room emptied of all its furniture to make way for tables and chairs, the kitchen expanded to accommodate added volume in food preparation. Tuke found Charlene hospitable enough, plus she made a mean mixed berry pie—blueberry, raspberry, blackberry. It was not unusual for Tuke to visit two, sometimes three times a month, usually on a Thursday, the week winding down yet still ahead of the weekend rush. Tuke ordered the mixed berry with ice cream and a tall glass of ice water, the July heat testing his stamina. Chester had apple, plain, with coffee.

"This is odd, wouldn't you say?" Tuke began, skipping any pretense of small talk.

"What's odd about a man wanting to speak with his father in-law?" Chester responded, wondering whether he could still consider the two of them as in-laws. Tuke shrugged a response, unsure as well how to characterize their relationship.

"So tell me what's troubling you," he offered, preparing for a barrage of questions concerning Dorothy, about how she was getting along, having shut herself off from the world. He had no way of knowing Chester had been by to see Dottie the other day, sat in her room and did the crossword puzzle with her, just like old times, Chester taking care not to give away anything Tuke might not know already.

"Trajan has been on my mind of late," Chester admitted.

"There's nothing wrong with Trajan. The two of us had dinner the other night—foot-long hot dogs on the way from Ocean Beach with hand-packed milkshakes, hunks of fresh strawberry clogging the straw." Tuke wished he hadn't been so liberal with details that might stir Chester's insecurities concerning rapport between his one remaining son and somebody else, even if that somebody was his son's granddad.

"I'm worried about him and me," Chester confided. "We hardly talk these days."

"That can't be entirely Trajan's doing. Give the boy a call."

Chester played with his fork, pushing the last bit of piecrust around the plate. "And say what?"

"Say you've been thinking about him. You're his father. The two of you ought to talk every once in a blue moon."

Chester had always admired Tuke's frankness, the way he had of telling it like it is, as only an old man can do. "There's no time for beating around the bush," Tuke said when Chester came to ask for Dottie's hand in marriage. He said something similar when he learned Chester was leaving. "You've got your hat; don't forget your coat."

Tuke had tamed some since then. Told Chester to go see his son. "I'm sure he's thinking about you too," he offered. "Now pay for my pie, and don't be stingy with the tip. I have a reputation to uphold around here." Tuke hopped back in his station wagon and set off for Preston, those last two lawns not likely to cut themselves.

A rut in a marriage is like a sinkhole pulling at the foundation, threatening to collapse the entire structure one day. Mrs. Quigley was ashamed of her behavior, but she took solace in knowing that she had survived any urge she felt toward a student in her charge. There had been other boys in her classroom. Some she found smart, charming, ambitious. But none was like Langston. Then none was like Trajan. She generally discovered resting at the base of every young man's ambition a certain cockiness, some latent insecurity that undermined however smart or charming he might have been. She saw nothing of the sort in Langston. He exuded confidence even in his wounded, altered state. Trajan exhibited more of an understated self-awareness. It required careful study to recognize his ambition. Part of it he'd inherited through close affiliation with his brother, having observed Langston's brand of cool put to good effect over the years. The rest he acquired through osmosis, filling in the cracks that Langston's ambition refused to reach. Life for Trajan became an endless string of measured endurances, periods of time spent waiting for things that he wished to have happen.

Trajan loved to run. The team practiced weekdays unless they had a makeup game. Soccer provided an unparalleled escape. The chalk lines and the matching team jerseys put Trajan's running into context for anyone observing from a distance, kept his incessant motion from appearing mindless. He had to endure a full day in the classroom before being set free on the field, that lush patch of green calling to him, its whisper growing more persistent as the hours droned on. Saturday was game day, weather permitting. Friday nights Trajan tagged along with Grandpa Tuke to his part-time job sweeping up cigarette butts and emptying ash cans at the casino.

Thursday was bowling night. Not that Trajan bowled. Gilbert Quigley bowled, leaving Trajan an entire evening in the company of his wife, Trajan's former fifth-period teacher.

Trajan wanted to know her maiden name, wondered who she might have been before she became his fifth-period teacher. Talbot, she told him. Before she married, her name was Rosalie Anne Talbot.

He asked what they considered themselves doing, as if he'd

played no part in their getting here, had just woken up knee-deep in their dilemma.

"I don't especially care to think when I'm with you," she finally admitted, her chin set on the impracticality of her position. "I've spent my entire lifetime thinking, always making the proper choice. With you, I want to feel, to live for a change."

"What about . . . you know." Trajan wanted to know his name too.

"Gilbert?" she surmised, decoding his stammering. "My Gilbert spoils me rotten. He caters marvelously to my needs, yet never seems to comprehend what I want. Doesn't seem to appreciate the things that most matter to me," she replied, having at last grown accustomed to smiling at him without feeling self-conscious.

"Then why all this?" he asked, her hand lingering against his forearm from the last thing she'd wanted to say.

"You're someone I can spoil," she said, shading a shy smile from open view. "And I enjoy being close to you even more than I like having someone to spoil."

Trajan had never told a woman he loved her. He practiced the words on Carmen the first time she let him kiss her fully. He rested his mouth open on hers, emulated the close embrace Langston and Angelica were wrapped in when he'd crept down the hallway to catch them. He couldn't figure what to do with his free hand, Carmen's shoulders plastered rail-straight to the high back of the love seat positioned along the wall in her parents' living room. They both kept their tongues to their own ponds, waiting for the kiss to be over.

"I love you," he told her. She said it was time for him to leave, startled by the sudden gush of emotion.

"I'll see you tomorrow, Trajan," she said, allowing him one last kiss full against her lips.

Carmen's mother urged her to slow things down with Trajan. She prayed to Saint Jude that her daughter would not be lost to the troubles that had come his way: a broken family, his brother dead at eighteen. She held no ill will toward him but wished he would see fit to steer clear of her daughter.

Sitting on the love seat kissing Carmen soon became old hat. They eventually worked out what to do with their tongues, though her shoulders remained plastered, leaving him to dangle one arm in the air, trying not to brush against her chest or to rest too high on a hip or thigh. The one time he'd gotten close enough to kiss Rosalie— eased in, his feet making their slow advance in between hers—she asked him to wait. "Not here," she urged, leaning in, wanting his mouth yet resisting, exercising restraint. The thing he'd begun to think would never happen eventually did.

Pride

Trajan had been taught to equate marriage with the words spoken at a wedding ceremony: to love, honor, and cherish until death do you part. But no marriage he'd seen ever ended that way, where love and undying commitment succeed in remaining on a consistent plane. He needed more seasoned insight. Langston would have been his first preference. If only Trajan shared their grandpa's ability to summon the spirit world, to consult his brother from the great beyond. Instead, he turned again to Grandpa Tuke for guidance. Tuke would set him straight without pressing for any information in return.

Odd jobs were among the many concessions the neighboring tribes had begun to extend in recognition of the Eastern Pequot having gained formal status with the state. Tuke accepted a weekend job. Trajan could have transferred to one of the tribal schools had he wanted, had he not already been nestled in a compatible school situation, surrounded by soccer and Carmen and BLT. Even Bunny merited consideration.

Tuke found a key fob adorned with the blue and white spinning propeller of a BMW insignia on the casino floor the week leading into homecoming. Homecoming marked the pinnacle of the high school football season, the consummate jock sport, sending the school slobbering all over itself in frenzied celebration. There was the obligatory pep rally Friday afternoon, followed by a school dance for underclassmen. Saturday was game day, followed by the homecoming dance for seniors and alumni returning on the five- and ten-year anniversaries of their graduation dates.

Ben had worked his brooding, blond-haired magic to score an invitation from one of the other cheerleaders, principally as a way to agitate Kelly Bergen. Bunny had plans to sneak in, using his brother's ID to blend in with the upperclassmen. Trajan assumed Lighty was staying home, the two of them not yet back on regular speaking terms. Trajan went to work as regularly scheduled alongside Grandpa Tuke. Homecoming was just another weekend, no different than any other. Rosalie's question continued to ring in Trajan's head, the slow procession continuing toward the real world beyond graduation.

Trajan and his grandpa strode across the parking garage to catch the shuttle to the employee lot. Tuke aimed the key fob and pressed whenever they passed a car he didn't know. "Unlock," he said underneath his breath, hoping to be rewarded by the low, swinging *byeeow-whoot* a BMW makes when the alarm system disengages. But no lock ever did respond.

He drove along Mohegan Sun Boulevard, Trajan at his side, the two having completed the Friday night shift.

"I can leave the house at ten o'clock, two o'clock, midnight, or noon, and I never catch this light," Tuke pondered aloud, presenting an opening for his grandson's first question.

Time together with Mrs. Quigley had afforded Trajan newfound perspective. He traded his ability to see a person about to be called home for a keen eye at spotting a marriage on life support, the plastic tubing attaching two people by the ends of their flared nostrils. Everywhere he turned he saw divorced fathers laboring through regularly scheduled visits with the pint-sized strangers in their lives, couples in distress hanging onto the hope of happily ever after despite an escalating churn caught in the throes of a rocky here and now, a grandfather pining away in silence over the only woman he'd ever loved.

"Why did Grandma Tuke leave?"

"You know your grandmother's dead?" Tuke responded, taking his eyes off the road to get a good look at his grandson. Respect for the dead was paramount for Grandpa Tuke. His dead didn't disappear to some distant heaven. His dead lingered close enough to hear and see you, to come back to touch your life again.

"Before she died," Trajan replied, qualifying his inquiry.

"Her parents never liked me," Tuke offered, blinking to ward off any emotion lingering in relation to the topic of his dead wife. "I wasn't who they had in mind for their daughter to marry."

"They must have gotten to like you in time," Trajan supposed. Tuke nodded in half agreement. "Besides, there's nobody around here who doesn't like Grandpa Tuke."

"I'm your family. You're supposed to like me," his grandpa responded, dreading where the conversation was headed.

"They were your family too. There must be something more to it," Trajan said, pleading for his grandpa to tell the story.

Tuke put up an initial smoke screen. "You know those towels some people have hanging up that no one is permitted to use? Your great grandma had some in her downstairs bathroom that I used to use all the time. She insisted that a proper gentleman should carry a handkerchief for such occasions. She gave me a monogrammed set one year for Christmas. Still, I insisted on using her good towels just to show that her daughter hadn't married any gentleman. Mind you, I treated your grandmother as well as I knew how. But the proud spirit in me wasn't going to allow her mother to train me into being somebody's houseboy." He blinked again, his emotions refusing to remain silent.

"Pride can be a difficult thing: have none, and you're sunk; have too much, and you're still sunk. Your grandma eventually got fed up with me constantly seeking to be at odds with her people and put me out. She went with them once they retired and moved back south."

"Didn't you love her anymore?"

"I loved your grandmother in a long trailing arc from the day I first set eyes on her to the first time I got close enough to catch the scent of her skin. I still love her to this day, even though these eyes can no longer see her, these arms will never have the privilege of holding her again."

Trajan resonated with Tuke's description of trailing emotion, running away from you in a way you can never quite manage to catch up with. "How do you hang onto that feeling, hold fast as the arc peters out?" Trajan asked, his curiosity shifting from his entanglement with Rosalie to the slow burn he and Carmen were still working to maintain.

Tuke worried again about propelling his grandson too quickly forward in life, but proceeded, preferring to be the one to tell him, his chest swelling with pride in knowing that Trajan had come to

210

him first, seeking advice on what to do with a girl. "Every relationship with a woman starts out the same—wanting to rip each other's clothes off. You eventually reach the point where so much is going on in life that neither of you can muster the energy for any clothes ripping. It's about that time somebody gets bored or lonely. The two can feel oddly the same. It takes a wise person to know it's the little things—compatibility, like mind-set, mutual regard for one another's feelings—that seal the bond between two people. That still won't keep the two of you from stumbling. But, without those things, you'll never survive the fall."

"How'd you get so wise?" Trajan asked, contemplating whether, according to Tuke's advice, his teenage flirtations could do anything to disrupt the bond Mrs. Quigley and her husband shared.

"I tried everything else first," Tuke responded.

WINTER'S FIRST FALLING

Few things inspire fear like something that the mind can clearly conceive but the heart has yet to anticipate: a person breaking into a sprint from the middle of a restless crowd; an indolent growl roaming uncaged beyond the shadows, an unseen monster threatening to rip you limb from trembling limb; steam rising from a heaping mound of snow, dwindling body heat intimating the last signs of diminished life.

Cadence

Trajan had come away from his talk with Grandpa Tuke convinced that he and Rosalie could pursue a physical relationship without compromising the closeness between her and Mr. Quigley so long as they minded clear boundaries, took care not to throw her compatibility at home too far off balance. His evenings together with Mrs. Quigley soon developed a familiar cadence, a rise and fall to them: time to become reacquainted, to settle in one another's company again, making way for a divine middle followed by a quiet period of cooling off before sliding back to their separate lives. Rosalie had schooled Trajan on the importance of not jumping straight to it, encouraging him to approach each encounter with fresh eyes, to maintain as best they could the wonder they saw in one another.

The winter months forced them indoors again, inside her house, on the vaguest assurances from her that it would be all right. Trajan was jittery with nerves his first time with Mrs. Quigley, unable to look straight at her even after sitting together a good while in her living room. She wore a pale yellow bodice hidden beneath a wool blazer paired with a denim skirt. He was certain he'd seen her wear the blazer to school, but the denim skirt was outside the norm for her. He liked it, felt obliged to tell her as much. She invited him to move closer to the fireplace, slid her arms free from the blazer to reveal soft, brown-flecked shoulders. The bodice cinched together in back in a web of black ribbing held tight by a thin snake of lace ribbon. He'd discover later that night that the ribbon was merely decorative, the bodice fastened up front like a gigantic, twenty-clip bra strap.

He reached for her as she slid the denim skirt past her hips, slipped her legs free one after the other. He wanted her next to him, but the curl of her lip said to wait, her chin nervous, her posture unsure. She had her own case of jitters still to overcome. Trajan continued studying her eyes for cues, content to follow her lead, permitting Rosalie to dictate the pace between them. He understood for the first time what had compelled his brother to spend any time he could alone on the sofa with Angelica Chu.

Trajan deferred to Rosalie's experience. Followed any instruction she saw fit to give with the attentiveness of an untrained civilian tasked with landing an airplane, defusing a bomb. "It's the height of every girl's idea of romance to wallow about snared in a loose tangle of her own undergarments," Rosalie had said, sufficiently direct to make sure he caught the sarcasm. She explained how a woman wanted to be undressed, admired in the eyes of whomever she'd chosen to allow in her bed. "Take your time, love," she added, smiling, boosting his desire to please her. "I'm not going anyplace."

He followed her lace panties to the floor, helped her out of them one dreamy leg after the other. She rested a hand on his shoulder, dictating the pace of his ascent. She stopped him at the midpoint of her calf, guiding him with her hand as he attacked her in slow, gentle nibbles along the back of her knee. She allowed him partway up her thigh, still nibbling, kissing outside then in, working up the back of one leg lifted in the air to allow him access. She rolled onto her belly, exposing a perfectly formed backside. He went to work again back around her hips, resting on the tender mound formed by her exposed cheeks. She rolled over again, placed him back between her thighs.

The prickly ends of his mustache combed soft pubic hairs. He sensed her moistness, licked droplets from his tiny whiskers. He breathed in deep to steady his nerves, prepared to take the plunge, to taste her.

"I'm too wet," she whispered, guiding him up her belly. He lay on top of her, her thighs spread on either side of his waist. He slid himself inside her and for the first time made love to a woman.

Trajan began maintaining a tally inside his head of the times they'd been together, of all the things they'd done. Rosalie kept tabs on the clock in order to maintain a comfortable margin of error with their cavorting. Rosalie generally made arrangements to pick Trajan up to save him the trouble of walking there and back. She would find some errand to run: a friend she needed to visit, a former colleague retired over in Ledyard or Gales Ferry, providing plausible excuse to be that far from home at night if something were to go awry—a car crash, a fender bender, a nail in a tire.

Trajan had nobody looking in on him, didn't need an excuse to be any distance from home. He would set out the same time Rosalie indicated she was leaving, his aim to make it to the near side of the bridge along Rte. 2 before her burgundy Volvo came rolling along from the opposite direction. She would U-turn alongside Trajan, waving for him to hop in before another car cruised past, someone who might recognize her at the wheel. She'd let him out at the back end of her neighborhood with a bit of woods plus a small creek to cross to reach her back porch. They took the reverse path home.

On a clear night, the moon that reflected off the gentle trickle of the stream led the way. His tennis shoes had committed the short path through the woods to memory by the time the creek had frozen over for the season, winter laying her cruel hand on things. Trajan used the crackle of frozen twigs beneath his feet, the shuffle of loose earth giving way to the stream's slick surface, to time his leap. From there, it was a short jog to the Quigleys' back steps, where he would be let in. On a night like this, the moon turned shy, thick cloud cover protecting its position overhead, and Trajan used the gurgle of the stream as it raced against dull rocks to find his way, winter still preparing to silence the flow of water trickling past.

Rosalie and Trajan were well past the period of getting reacquainted and on their way to the divine middle phase when Mr. Quigley called the house phone to say he and the boys were calling it an early night on account of the storm threatening—a nor'easter, he reckoned. He said he wanted to get home before the roads got slick, his voice stained with the heavy covering of one last beer, swallowed fast before venturing back on the road.

"Are you sure you're okay to drive, Gilbert?" she asked.

"I'm fine, Rosalie. I'm in much better condition, quite frankly, than the rest of these imbeciles. I'm going to shove off before any of them gets out there. I'll see you shortly."

"Drive safely, my love," Rosalie said into the phone before hanging up.

Trajan witnessed her in that brief exchange make her way from heated lover to concerned spouse to calm coconspirator, calculating the moves needed to remain above suspicion.

"Trajan, I need you to gather your things," she announced, thrusting him back to fifth-period early American history, her lecture about things that had never before concerned him suddenly a matter of life or death, the future of all mankind depending on how he conducted himself at this precise moment in time. "You'll need to leave through the back. And, sweetie, I'm sorry, but I can't afford to drive you back across the bridge to Preston. A light frost has begun to set up on the driveway. Gilbert is sure to see tire tracks if I pull the car from the garage at this late hour. Stay warm and do get home safely." She kissed his mouth long and soft indicating that this was a hardship for her too. Then she hustled him out the door, switching off the porch light before he reached the edge of the yard, the back lawn certain to show prints as clearly as the frost-covered driveway.

218

Spirit Gods

Trajan started in the direction of the highway. *This is going to suck,* he thought, pulling his jacket closer around his neck. *It sucks already.* He drummed up ways his night could have turned out worse to distract himself from how bad it was already. Mr. Quigley might have skipped that last beer, heading straight home unannounced. He would have found Trajan bare-ass naked and stretched out on his living room sofa, a fire crackling from wood split with the effort of Mr. Quigley's two hands, the supple contour of his wife's shapely thigh draped across Trajan's thin frame. The storm might have reached its full potency before he could make his escape, trapping him there, Mr. Quigley joining Trajan and his wife in front of the fireplace, his two hands at work against Trajan's windpipe.

Trajan began to think he'd gotten off easy when it started to rain. The kind of rain that's falling only to allow time for the temperature to drop, for that penetrating chill to set in, to summon the sleet to follow. It's like the sky was filled with machinery, and the part responsible for wrecking Trajan's night was just winding up.

A great white owl whispered past as he reached the roadway heading back across town, the cut of its wings angled for distance, not for stealth. The owl carried in its talons a long, delicate string, pulling in its wake a sheet of white snow. Ghoulish flakes cloaked the night sky in dense, fluttering swells that littered Trajan's path in a haphazard pattern of inverted paw prints layered on top of one another in any place the ground was already moist, the clouds needing to shed excess snow production before a normal fall could proceed.

Trajan took a shortcut through Fort Shantok, the Indian burial ground, figuring the heavy tree covering would protect him from the sky's wrath. He hoped that Grandpa Tuke's ancestors would find some way to excuse his transgressions. That they might safeguard the balance of his journey home. He came upon a deep mound of snow as he listened for a response, the wind rustling the tree branches to acknowledge his pleas. A fallen animal, he surmised, caught unaware by the sudden onset of winter. As he stepped to get a closer look, he tumbled across a second mound, heavy like the first, only bigger. He scrambled to his knees, struggling in the dim light to make out the animal, the full length of its body crumpled on top of itself, appendages strewn at crazy angles showing the desperation of its failed attempt at flight, the violence that marked its fated end.

He crept over and knelt beside the thing, looking for a snout to see if its muzzle was still warm. He pulled at the end he presumed was the animal's head to find the sleeve of a yellow goose down jacket. A bulky silver watch hung loosely at the end of a slender wrist turned over on itself, cracked in two from the impact. Trajan rocked back on his heels to get a broader view. The man's knees were tucked beneath him, his hips angled skyward like he'd been rear-ended by a train, death stomping life into the dirt and leaving its latest victim in a crumpled heap. Pools of dark blood stained the shell of the man's yellow jacket, ketchup in eggs the way Chester and Grandpa Tuke liked them.

Trajan spun backward, stumbling over his feet, trying to put distance between himself and the dead man. He turned back in the direction of the first mound, noticed steam rising from it. The mound was still moving, still working to escape. He found a woman lying beneath a beard of blanketed snow—a second victim—one eye begging for it to be over.

Trajan crouched beside her. "I'm not going to hurt you," he whispered, brushing snow from the woman's face. She let out a gasp as Trajan lifted a thick tangle of braids from around her neck, sending a small flurry of snow into the air beneath her. He rolled the woman over on her shoulders, positioning her faceup to help her breathing.

"I'm going to get you some help," he assured the woman who lay expressionless, both eyes trained on him, when the pounding of feet came charging from the direction of the park entrance. The chatter of a police radio was evident above the sound of the officer's hard charging, implements of his trade jangling beneath the waist of his short coat, indicating that winter had also caught him unprepared for the season's first earnest offensive.

Trajan made himself small, light as he darted toward the woods in search of cover. He noticed prints in the snow ahead of him as his feet left the gravel footpath. Heard feet shuffling for position along the thin ledge resting a few footfalls beyond the jagged edge of the pathway. He took heed as hushed whispers in Haitian Creole rustled in the darkness. Trajan didn't speak Kreyol, but owing to a couple of recent recruits to the soccer team, he recognized it when spoken.

Trajan retreated in the direction of the police chatter, hands above his head, screaming at the top of his lungs, "I didn't do this. It wasn't me."

"Stop where you are," the officer commanded, his weapon drawn. "And keep those hands where I can see them."

A second officer arrived, placing himself between Trajan and his partner's gun sight. "Give us your name, son," he instructed, a hand resting loose against the butt of his 9mm. Trajan mostly saw the uniform, the proximity of his hand to his weapon, the flop of his tongue as he spoke, his lip lost beneath a heavy brown mustache, the dusting of snow gathering atop his hat. He refastened the buckle on his holster and extended a hand, pulling Trajan to him. He told Trajan to put his arms down after a brief search of his pockets. Asked him to produce some ID.

The other officer closed in on them, his gun lowered but still resting firmly in hand. "Do you care to tell us what you're doing out here?" he demanded, adrenaline filling his voice with an abundance of undue energy.

"I was taking a shortcut home," Trajan responded, fidgeting, wondering when they would ask about the woman lying a few short steps away.

"What shortcut? Sylvia Lane is that way, little homey," he scoffed, pointing over his shoulder with the barrel of his gun.

"Stand down, Rodriguez," his partner instructed. Rodriguez threw up his hands.

"I'll leave yous to it," he said, turning his back to them. He holstered his gun then lit a cigarette. He continued to turn small circles in the snow a short distance away from them, smoke from his cigarette mixing with the crystalline night air. Officer Rodriguez was a local product, having grown up in New London in the shadow of the Crystal Avenue Apartments—his own Sylvia Lane, a short drive away—breeding contempt for all he mistook Trajan to represent. He had been cited twice for overzealousness in carrying out his duties, the department receiving countless citizen complaints on the heels of his antics. He had never fired his service weapon in the line of duty, though he desperately hoped for the chance to fight crime someday and have the boys in blue come out on top.

Officer Haley resumed questioning Trajan. "Where's your home, son?"

Trajan pointed to the far end of the park. "I live in Preston."

"Do you know the deceased?" the officer questioned.

"No, but I think the woman is still alive," Trajan responded, starting toward the place he'd left her, lying faceup, laboring with every breath.

"Stay here," Officer Haley advised, grabbing Trajan by the shoulder as Officer Rodriguez charged ahead of them, his weapon again in hand. A lit cigarette lay smoldering inside a series of neatly drawn circles that Rodriguez had made in the snow with his feet.

He checked her pulse with one hand while the other hand scanned the tree line for movement along the barrel of his gun. Rodriguez circled the air with his finger, signaling to his partner that the woman was still breathing. Haley radioed for an ambulance. "I need you to run full sirens," he advised, encouraging EMS to hustle.

"We may have a live victim." Trajan recognized that he meant to say witness, the woman's condition having been of marginal interest just thirty seconds prior.

Within minutes, the park was swarming with activity: firemen, paramedics, police backup, the squadron leader. Even if the victims were of little consequence, efforts to identify the person or persons responsible for the shooting drew loud ministration.

Officer Haley held Trajan apart from the commotion. Meanwhile, Officer Rodriguez buzzed around the scene, working to keep himself at the center of attention. Trajan watched as paramedics unfolded the man's body, scooped the remnants of the train wreck into a dark plastic bag, zippered it shut. Trajan thought about his brother, wondered if Langston had seen the inside of a body bag, as they loaded the man inside a coroner's van.

Trajan caught sight of the woman again as they wheeled her on a gurney toward a waiting ambulance. They locked eyes one last time. Her eyes thanked him and didn't thank him. The care he showed for her well-being had been generous, but he had done her no kindness, leaving her to stand witness for a crime that had nearly succeeded in taking her life, her man bagged and carted away. She, too, may have been better off dead.

Bred'ren

Officer Haley had a patrol car drive Trajan across the river to the town line. When the car had left, Trajan continued on foot, the snow having found a steady rhythm beneath a cowering sky. The soft snow cover absorbed any semblance of sound, wrapping Trajan in a heavy cocoon. He used the layers of white to silence his anxieties. Each footstep seemed to last a small eternity. He'd imagined death a hundred times, had pictured countless victims on the verge of slipping free of the hold their earthly existence had on them. He had never before encountered a dead body in the flesh, a person there in one instant and then gone the next. He tried to erase the image from his memory as he continued toward home.

A hundred yards from his mother's front door, a white Mercedes approached him.

"Big guy," a voice called from the passenger seat as the window slithered open. "Let me chat with ya. What you seen back there in the park tonight needed doing, simple as that. But that don't make me no bad man. You understand?" The man's heavy accent rested beneath a tongue accustomed to speaking Kreyol almost exclusively.

"You did good, Bred'ren," he offered. "Placing tracks on top of my tracks till I ain't had no tracks. I am in your debt, *mwen frè*, my brother. Call on Luscius should you need anything." The car U-turned in front of Trajan, creating a pair of high rooster tails as the rear tires scrambled for grip, then eased off, its paint blending with the falling snow like a ghost ride, there and not there when you looked for it a second time.

Fell Swoop

Rosalie blamed the decision to bring Trajan into their home on the wind, on the feel she got of dancing and flying, of setting her mind free the time he'd convinced her to venture a ride on his skateboard, his arms wrapped tight around her. She studied the possibilities brewing between them, came away with the sound rationalization that a careful excursion beyond the bounds of convention would relieve the tension building steadily with each new encounter together. She would give in to the notion, let the air out a bit at a time until she was over it, had gotten the urge out of her system. If only a thing like that could be tamed. She had hoped that surrendering to her feelings, slipping free of her obligations on calculated terms, would minimize the potential of a rampant tear, railing unchecked against all things sacred, held to disrupt everyone's existence, happy or otherwise. She had never behaved so irresponsibly in all her years.

She held onto the idea through several more visits in the parking lot together before springing it on Trajan, an errant star validating her way of thinking with a convincing twinkle. Part of her wanted to believe she'd imagined the closeness between them, had dreamt the whole thing. She worried that a middle-aged woman had seen a darling young man smile her way and let it upset the only truth she'd ever known. Her Gilbert loved her, and she loved him. She'd been a devoted wife, a dedicated teacher who placed the needs of her students above all else, committed to doing what's right her entire lifetime only to wind up here, threatening to throw it all away in one fell swoop.

She thought on several occasions to confront her husband, to air their differences. "Gilbert, you hardly know me anymore, barely recognize the person I am transforming into," she would assert. "Yes, but I have every confidence that I will adore whoever that turns out to be," he would muse missing the gravity of her concern. Yet, after twelve, fifteen, eighteen years of marriage, she had learned to set aside any differences that didn't pose an immediate threat to the peace and harmony between them, even though her interests had strayed.

She weighed the choice put before her, spanned the range of consequences inside her head, utter catastrophe the most likely outcome. Nothing succeeded in quieting the yearning. She'd held onto what she had, took comfort most days in knowing she had given the best she had to give. Contemplated why on other days the urge to give eluded her. There are times when it rains, a warm, inviting rain sent to nourish, to remind us what it means to be alive on this earth. Other times, a steady rainfall proves depressing, its ability to foster new growth turning against us. We long for the return of sunny days, hoping to be set free. Rosalie had reached a point where she no longer cared about the rain, sought other means to nourish a withering spirit.

Rosalie didn't sleep that night. Time would not permit her the warm bath, the hot cup of tea she'd adopted as part of her Thursday ritual to quiet her insides. She showered, tracking the time since she'd hung up with Gilbert, did a quick load of laundry, putting away anything out of season like sheer hose and silk lingerie reserved for birthdays or Valentine's or something else on the calendar. She sat at the kitchen table in a terry cloth robe, her heavy winter gown, a pair of fuzzy worn slippers to keep her feet warm as she waited for Gilbert to return.

Gilbert burst in the door with a bluster of wind, the short walk from the garage reminding him why he'd headed out early. "It's really coming down out there," he remarked, stamping his feet to rid his boots of loose snow. "It's all I could do to keep my truck from veering into a ditch. Snow was falling so thick at one point I had to resort to navigating by way of the centerline," he boasted, looking to impress his wife with his resourcefulness. "Once the centerline vanished, I used the tracks the snowplow left on its latest pass to guide the way—guardrails piled high on either side marking the roadway."

She helped him out of his coat, unfurled the wool muffler from around his neck. Hung it next to his hat on the French country hall tree that sat opposite the kitchen door. He took a seat on the wooden storage bench and proceeded to unlace his boots. She asked whether he wanted anything—something to eat, something warm to drink.

"Truth be told, darling, your old man is spent. I'm heading off to bed. You coming?" he asked as he made his way toward the back, switching on lights everyplace he passed: the dining room, the narrow hallway, the hall bath adjacent to their bedroom.

"Umm-hmm," she replied, trailing behind him, switching off any lights he'd turned on. She lay next to him in the bed and waited for the familiar sound of his snoring to smooth the ragged edges she'd managed to unearth in their quiet existence together, to bring an end to a fitful night, to erase any last trace of wind from her hair.

She opened the drapes the next morning on a perfect postcard world, the whole planet cloaked in white from the scraggly, naked tree limbs to the snow-covered hump vaguely resembling the gross geometry of a child's tricycle that the neighbors had left in their front yard. She scanned the area around the fireplace for remnants of last evening's escapade with Trajan. Everything was in its proper place. The cushions were arranged in an orderly fashion on the couch, the fireplace utensils were hung in their rack, the coffee table stood centered neatly on the blue chenille area rug. She shuddered at the sight of it: her home put back in perfect order, good housekeeping at work to disguise her gaping indiscretions, the impending break in her marriage. She sank with the realization that she had become proficient, skilled in her deceit, a new knot twisting inside a stomach already cramped with worry.

She switched on the television resting on a shelf in the kitchen next to the microwave oven, in search of background noise to keep her company as she prepared a pot of coffee. Waded through a barrage of school closings, waiting for the announcer to resume with the inevitable stream of incident reports: fallen tree limbs, downed power lines, stranded motorists. How else would she know what had become of Trajan? Who could she call?

She thought she heard the dreaded headline being read, her

mind playing a cruel trick beneath the incessant churn of the percolator spewing brewed coffee back on itself: *A young Preston man became lost in the wilderness, buried in snow.*

A delightful young man with the most beautiful mouth, Rosalie thought, adjusting the newscaster's account. *Eyes so clear you'd think they were painted into his head by the hands of an artist.*

How could she be so reckless, so self-absorbed? To send him out into the night ahead of a storm that had only just delivered her Gilbert, returned him to her? That she allowed Gilbert out in the first place knowing the weather forecast, recognizing the threat that loomed, underlined how desperate a hold the desire to be with Trajan had placed on her, how much she had forfeited already.

FOUR

Trajan grew in spurts. By senior year, he was half a head taller than his brother had been at the same age. He'd even gained an inch or two over Chester. Dottie was uncommonly tall for a woman, though Trajan was confident he'd passed her up as well, leaving Grandpa Tuke the official runt of the family.

CLOSE-KNIT TIES

Home for Trajan became increasingly transitory: a place to shower, to grab a change of clothes, a bit of shut-eye, something to eat. Then he was out the door again, letting the wind carry him whichever way it might choose to blow, at times cognizant of his desperate yearning for human contact, other times oblivious to the need.

Trajan developed individualized means of communicating with the people in his world. It got to the point where he knew who was calling by the way the person tried to reach him. Tuke was a horn honker. He'd sit outside the house, give a few quick blasts, and then drive off if Trajan didn't show up within the next couple of minutes. Tuke recognized the move was disrespectful but felt that as an old man he was entitled to certain allowances. He warned that he'd put a foot in Trajan's backside if he caught wind of his grandson honking outside anybody's door, seeming to forget Trajan didn't drive. Trajan thought he might get a horn for his skateboard, a big brass thing—the kind little kids have attached to their bike handlebars that you squeeze a rubber clown nose to honk. He would press the nose flat with his foot to get someone to look his way.

Conversations with his mother remained one-sided. When she did answer—her voice sounding upbeat, cheery like her old self—she still refused to let him in, quite unlike her old self. Chester was the only one who called the house phone anymore. Carmen called the library on the off chance she needed to speak with him, to confirm he was heading over on any given night.

Mrs. Quigley had gone all secret squirrel on him. She would drop by the library before closing, mill around the biographies awhile, pretending to browse. Trajan walked the stacks each night, his first duty to right anything that had fallen into disarray over the course of the day. The librarian was insistent that no one rearrange the shelves; that was her responsibility, the Dewey Decimal System evidently beyond anyone else's capability. On nights Mrs. Quigley had stopped in, Trajan would find John Quincy Adams turned around, the book's leafy pages facing outward in place of the broad expanse of its spine. John Quincy Adams was her favorite early American hero, one whose honor she risked defacing as a signal to Trajan.

It meant she expected to have the house to herself that night. She would meet him on his way back from Preston.

A flood of Thursdays passed and still no sign of her, John Quincy Adams's proud spine staring back at him whenever he passed the biography section. She got like this at times, guilt knotting new ties to home—their anniversary alone buried her a couple of weeks at a time. The winter months were particularly sketchy. The bowling league suspended activities through the holidays, their hiatus lasting well into the start of spring. Trajan walked the stacks week in and week out, desperately awaiting her return.

Extracurricular

BLT broke up at the start of their senior campaign. Ben suffered a meniscus tear during a preseason exhibition match, bringing his high school soccer career to a decisive close. Lighty was recruited to join his father's paint crew after a hired hand fell from a ladder and fractured his tailbone. Coach Beckford asked his returning seniors to prepare a schedule of their daily activities, weekends included. His aim was to have them consider their chosen path in life and how choices made in one's daily routine can influence future prospects, to picture how far they might come this time next year with proper focus. He was a walking after-school special in that way.

Trajan gave his schedule added spiffiness. He got straight on his homework before work got started, suggesting he was diligent. That

235

he had a part-time job in the first place meant he was industrious on top of being diligent. He listed soccer and skateboarding as extra-curricular activities, neither of which should come as a surprise to anyone who knew him, the head soccer coach especially. He spared mention of lessons on flying, of having taught Rosalie to skateboard, the things she had helped him discover in return.

Trajan had gotten in the habit of waiting with Bunny for his uncle's van to pull up, stood in the dark alongside his childhood friend whether he was planning to ride home with them or not. This way he could eliminate the possibility of crossing paths with them some distance from the library, giving away his whereabouts outside the list of sanctioned activities, Coach Beckford's approval a minor consideration amid a long list of more imminent concerns.

"You going to see Carmen?" Bunny asked.

Trajan wagged an in-between nod with his head, unwilling to commit one way or the other on the prospect of seeing Carmen.

"I'm beginning to grow on her friend Maria. Wouldn't you say?" Bunny inquired. *Like a fungal infection,* Trajan thought.

"Are you heading straight home afterward?" Bunny continued to press.

Trajan gave another head wag, recognizing the sudden creep in interest, Bunny angling for an invitation to tag along. He toed the curved tail of his skateboard, let the board roll away from him before catching it with his foot. "I might just hang around town," he said. "Cruise past the shop windows, see what's new." Mention of cruising was intended to put Bunny off any ideas he had of joining Trajan for the night. Bunny was a homebody, preferred the remote stillness of Preston to any amount of bustle in town. Trajan didn't need the company, plus Bunny had never been much of a skateboarder. He trailed behind on foot, Trajan resisting every urge to ditch his little buddy, take a sharp downhill turn and place serious distance between the two of them.

The Otis Library sits at the base of downtown Norwich, ensnared in a maze of one-way streets leading to and from the marina in every direction. Trajan took the short walk up Franklin Street after Bunny and his uncle pulled away from the curb, his skateboard dangling by his side. Standing high atop the river valley, the world was his oyster. A roll in the direction of Mohegan Park led to the high school. A short push farther along Washington Street brought him to the neighborhood where Carmen and her parents lived. A glance in the opposite direction revealed Norwichtown, marked by a dense cluster of light shimmering in the distance. Rosalie lived farther still, on the way to Bozrah. Trajan left his skateboard at home anytime he was planning to see her. A plaything, it stood in the way of the adult thing they were attempting to do, drew unneeded attention to the countless gaps between them, the difference in age in many regards the least among them.

237

Fare Thee Well

E-Z graduated NFA by the slimmest margin. Principal Adams

modified his standard send off—*fare thee well, graduate*—as E-Z crossed the stage to receive his diploma. "Do your best out there, son," he said, giving E-Z's hand a brisk shake.

Mathieu Sessions was proud of his son the way a father should be proud. At the same time, he sat filled with anxiety, knowing this was the last hold he would have on E-Z. Mathieu had settled into his position as a welder, second shift. He earned an honest wage, but his work did not save lives, as he'd once pretended as a way to entertain the boys. At most, his job, if poorly done, might cost lives, and even then it would only cost Mathieu his job. There were plenty of men standing in line behind him to do the job better, faster, cheaper if he were to ever slip up. He wanted better for his son.

He was resigned to never playing major league ball. But he had put forth the effort, set a goal for himself, and then given all his might in an earnest attempt to get there. He wished to see E-Z do the same. If not his father's sport, find another pursuit: football, soccer, cross-country, lacrosse. If athletics were not his thing, work to become a star student, earn top marks. Instead his son tumbled headlong toward the finish line, making it by the skin of his teeth. Still, Mathieu couldn't help but stand proud, cheering as loudly as any parent at the graduation ceremony. E-Z was, after all, his firstborn son.

Life for Mathieu had taken a hard left turn, derailing any ambition he had in the world. Through it all, raising a family had for the most part been worth the sacrifice, though he struggled to see the impact he'd had on their lives. He might have made better choices had he recognized the influence he would have in shaping the people they would grow to be, had he understood the impression his example would make. He might have leaned in, accepted the hand fate had dealt him more graciously, kept the yo-yo at the top of the string. His big guy finishing high school punctuated a stretch of time that neither of them could ever hope to retrieve. Whatever ambitions E-Z was destined to pursue, he would now have to get there in his own way.

Everything happens in its own time, Tuke was fond of saying. E-Z stepped into a time and space handpicked for him to excel in the career he chose. A trend in the direction of increased criminal activity began to encroach on the casinos, disrupting the steady flow of out-of-town gamblers flush with cash. Rising concerns over the safety of the casino patrons necessitated an especially heavy recruiting class in all branches of security that coming fall. E-Z was accepted on his first application to the Foxwoods Tribal Police Force in light of new evidence indicating his mother was at least one-sixteenth Mashantucket, a marriage certificate linking a great-great-grand to the Hadley brood. Who was to say otherwise?

The Sessions had only ever acknowledged ties on their father's side to the Franco-Caribbean island culture of St. Martin. They encountered Grand-mère tucked in a corner beside the kitchen table any time Trajan followed Bunny home from school, the quiet at Trajan's house having grown deafening. She spoke to them in crusty old French, her tongue maintaining allegiances to home despite her move to the States appearing to have become permanent.

239

"*Qui est-il?*" his grandmother asked, aiming with a finger bent from old age.

"That's Trajan, Grand-mère. You met him before," Bunny explained.

"Ah, *oui. Je me souviens.*" She remembered him. "*Son frère, il est mort. Si triste.*"

"She's sorry to hear about your brother," Bunny said, placing a hand on his grandmother's shoulder as he bent to kiss her. "We'll see you soon, Grand-mère."

"*À bientôt, mon petit-fils.*" She waved good-bye to her grandson with more curled fingers.

THE BOOM BOX

In the beginning, there were two turntables and a microphone. Before there was gangster rap, conscious rap, before your favorite cereal box showed up rapping in TV commercials, back when rhymes were funky fresh, there was a DJ spinning records on the turntables providing loud backdrop for the Master of Ceremonies controlling the mic. A band of entertainers descended on the Norwich/New London area from New York and started hosting block parties the summer Dottie and Chester turned Trajan's age. They called themselves the D&D Wrecking Crew after Derwin and Davonte, the crew's DJ and MC, respectively.

Derwin billed himself as DJ Diamond D. Davonte went by the stage name Divine. D&D were accompanied by a ragtag crew of poppers, lockers, break-dancers, and the occasional beat box artist. They were the hottest thing to hit the river valley. D&D threw the flyest parties and ran the tightest crew, amassing a minor cult following, the girls in the valley drawn to the beat of their rhythm.

In time, Derwin fathered a child or two or three beneath the dim light of the basketball courts across from Sylvia Lane or the Crystal Avenue Apartments, his turntables robbing the street lamp for energy. He made his home in Connecticut, wanting to remain in reasonable proximity to his kids. He eventually adopted the regular-Joe routine and got a day job, deejaying clubs and private parties when he could drum up a gig.

Divine returned to the city. He found mild success promoting fledgling rap groups as an appetite blossomed for all those cereal commercials. He had a hand in a couple of mid-range hits before hanging up the mic. He thought about the regular-Joe thing, too, when the casinos landed, a development that sparked a sense of rebirth in the valley, resurrecting the D&D partnership. D&D opened The Boom Box, among the string of after-hours spots that cropped up along the outskirts of the casino grounds, siphoning off the tribes' success. Baltic Street provided a place locals could go for a night on the town without getting fleeced in the tourist trap, a collection of social clubs designated BYOB, permitting them to do as they pleased as long as no one was assaulted. Everyone from eighteen to eighty found something to like at The Boom Box—that was the promise Derwin made to the crowd each night from his place behind the turntables.

Signing on with the police force afforded E-Z added freedom. Never mind the badge and gun, the uniform with its put-on authority. As an appointed member of the patrol squadron, he was given unrestricted use of an official police vehicle, an oversized SUV meant to scale rocks and climb boulders with enough space in back to cart away any obstacle the truck proved incapable of running over.

E-Z invariably found himself in need of some diversion to wind down his adrenaline before heading home at the end of his shift. He hopscotched his way through the clubs along Baltic Street. The Boom Box offered the only relatable music selection, a live DJ mixing hip-hop with the occasional slow set to satisfy the female clientele. He eventually dragged Trajan and his brother along for the night, tired of being the youngest face in the crowd. The man working the door allowed the boys entrance to the club on the condition that they not do anything to draw special attention to themselves, a feat they recognized Bunny was the least capable of. They had hit the big time, out on the town, E-Z let loose behind the wheel.

Bunny hadn't wanted to go. "The place is going to be full of old biddies," he complained. They couldn't get him to leave after one or two of those old biddies let him slow grind against her in between fast sets. Trajan sat lost in the music: Run DMC, The Jungle Brothers, EPMD, Tom-Tom Club, Mantronix. His arms showed goose bumps as Afrika Bambaataa issued that hypnotic chant—*Party People, can y'all get funky?* This is the music that had filled their household when he was growing up, the walls pounding with cuts from his father's milk crate collection on wax, Chester for the first time cool, funky fresh in Trajan's eyes. The boys developed a new weekly routine, old biddies and old school hip-hop receiving equal billing.

Good Riddance

Carmen didn't mind that Trajan had stopped showing up Thursday evenings. She seemed to prefer the break. Found it helped ease tensions at home, Mrs. Padilla having taken to mothering Trajan indirectly through increased restrictions placed on her daughter. If Carmen was to continue seeing Trajan, it was to be on Mrs. Padilla's terms.

Mrs. Padilla had her bubble too, one based in a traditional upbringing in Puerto Rico where no upstanding young girl would be left unsupervised with a boy, and her eavesdropping from the other room would hardly be considered an intrusion—*¡Ni hablar!*—don't give me that. Trajan would graduate in a few short months with Carmen a year behind him. It was time to make intentions between them clear. Who were his people? What was he planning with their daughter once the two were off on their own?

"We should have your family over for Easter dinner," she announced from the kitchen, ignoring hints that the two of them would prefer she head off to bed. "I'm preparing baked ham and roast leg of lamb with rice and peas and potato salad." She checked the items off inside her head, flicking a finger in the air to keep accurate count, before pausing to ask: "Your family eats pork, don't they?"

Trajan said he believed they did, but he would be sure to ask when he got home.

"You'll let us know next time we see you," she said, poking her head out of the kitchen door. "Have a good night," she bellowed at him over a loud banging of pots, showing little inclination of abandoning her watch for the night.

Trajan fidgeted awhile longer on the sofa next to Carmen and then headed out, marking another silent victory for Mrs. Padilla in her escalating offensive against free reign over her daughter's idle time.

Trajan considered the prospect of his family coming face-to-face with the Padillas. He might convince Carmen's mother to set up dinner on a card table outside his mother's bedroom door, celebrate the Son's resurrection in the cramped space across from the hall bathroom. He could invite Chester, drag Callie and Paulo along for good measure, to help bridge the gap in cultures.

Trajan was surprised to learn Callie didn't speak Spanish. (Paulo knew only curse words.) Trajan wished Callie and his father a Happy New Year in the way Carmen had taught him in hopes of charming her mother—*Feliz Año Nuevo*. Callie looked him off. "I don't speak that," she said, feigning offense at the gesture. Doesn't speak what: her parents' native tongue, or her hope of a year filled with

245

happiness? Trajan suspected the former, but considered both equally probable, having gotten a glimpse at life in their household, Paulo and Chester constantly at one another's throats.

Trajan became increasingly scarce as Easter Sunday approached, telling Mrs. Padilla all she needed to know about him. *"Es para lo mejor,"* she told Carmen—it was for the best.

Trajan took to the road again, the lonely walk home furthest from his mind. He couldn't get Rosalie out of his head. He compartmentalized the intimate knowledge he'd acquired, secrets amassed through stolen moments alone with her in front of the fireplace, confined them to the shelf furthest back in his subconscious. Still, she crept into every waking moment apart from her. He could only take so long sitting on the couch with Carmen before the need to be in the company of a grown woman again took hold. Even a woman he didn't particularly care for struck him as roundly compelling. He headed to The Boom Box on his own, content to blend into the woodwork and soak in the sad intermingling that passes for courtship among people his parents' age.

Trajan entered a narrow space that was wall-to-wall movement. The DJ was rocking; the dance floor was rocking. People were rocking in their seats unable to keep their legs still, their heads nodding in hypnotic agreement. Trajan had found a home. Rosalie showed him how to two-step in the middle of her living room in time to an endless 1–2–3 beat, their backs as stiff as boards. The D&D groove started low in the hips, causing feet, arms, legs to move in syncopated rhythm.

Middle-aged women in a nightclub exhibit a characteristic earnestness that makes them appear more or less the same: lips too plump, too red to be real; eyes colored dark, smudged at the edges to conceal a universal desperation. Outlandish hairdos stand at odd angles, teased in every direction except the way the hair wants naturally to go. Tight dresses cling to snug undergarments whose sole purpose is to hide their bulges and to allow a close-fitting dress in the first place. But Trajan found the scent of their perfume, most evident when dialed in close, deeply intoxicating. Even the most overdone spinster was sure to afford him a tiny whiff of heaven, upping the ante on the bet that her desperate yearning on that given night was, after all, not for nothing.

Trajan was invariably the only unattached male in the place. He surveyed the crowd, pairing couples inside his head to avoid stepping on anyone's toes, asking the wrong woman to dance or eyeing the backside of the wrong clinging skirt too eagerly. The side tables seemed reserved for people who preferred to fade into the shadows, seeking the cover of dim light to conceal an affiliation whose propriety beyond the club doors lay in question. A few sailors would wander in, home on leave, hoping to stretch their meager pay a bit further than the casinos would permit. They'd step inside the club, sum up the sad state of affairs, and then shove off, their lack of appreciation for old biddies seeming to rival Bunny's before he dis-covered otherwise.

Trajan was more than happy to fill the void. Bunny's cousin had let them slow dance pressed tight against her one summer in the dank clamminess of her parents' basement, Patrice as much the aggressor in any grinding as either of them. Rosalie instructed him to hold her close around the waist and lead her, one simple step after the next in time to the beat of the music. It's like she was prepar-ing him, molding him into the kind of man she believed the world needed more of: considerate, attentive, sufficiently versed in the art of romance to want to hold a woman on the dance floor before get-ting down to business.

Trajan slow dragged one sanguine lady love after another around the floor, Rosalie's two-step proving serviceable, his sole ambition to spend time pressed next to her, his nose lost deep in the musk of her smell. The walk home was the slightest bit sweeter, music ringing in his ears, his skin permeated with the scent of fresh perfume. He didn't know what he'd done to brighten those women's night. They couldn't know all they had done to lift his spirits.

Sharkskin Suit

A fellow cadet at the police academy advised E-Z to give the psych board something, a solid hit as the only way to get them to stop digging for buried personality defects. No animal cruelty, no devi-ant sexual stuff, no two-headed monsters visiting your dreams. He suggested the death of a family member, somebody close. The board was going to want details.

E-Z had grown up in the shadow of Trajan's brother, Langston. Anything E-Z knew of his death he'd learned second- or thirdhand as word of the tragedy spread across town, acquired new texture as urban legend grew throughout his high school tenure. But E-Z knew Mr. Gurley, had visited with him every night for a whole year, if not longer placing plenty of details at his disposal, from the food-stained coloring of the ratty old sweater Mr. Gurley wore around the clock to the pantsuit his niece's lesbian partner was wearing at the funeral, gray sharkskin hugging the insides of her thighs until E-Z could make out every detail of the narrow crevice between her legs.

The two had driven down from Providence in the niece's Range Rover. Parked it underneath Mr. Gurley's carport like they were home to stay. That night, E-Z watched the two from his bedroom window locked in an embrace, leaned against a stretch of counter that extended from the kitchen into the living room. The niece stood with her back pressed into her partner, her blonde ponytail flipped across her shoulder to avoid crushing against the lapel of the woman's sharkskin suit. It took something as small as that for E-Z to know the two were lovers, one sent to comfort the other, staring at the back of Mr. Gurley's empty chair, soaking in silent memories of him as the two alternated sips from matching wine glasses.

E-Z neglected the part about the sharkskin crevice between Mr. Gurley's niece's lover's thighs when asked to tell the story in front of the psych board, recognized the potential for that particular detail to be misconstrued as a proclivity of some sort. He did, however, mention the embrace. Described it as tender, natural for two people who had shared a loss—again, on advice from his fellow cadet, be sure to show compassion for your fellow man whether that's what you're feeling or not, the review board having grown wary of sending unfeeling robots out among the populace.

Reckoning

Trajan encountered Bunny's brother on his way past Fort Shantok one night in early June, a dozen or so snow days left to burn off the only thing standing in the way of graduation. E-Z pulled up as Trajan started the long walk home, motioned for him to hop in the truck beside him.

"You been to The Boom Box?" E-Z asked.

Trajan nodded. "Things were about to wind down for the night," he volunteered.

"You get any numbers?" E-Z teased, looking to get a rise out of him.

Trajan focused his attention out the side window, beginning to regret having accepted a ride.

"You tired?" E-Z asked.

Trajan shook his head. Trajan never said he was tired whether he was tired or not, always looking to keep the night going.

"I know another spot," E-Z offered as he pushed the truck hard up Rte. 32. They rolled along Thames Street in search of a storefront backlit with lingering activity still burning inside. E-Z's mind raced back to a card game he'd stumbled across one night just as it was breaking up. The hostess at Bella Sera was losing badly at strip poker to some of the kitchen staff, on purpose it seemed, her face hungry to have their eyes on her. Long strands of chestnut hair that hung loose across her shoulders provided the only modesty. Rumor had it she'd been having an affair with the restaurant's owner and that she'd had a minor meltdown when he broke it off.

They found the windows of Bella Sera had gone dark already. The whole town appeared shuttered for the night. E-Z made a second pass to be certain, then turned in the direction of Preston, prepared to give up the quest, when a rattly old pickup truck shot past them, its fenders and hood mismatched and the truck bed covered in gray primer.

The truck clipped the shoulder, making a wobbly turn on its way out of town and barely managing to stay upright. E-Z gave chase. He checked his side mirror to make sure no one was on the road behind them before giving the siren a blast, the lights twirling against the flat rectangle of glass in the truck's back window.

"You taking them to jail?" Trajan asked, preparing to be let out to make room for a drunk transport.

"Nah, I know these chicks," E-Z answered, his eyes gleaming. "Just going to give them a little scare, get them off the road awhile."

The truck rumbled to a stop, a cloud of dust swirling in dim columns of light projected in reach of the ineffectual headlamps, yellowed with age. E-Z jumped out, trotted up to the driver's side door. He made a couple hand gestures over his back and then reached for the door handle. He helped three leggy young things down from the cab of the truck, extending a hand Prince Charming style as the girls stumbled in line along the shadow of his high beams. They were dressed alike: ankle-high boots, miniskirts, cut-off shirts tied high across bare midsections. Go-go dancers, E-Z felt obliged to explain. They trailed E-Z back to his patrol vehicle and piled in behind Trajan, an open bottle of vodka jangling loose between unsure hands.

"This is my buddy Trajan," E-Z said, slipping an arm around Trajan's neck to feign a level of familiarity between them. The girls said their names: this one, that one, the other one. Deanna was the only name Trajan took care to remember. She appeared the one most in need of convincing to be there. Trajan thought to wave to her on the sly, away from E-Z and her friends, to see whether she would wave back, to gauge where she was in the backseat of her mind.

E-Z had a terrific brainstorm. "Whaddya say we head out to the falls? It's been raining like mad. We can splash around in the over-flow from the pond."

Within minutes, they were standing at the edge of the shallow pool that builds along the tracks during the rainy season. Trajan crossed the train bridge. He set up along the rocks on the far side of the pond as E-Z persuaded the girls to take a dip. He slipped his arms into his jacket, pulled the hood over his head. It was still too cold outside to swim.

"We don't have suits," their pack leader complained, the vodka in her belly counteracting any ill effects of the damp night air.

E-Z suggested they swim in their bras and panties. "What if we're not wearing any panties?" she cackled, leering in the direction of her girlfriends as they started to undress.

Trajan hid his eyes in the shadow of his hooded sweatshirt as the girls slipped beneath the moonlight into a pool of mint green water. The bit about not having any panties was a lie, but if they'd had bras, they'd slipped them off together with their cutoff shirts as they folded their arms above their heads. They paddled away from E-Z, slipping onto their backs, wedges of white flesh highlighting bright pink nipples shielded from the sun by a lifetime spent in proper bathing attire, triangles in light toast missing from each breast.

Trajan worried the girls might become self-conscious bobbing in the water alone. E-Z looked to be toying with the idea of joining them. He'd locked his belt and gun away in the truck's glove compartment, leaving the tail of his shirt hanging loose about his waist, a free hand at work beneath his undershirt rubbing the hair on his belly to channel his enthusiasm. His ill-fitting uniform struck Trajan as belonging to someone escaped from an institution, a narrow green and orange stripe running the length of his pant leg.

The Norwich State Mental Hospital sits opposite the Mohegan Sun on the Preston side of the river. The spirit of the eternally damned presides over the river valley from the hospital's perch high above the Thames, the facility sitting unoccupied since its closing in 1996. Grade school folklore—passed in hushed tones in the shadow of the monkey bars on school playgrounds across the land—propagated the belief that any patients present at the time of the facility's decommissioning had been released onto the streets, and many could be found roaming downtown Norwich to this day, looking to find a way home. Another particularly chilling account told of an orderly drowned while attempting to rescue a patient who'd slipped free from his ward and then thrown himself into the river. The man gripped his would-be rescuer so tightly along the collar of the orderly's white coat that the orderly fell victim, unable to escape the silent undertow. Afterward the man swam back to safety, pulling himself ashore where he waited, cool as a cucumber, to be escorted back to his room. Now that's crazy.

Trajan began to suspect that he and the trio of go-go dancers had fallen into the hands of a lunatic, minus the dull tin star pinned to his chest. (A state mandate required that polished brass be reserved for municipal jurisdictions, a concession with which the tribal governances were forced to comply for the privilege of operating separate police forces within the confines of the reservations, relegating their officers to little more than armed security guards when encountered at a distance.)

The earth surrounding the bridge shifted, drawing Trajan's attention to more immediate concerns. "Train's coming," he announced, easing further up the granite outgrowth that lined the pond. Rumors persisted around school of vagrants who'd been hit by the train near the falls at Indian Leap, launching their bodies a hundred yards into the woods. When asked whether any remains were ever found, the storyteller insisted that wolves had dragged the bodies away, spiraling down another layer in misinformed speculation. Trajan knew from ventures into the woods with Grandpa Tuke that even with wolves, there would be evidence left behind: droppings strewn with bits of clothing, strands of hair, chunks of jewelry that survived the animal's digestive system unmolested.

"The train runs at midnight. Twelve-thirty latest," E-Z answered glibly, sounding a wee bit overconfident.

"The train comes when it comes," Trajan yelled into the space between them, repeating part of a lesson Tuke had shared with Trajan and Langston: *You can move out of the way according to any schedule you like, but that won't stop the train from knocking you flat.*

Tuke used to bring Trajan and his brother out this way when he wasn't in the mood for fishing. He enjoyed full command over every bit of land in the valley, made himself at home anywhere his people had once set foot, despite the state having thus far deemed otherwise. Bullfrogs were especially abundant after a heavy rainfall. The passing train sent the frogs scampering, a dozen or so unfortunate souls—the ones less swift with their leap—left floating bright belly side up in the train's wake, knocked unconscious by the percussion of tracks vibrating beneath the water's surface. Tuke waded into the pond ahead of his grandsons, turning over one frog after another, coaxing them out of their stupor before any of them drowned.

The boys asked if they could bring home a few of the frogs they'd rescued. Tuke didn't believe in keeping pets, not any animal taken from nature. It made as much sense to him for a pack of wild animals to take in one of us, raising us as their own. "Let them be," he said, intuition leaving him leery of things a group of bored kids might think to do with a bunch of punch-drunk bullfrogs. He'd heard tales of Bunny and E-Zs' exploits with stray animals they found, tales usually involving fireworks. "Our work is done here. The ancestors will not be pleased if any further harm comes their way."

It was a particular thrill for the boys to arrive in time to see a train passing. It starts out like the wind howling, a sound that's familiar yet remains elusive, prattling in the distance. The spill from the waterfall distorts the perception of sound. The drop in air pressure and the crash of the water cascading on the rocks below smothers any words uttered at eye level with the field surrounding the pond. At the base of the falls, the sound from up top is all you hear, stolen echoes boosting the volume above the tumbling rapids as a stuttering stream of white swell proceeds along the jagged riverbed. According to Tuke, by the time the sound of an approaching train registers in your brain, the churn of steel wheels glistening along thin rails as the train gathers speed, its locomotive breathing heavy as it breaks across the stand of shallow water, it's too late. You should have been gone already.

Trajan took cover away from the end of the train bridge. He rubbed an anxious finger across his brother's buffalo head belt buckle, Tuke's instruction filling his head. Survival instinct says to stay clear of the falls, to fight the pull in the downstream direction that sends anyone still in the pool scrambling for cover underneath the rusty train bridge, the place where the train's assault is at its worst, the crash of falling water nothing in comparison to the swirl of eddy currents stirred along the bridge supports. Tuke used to point out bunches of frogs scrambling up either embankment, having managed to swim across the undertow to safety, Mother Nature offering a valuable lesson put on live display in the shallow wading pool overlooking the falls—you may have to cut against the flow to make it, especially in dire times.

The Call of Home

The train was on the girls before Trajan could issue a second warning, a battering ram set loose in the middle of the pond wailing a hundred miles an hour. Trajan kept to his hiding place, listening for the last car filled with furniture, livestock, replacement auto parts, kitchen utensils to pass. He waited for the rails to stop squealing, for the bridge to stop swaying, to cease swinging in place, to rock itself back to sleep.

Trajan saw E-Z climbing the opposite bank once the commotion settled, a drenched go-go dancer close on his heels. The other crouched at the edge of the pond, her head stuck between her legs, retching up remnants of their ordeal.

E-Z did not fare well in any situation he could not bully, his impulse to flee taking command over his logical reasoning, limiting the sphere of possibilities he might think to pursue. He trudged back toward the one still crouched on all fours, pulled her up by the arm. "Come on," he urged. "I need to get you out of here. The lieutenant's gonna have my ass if he catches wind of me with a carload of civilians this far off post."

"What about Deanna?" the girl moaned. "We can't leave her."

"She probably went out the other side," E-Z offered, scanning the pond's surface for movement.

"With your buddy?" she questioned.

"Sure," E-Z conceded. "Trajan's real familiar with the trails back there. He'll take good care of her."

E-Z continued reassuring Deanna's girlfriends as they hopped in his truck and sped away. "You should head home," he said as they approached the corner where the girls had parked. "I'll double back, look for Trajan and your friend."

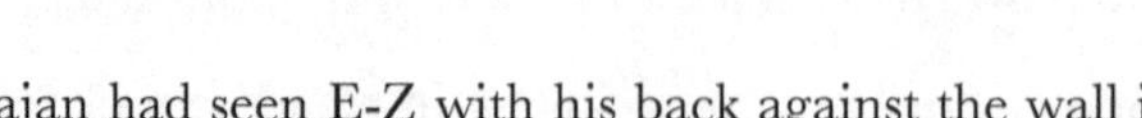

Trajan had seen E-Z with his back against the wall in the past. Any action he might consider taking at this stage, short of hopping into the truck when E-Z returned and fleeing along with him, would only place the two further at odds. It was irresponsible of them to have driven the girls out here in the first place. E-Z was not bound to stand by and let Trajan play the unwitting sidekick while charges were leveled against him: dereliction of duty, misuse of an official police vehicle, failure to render aid. Fortunately, Trajan's logic was rooted in the outlook for another living being, something Tuke had instilled in him and his brother, Langston. He eased into the water and began poking around beneath the bridge, waiting for Deanna to surface. She came to with a startled gasp for air like she'd been breathing the whole while inside her mind, waiting for his hand to pull her back into the conscious world. She spat up a lung filled with pond water mixed with vodka and whatever little food she'd eaten that day.

Trajan helped her up the granite embankment, slipped his jacket around her, zipped it shut to cover the brightness around her nipples. "I want to go home," Deanna muttered as the grogginess began to wear off. "Will you take me home?" She asked it like home was the answer to all her problems: her poor choice of friends, a gig she could no longer stomach, her close affiliation with girls who didn't mind jiggling their asses for tips that had landed her the job in the first place. Trajan envied her way of seeing things. Life for her was like the game of freeze tag they used to play during the summertime while waiting for the streetlights to flicker on. She'd nearly drowned tonight, but as long as she reached home base, everything would be all right.

Trajan wondered how long E-Z would wait, knew he would circle back to see for himself what had become of the girl he'd left behind. Trajan gambled on the innate laziness that E-Z and his brother both shared. He thought to himself: *What would Bunny do?*

Trajan kept low as high beams swerved into the gravel lot again. He held Deanna down alongside him while the spotlight mounted to the side of E-Z's patrol truck swept back and forth over their heads a couple times and then switched off. The truck scrambled from the lot. Trajan guessed E-Z would set up along the roadside and wait for him to break toward Preston—or toward Ledyard to take Deanna home if she'd managed to survive the pond.

Deanna pushed her arms through the sleeves of Trajan's jacket, reached for his hand as he helped her to her feet. She was still unsure where she was and how she'd gotten there, but she recognized that he meant her no harm. She was, however, quite certain she was not getting back in the water. And there was nothing Trajan could say to persuade her to follow him across the train bridge and leave the same way they'd entered. It was just as well. E-Z would be waiting, weaving back and forth between the few roadways that crossed the river if they attempted to head straight home.

Trajan started toward Sylvia Lane, Deanna dragging behind him, tugging at his elbow about needing to get home. They trudged deeper into the woods, heading in the only direction Trajan knew to go: farther away from E-Z. A smattering of light eventually came streaming through the thinning tree line: shiny things, man-made things, things that might see them home safely.

They swashbuckled their way down a grassy slope at just past two in the morning, angling their descent, reaching the pavement thirty yards from the place where they'd exited the woods. The courtyard outside the apartments was teeming with activity, the drug trade in Norwichtown obeying no fixed schedule. Trajan approached the first face he came upon.

"Do you know where I can find Luscius?" he asked.

The face paused, searching the skin and bone of him, the half-dressed white girl tagging along beside him. "I don't know any Luscius," the face responded in the darkness.

Trajan continued between clusters of people. His question was met each time with the same shuttered ignorance, nobody willing to claim knowledge of the man for whom they were no doubt busily plying their trade.

A pair of eyes followed him, had been on him since he and Deanna entered the courtyard. "Young boi, what you doing out here?"

"I need to find Luscius."

The man's eyes took their turn to study him, to survey his frazzled sidekick. "You know Luscius?" he asked, not waiting to hear Trajan's response. He produced a phone from his pocket and began speaking fast and low in Kreyol.

"I helped him once at Fort Shantok," Trajan added, pleading his case. "Turned tracks for him in the snow."

The man turned to the phone again, relaying the bit about the snow. "Bred'ren," he offered, echoing the words spoken on the other end of the line.

"Yes!" Trajan answered, beaming. "He called me brother, said I should come see him if there's anything I needed."

"What is it you need?" the man asked.

"To get home," Trajan replied, Deanna still antsy by his side.

The man spoke into his phone one last time. "Wait here," he said.

Within minutes they were in the backseat of the white Mercedes, Deanna snuggled next to Trajan like she was afraid to leave any open space between them. She poked her head out from beneath the hood of his jacket every so often to give directions. They pulled up in front of a dilapidated farmhouse. A broken-down pickup truck similar in vintage to the one her friend was driving sat in the open space where the side lawn should have been.

Trajan walked Deanna to her front door. "Give me a second," she asked. She returned wearing baggy sweatpants and an oversized T-shirt. She handed him his jacket, gave his neck a long squeeze. She moistened his cheek with a damp kiss as she pulled away from him. "Thank you, Trajan." His was the only name she'd bothered registering as well.

Trajan sat in the back of the car as Luscius directed his compatriot along the string of unlit, tree-lined country lanes that led toward Preston. The two spoke sparingly, if at all. Trajan took heed, sensing Luscius was the kind of man who appreciated his silence, who like Grandpa Tuke had little use for idle conversation. Trajan sank deep into the heavy cushion beneath him, for the first time in many months felt protected, looked after in a distant way, absent any undue emotion. He took it in the spirit in which it was intended, care for his well-being imposed out of obligation, a promise made in the swell of a snowstorm outside his mother's front door dictating any kindness thrown his way.

"This the way, Bred'ren?" Luscius asked as they approached his block.

"Just ahead on the right," Trajan confirmed, motioning with his hand. He turned as he headed up the walkway. "She's just someone who needed my help tonight," he started to say.

"No need to explain yourself, Bred'ren," Luscius offered. "Besides, if you tell me, I may owe you another promise, and Luscius is not one to go back on promises."

The Mercedes eased off, the night sky doing little to conceal its paint, absent the aid of heavy snowfall. E-Z lay in wait at the end of the street, sat in the shadows to observe Trajan delivered by the hand of the Thames River Valley's most nefarious outlaw.

THE HOPPER

Lacking sufficient resources to pursue every criminal, to police every crime, local authorities instituted a lottery system of their own. Luscius Brand's name came up in the hopper every now and again. The bigger the charges against him, the greater likelihood his number would hit. Luscius did not promote violence, but he recognized its necessity, given his chosen line of work. You cannot breed men to be violent. Violence is a trait a man must possess from his deepest core. Luscius surrounded himself with such men, sought use of the violent tendencies in them when necessity deemed extreme use of force inevitable. He recognized that only on rare occasions is justice truly blind. Other times, justice possesses sharply honed insights, doling out her punishment with exacting precision, wiping the offender from existence anytime the crime warrants such measures. There are times justice sees fit to punish both sides at once, the accuser suffering the same lumps as the accused, if not bigger.

Luscius had handed out his fair share of hard lumps. He held responsibility for several lives taken: some by direct oversight, the act committed on command of his word, others by his own hand. The first man whose life he took never saw it coming. He was sent to meet the devil with eyes wide open. Luscius hoped to be afforded the same mercy, a white-hot flash marking the instant his time came due.

Luscius arrived from Haiti with the one friend he had in the world—Jean-Pierre Marchand. Orphans of the same system, Luscius trusted Jean-Pierre with his life. The two were sent to stay with Luscius's mother's cousin in West Haven. Crack cocaine had taken hold like wildfire, and the cousin had sent word by way of relatives in Port-au-Prince soliciting sorely needed help in order to ensure a continued flow of funds back from the States. Who better to trust than family in a time of desperate need? He remembered Luscius as a calculating lad, rail-thin yet not one to be taken lightly. The work was blatantly manual, suited to the limited skills of his new recruits; their task was to break cakes of cooked cocaine into rocks, to put the rocks into vials, to bag the vials for transport down to the street.

Haitian youth grow up believing that the streets of America are paved in gold, its citizens luxuriating in palaces surrounded by riches the likes of which the eye would not believe. Luscius and Jean-Pierre arrived by train from Newark Airport to find the mother's cousin living at the bottom of the bottom, a palace for rats and roaches, a shithole for humankind. A man entered their apartment in the wee hours of the morning, pushed the door in with a foot followed by the weight of his shoulder. He fired two shots into the window frame as the cousin went crashing through in a spray of glass and splintering wood. The last Luscius saw of his second cousin, he was running along Washington Avenue in his stocking feet, his fists pumping the air for extra locomotion.

Luscius hid himself in the sag of sofa cushions, their batting having long ago lost its resilience. Jean-Pierre lay asleep across the room, his head buried beneath a mound of blankets, cold penetrating every corner of the room through cardboard thin walls. The man laid his weapon on the sofa, dropped to one knee, and began stacking bills. He produced a knapsack from inside his waistband and then spread the bag open beside the mountain of cash.

Luscius's hand found its way to the gun by sound alone, by memory of the low thud it made as the man let it fall in easy reach of Luscius's head, believing he was in the room alone on the cusp of an easy payday, his play in the game to rob street dealers at the end of the night when their coffers were overflowing. Luscius delivered a single shot to the back of the man's head. He knew by instinct not to give a man a second chance to think of killing you. You take careful aim and hope to kill him first.

That was Luscius's first offense against humanity. Now there

267

are twelve bodies to his credit, number twelve's woman—Mrs. Yellow Goose Down, the one Trajan found on his way through Fort Shantok that night—having narrowly escaped becoming lucky number thirteen.

Luscius stepped carefully with every move he made, recognizing that the consequences of his actions were usually permanent. Yellow Goose Down had made a move against him, had begun skimming off the top, stockpiling product to fund his own venture. That in itself was recoverable, a chop to the body in the form of an increased levy imposed on his crew, a reduction in responsibilities plus the promise of renewed commitment, and they would be square in no time.

But Yellow Goose Down had ambitions beyond his own piece of the rock. He had begun making inroads in search of an out-of-town connect to compete head-to-head against Luscius. Again, fair enterprise is fair enterprise, even among a den of murdering thieves. But he'd gotten reckless. He and that woman of his had begun to mistake the turn toward rational thinking as a sign Luscius had lost his edge. The connect they sought had ties back to Luscius by way of a couple of crooked local police who were sympathetic to Luscius's cause for their own selfish reasons.

Yellow Goose Down's ambitions had drawn unneeded attention. What presented itself as an out-of-town connect was instead federal drug enforcement working to set up a sting. It would have been fair punishment to let Yellow Goose take the fall. But few men have the resolve to fall alone. Yellow Goose couldn't be trusted to take the full weight without letting Luscius's name spill from his tongue with the slightest pinch. So Luscius and Jean-Pierre did what needed doing— with Bred'ren on hand to witness the results of their handiwork.

3 A.M.

Trajan noticed the light on at the end of the hallway as he turned to lock the front door. Dottie spoke to her son at three in the morning the same as she would at three in the afternoon, Trajan just coming in from school. Conventional wisdom said to track a child's every move. Practical experience had taught her that a child's whereabouts mattered little so long as no one called to say he was never coming home again.

She stayed clear of the phone any time Trajan was away. Aunt Sherry knew to call only when asked to do so. *Call you at ten tomorrow,* they'd agree, and Sherry wouldn't call a minute sooner. Chester had access to a key, limiting his need to reach her by phone. Tuke made use of the same key Dottie had directed Chester to use, though she had yet to clue her father in to her renewed association with her ex-husband.

"Did you hear about Dimitrius Giannakis?" Dottie asked as Trajan's shadow slithered past on the way to his room. She couldn't track her son's every move. She instead sought opportunities borrowed from the local newspaper headlines to keep tabs on the places he might go, her outlook for her son's well-being based in the premise that bad things befall good people in isolated spurts. Collecting newspaper clippings was her small way of gauging the level of threat that might land his way. If only Trajan could afford to wait for the headlines to catch up with the turmoil in his world—Ezrah Sessions, lingering difficulties with Carmen, Mrs. Padilla clocking his activities on her love seat, his connection to Luscius Brand, to Rosalie Anne Quigley, his recent affiliation with a trio of scantily clad go-go dancers—his mother might be in a better position to lend her perspective.

Trajan imagined hearing the story told, someone describing what they'd heard. He and E-Z had gone off-road with some girls they picked up coming from a club in town, dragged them into the woods. Had them out there doing God knows what and then left them for dead, hit by the train as far as either of them was concerned. He came out no better than E-Z—until you took Deanna into account, considered that she had made it home safely, that Trajan had gotten her there. He tuned out the thought in his head as his mother continued to marvel over her newspaper story.

"The *Bulletin* says he was assaulted in a robbery attempt at his family's pizza restaurant. The place on Rte. 12. You know which one I'm talking about?" Trajan knew the place. "You stay clear of there."

Right, Ma. Trajan thought to himself. *Boycotting Greek pizza is the best way to fight the rise in crime around town.* "I will, Ma," he replied, leaving her in the room alone, the newspaper lying neatly across her bedspread.

Local authorities took false comfort in affixing labels to any offense committed within their jurisdiction whether or not they understood the nature of the crime or had succeeded in deciphering the relationship between perpetrator and victim. They would have a panic on their hands were they to leave their constituents alarmed by the prospect of armed gunmen going around assaulting ordinary citizens without cause. The robbery was labeled an attempt, owing to the fact no money had changed hands. Spiro Giannakis ran an upstanding family business. The responding officers couldn't find any other motive for gunmen to enter the restaurant and put their hands on his son, Dimitrius, bringing their investigation to a swift close.

Dimitrius had graduated with Langston and Angelica. His sister, Diana, was in E-Z's class. Had he bothered to ask around, Trajan would have been sure to learn that the apparent assault was a botched attempt to collect payment for a brick of cocaine bought on consignment, the rumor mill at NFA in touch with sources beyond the reach of the police. Having crashed and burned at Central Connecticut State University, the years looming—stuck in his father's shadow spinning pizza dough above his head—Dimitrius set his sights on making his own way in life, the same as his father had done before him.

An Internet crash course plus an abundance of rap lyrics, spat recklessly close to true-life events, provided ample instruction on how to cook cut powder into hard rock. But there is no crash course in heart. Dimitrius lacked the charisma to recruit local talent to help move his product, was frightened out of his wits to stand alone at night mingling among the derelicts and fiends alongside committed players. He found himself caught in a classic hood dilemma: a choir boy saddled with an excess of crack rock to sell—for which he couldn't very well traipse back to Sylvia Lane and demand a refund—and all his money spent. Securing funds to repay his debt would require alerting his father as to the illegal enterprise he'd exposed the family business to. Shorting a legion of commissioned drug heavies offered better odds.

Intransigent Worry

Dottie knew nothing of Dimitrius's descent into the drug trade. Had no cause to fear that her son had gotten mixed up in any affiliated distress. When Dottie worried, she worried by association. What might someone influence her son to do? Langston hadn't ventured out to the Singer factory entirely of his own volition. It took some fast-in-the-behind little girls to lure him there under false pretense of a party. Never mind whether they meant him any harm. He wouldn't have been there in the first place if not for their meddling influence. She worried about E-Z carrying a loaded weapon loose about town, Trajan riding along by his side. What business did a rookie officer have with use of a patrol vehicle at his disposal in the first place, off-duty hours included? That they could afford to do it, buy each officer two cars if they wanted, was the only plausible justification, money flowing into the tribes to the point of masking rational thinking.

She couldn't help but see them as kids up the street playing, related anything they might do to what she had known of them in grade school, struggling in the classroom. A tiny wrinkle of intuition into the worst any of them might do stretched as they grew into their individual selves, afforded a deeper view into the chasm of wayward impulses her son and his friends might gravitate toward. E-Z was the less mischievous of the Sessions brothers and was, for that reason, all the more troubling. Bunny couldn't help his ways. It's like the one wire inside his head that said *don't say this* or *don't do that* had gotten detached, leaving him to fly open loop, his feedback mechanism on permanent override.

E-Z, on the other hand, had full command over his actions. He was lazy in the classroom, proved impossible to motivate, though he didn't entirely lack ambition. He managed to hold himself in line long enough to survive the state-administered police academy, serving to lend further evidence in Dottie's eyes to the deficiencies

275

in initial screening that had netted the likes of Officers Dooling and Wendt. Dottie added Ezrah Sessions, sworn peace officer, to the list of men she didn't wish to see her son grow to be.

Bedfellows

Trajan's schedule turned exceedingly no nonsense. He preferred to stay put after Bunny's uncle dropped him off each night. Time with Carmen was relegated to hallway visits in between classes, Trajan no longer in a position to risk another misadventure with E-Z on the trek home alone after an evening spent in her parents' living room.

E-Z had also begun keeping to their side of the river, having seen Luscius drop Trajan at home, go-go dancers and old biddies left to muddle along without him. He spent the balance of the night sitting upright in the squad room listening for reports of a drowning victim, a missing go-go dancer. Now he regularly hung back in the station house to conduct research on the police computer to curb the restlessness at the end of each shift. He needed to know who he was dealing with—Luscius Brand. No charges had been filed against him. The active investigation open in his name was password protected, leaving him to consult other sources.

E-Z tasked Bunny with texting him at the end of the night to say whether he was heading straight home. (Chester had never permitted Trajan to carry a pager, not after Paulo's mother found one buried in his laundry. Wannabe gangsters carried pagers, drug runners, new police. Chester was determined to keep his son from falling into such a dismal string of limited possibilities despite the distance between them.) Bunny mistook his brother's sudden interest in his whereabouts as being about him; maybe E-Z was contemplating another trip to Baltic Street, time spent in the company of his little brother more palatable as graduation approached. E-Z's next question was always the same, deflating Bunny's spirit a bit further: *Trajan with you?*

"Trajan, you feel like going out tonight?" Bunny asked, his fingers poised to tap out a response to his brother's inquiry.

"Nah," Trajan responded, hiding his anxiety beneath a manufactured yawn.

"Me neither," Bunny replied, feigning a similar bout of fatigue descending on him from out of nowhere. Another question struck him before his fingers could type. "You gonna want to go out tomorrow night?"

Trajan's answer was again a bedraggled no.

"I didn't think so," Bunny responded. "I'll just tell him we're too tired to hang." His fingers finally went to work, pecking out a reply.

Mrs. Sessions insisted that Trajan accompany them anytime Bunny went out with E-Z. Bunny loved to show off, took advantage of every opportunity to impress his older brother. She hoped he would follow Trajan's lead and not cut up too badly.

Trajan had little concern for Bunny's antics at this stage. He summoned his grandpa's spirit gods again. The universe left nothing to chance. Every encounter in life has its purpose. Trajan was meant to be there for Deanna, just as Luscius had been placed there for him to call on in a time of need. What purpose could be served hounding Trajan over a girl to whom neither he nor E-Z had any serious connection, had no intention of pursuing further? He hoped E-Z would let the whole thing go. They'd had a scare, had survived the closest of calls. Trajan wasn't inclined to speak out of turn, even if he did hold E-Z partially responsible.

E-Z had other worries. Trajan could say anything he liked to the proper authorities. He had his story straight: An inebriated go-go dancer found herself out of sorts in the middle of the pond overlooking the falls when a train passed, considerably late according to the advertised schedule. It's all he could do to rescue the first two. Provided Trajan went along, he could play hero too, having risked life and limb to save the third dancer. If Trajan decided to buck, contradicting E-Z's account, he'd be a ready scapegoat. Trajan had ventured to the far side of the pond, lured one of the girls to swim across and join him, naked save for a pair of skimpy panties. No one would believe Trajan over him, the band in blue closing ranks to preserve the integrity of the force—the band in green and orange stripes.

Luscius commanded a different respect. There was little E-Z could do to sway opinion in his favor if anybody went to Luscius instead of the proper authorities. He continued monitoring the police blotter: still no mention of a missing person. Maybe she had gotten out after all.

That didn't explain why Trajan had begun acting so peculiar. He stopped carrying his skateboard everyplace he went. He stopped going anyplace, beating a neat circuit from school to work, then back home again. Soccer had been cut from his life, the senior season having come to a close. It wasn't evident when he would play again or where, his plans beyond high school still up in the air. He'd become a prisoner in his own little world at a time when he should be chasing new bounds.

Every police organization maintains an innocuous circle of checks augmenting internal investigation in an earnest attempt to preserve harmony within the community it serves. The commissioner appoints dedicated staff to police from within, while a Citizen Review Board monitors activities from outside the commission. The CRB investigates suspected cases of police misconduct, civil rights violations, and complaints of harassment and abuse of authority to balance interests in public safety against the rights of its citizens, those of the accused included. Everyone is bound by a code of ethics—the criminal most especially, in hopes of steering clear of undue police scrutiny. The more crafty the criminal, the more inclined he is to enlist an investigative team of his own. He polices the police in that regard, helps set bounds within which to operate.

A Little Bird

Word got back to Luscius that someone outside the normal jurisdiction had been nosing around in his file. A little birdie told him. Luscius privately helped fund a youth soccer league run out of the community center, one that predominantly served residents of Sylvia Lane. The Greater Norwich Youth Soccer Association was organized in partnership with the police commission to promote a drug-free outlook among local teens, an initiative to which Luscius wholeheartedly subscribed. He, too, had been a youth full of drive and ambition, soccer the only thing keeping him in line back in his native Haiti. The drug trade provided a springboard that was instrumental in his ascent in America, a means to an end. Who better to understand the obligation to protect our youth from the evils that men do than the man himself?

Retired from the *Norwich Bulletin*, Ned Turner had worked the police desk the vast majority of his career, witnessed the subtle transformation of the town's criminal activity over the years from petty offenses to tiny sprees of disorganized crime to the recent outcropping in criminal enterprise, spawning entanglements so pervasive that no one's integrity was beyond reproach. He knew the likes of Luscius Brand. Knew the Luscius before him and was bound to know the Luscius to come, provided he kept his nose to the wind. The Lusciuses of the world fill a void that doesn't go empty long. Better somebody open to candid exchange than one closed to any idea he hasn't come to on his own.

Ned's first several conversations with Luscius were like trying to coax warm soup from hard stone. The two had since formed a tenuous alliance. As a fellow Youth Association board member, Ned felt compelled to apprise Luscius of the occasional rise in tide against him. Took it as his role in the cat-and-mouse pattern of engagement between the police and the reputed drug lord who, some might argue, appeared to have grown a heart. Luscius, in turn, notified Ned of the influx of any insidious chem lab activity, crystal meth, and other home-brewed narcotics. Luscius considered his to be a roots-rock drug enterprise, the purveyor of product aimed at getting you high. That chem lab *ish* put you out of your mind. Anything that didn't come straight from mother earth had no place in his jurisdiction.

"Someone has been asking about you," Ned mentioned in passing at an awards banquet marking the end of the spring soccer season.

"Somebody wants to know Luscius?"

"They appear to know of you. It seems they would like to know you better," Ned reported.

"You know this person?" Luscius inquired.

"Only a name: Ezrah Sessions. He's known on the streets as E-Z."

"He is police?" Ned nodded, affirming Luscius's suspicions. "And who is his sergeant?" Luscius asked in order to see whether that bread had been buttered already.

"The inquiry came from outside the municipal jurisdiction," Ned replied, confounding Luscius's concern.

"Not Norwich Police?" Luscius asked, perplexed.

"He belongs to one of the tribal forces. His post is located at Foxwoods Casino," Ned added, feasting on the prospect of a new wrinkle to trail, the newspaperman in him forever on the case.

"Why would Mashantucket police want to know Luscius? I did no dirt on their watch," he insisted, agitation stirring behind silent eyes. "Give me the name one more time," Luscius asked.

"Ezrah Sessions," Ned complied. "Goes by E-Z."

"Give me a couple days," Luscius said, taking Ned by the shoulder. "I'm going to see what there is to learn about this Officer Easy." Luscius enlisted the aid of Jean-Pierre, his first lieutenant. "You want I should pay this man a visit?" Jean-Pierre asked.

"It's too soon for that," Luscius responded. "Put a couple feelers out, see what comes back." He chuckled to lighten the mood. "Perhaps our fine officer is looking to contribute to the Benevolent Order of Luscius Brand."

"More likely looking to make a withdrawal," Jean-Pierre suggested.

"We can deal with that too," Luscius replied, his eyes fixated on a spot along the horizon he consulted in times of serious thought. "*Lè yo ap di, mwen frè*—time will reveal."

Renewal

Tuke let Trajan drive him home from the casino Friday nights. Trajan had never applied for his learner's permit, but then Tuke had never been one to follow any rule he felt he could get away with breaking. He sat pressed against the side door, his elbow perched on the armrest. He put his hand to work inside the passenger window directing traffic around them.

Tuke relished the extraordinary freedom the passenger seat afforded him to gaze, passing along familiar routes, soaking in waves of new detail. He allowed Trajan free reign over the car stereo as long as his grandson kept the volume well below mid-range. The WRIU mix, bubbling barely audibly over the strain of the car engine, went nearly imperceptible each time Trajan turned the car in the uphill direction. A stray bump or two rose above the whir of soft tires on the roadway—a soft pinging like those hearing tests administered by the school nurse as part of the annual physical required of all student-athletes. Then there it was again: *thump, thump, thump, thump,* the song impossible to identify at this volume.

Trajan sat stiff behind the wheel, his hands at ten and two, from the corner of his eye registering Tuke's body language. A clenched fist meant to brake; an open hand that it was safe to proceed, his

285

fingers extending down the roadway. Tuke tapped his foot in time with the metronome clicking of the turn signal, focused a narrow finger to ward off opposing traffic—*Back off, you. Keep out of my lane.*

"Whatever happened with the situation on your hands?" Tuke asked, his eyes still lost on the world outside the passenger window. "Your woman troubles."

"What woman troubles?" Trajan asked, working to gauge the breadth of his grandpa's suspicions.

"She's your woman," Tuke shrugged. "How am I supposed to know?"

Again, Trajan wished he'd said girl. "Oh, that. It fizzled."

"Fizzled before getting off the ground, or have the two of you already had your fill of one another?"

"It just wasn't meant to be," Trajan conceded.

"That sounds like grown-up talk. What about you didn't her folks like?"

Trajan did a quick recap inside his head. The situation with Mrs. Quigley seemed to have collapsed under its own weight, bloomed fast only to wither just as quickly. Things with Carmen had settled into a permanent holding pattern, her mother dictating every move between them or the lack thereof.

"It was just bad timing," Trajan admitted. More grown-folks' talk.

"I'll tell you like someone once told me: It's better to be out and know you're out than to stand around trying when you've got no chance of getting back in." Trajan took note of Tuke's tone, the sentiment offered in obvious reference to his wife, Estelle. Trajan silenced his tongue, another lecture on tap about stirring up the dead had he elected to probe further.

"Sometimes all you're left is out," Trajan answered, melancholy of his own at work inside his head. He started to tell his grandpa. Saw an opening to shed the burden collapsing his spine, his desire to remain at odds with the world buckling under. But a nervous unrest intervened, Chester's general sense of distrust encroaching on his son's perspective. How might Tuke judge him in the end? Would he run and tell Dottie where her son had been?

"You know the trouble with youth?" Tuke wondered into the narrow space between the car's front seats. "You're in too much of a hurry to get beyond where you are in life to enjoy what you have. Life experience teaches a man to slow down, to appreciate the road along the way as much as the destination. You have plenty of time for misery. Don't use it all up while you're still young," he advised his grandson.

Tuke reminded Trajan that everything is renewable, even a wounded spirit. "You'll have ample opportunity for heartache, heartbreak hopefully with a fair share of joy mixed in to justify the ordeal you must endure on the way to finding your one true love. Just make sure you don't get pregnant along the way."

Tuke intercepted a minivan threatening to turn right on red in front of them. Snapped his fingers on the van, held it fast, pointing with exaggerated authority: *Stay back, you. Let us pass.*

Strange Associations

Jean-Pierre returned with surprising findings: (1) Officer Easy was new police, fresh out of the academy. Luscius seemed a big fish for a rookie to want to land. At least he had aim. (2) He had a younger brother set to graduate that spring from NFA.

"So what, this younger brother wants a cut of the benevolent fund too?" Luscius asked. "This family is full of ambition."

"*Sa se pa tout*—that is not all," Jean-Pierre added. "This brother is good friends with someone you and I have come to know quite well, rides with him every day from Preston."

"Bred'ren?" Luscius snapped his tongue, cocked his head casting a sharp eye on *zanmi l'*—his best friend. "This cannot be."

"We cannot say for certain that the two situations are interrelated. But the boy has a way of showing up under the most unusual circumstances."

"*Wi, li pa nòmal,*" Luscius concurred. It is not normal.

CAT AND MOUSE AND
EVEN BIGGER CAT

Run from your troubles, and there's no place the devil won't find you. Stand your ground, and the devil just may go nosing around elsewhere. Words spoken by Granville Hastings to his son-in-law, Alonzo Tooker, on the prospect of his family splitting apart, wisdom that Tuke, in turn, passed to his grandsons.

Equanimity

Rosalie set about a ritualistic pattern of withdrawal. She steered clear of the library, wishing to see Trajan again only if he came to see her. She trusted her ability to judge character to tell her that he would not be so careless as to show up unannounced. She suffered her need for him in silence, bore responsibility for her role in their affair with quiet equanimity. She would carry to her grave how she had betrayed Gilbert, the disgrace she had brought to their home. She could not begin to imagine how he might forgive her if he were to find out.

Thursdays with Trajan were a thing of the past. It was like walking away from a traffic accident, the whole intersection turned at odd angles. Only those at the wheel know what they were intending, where they were heading before the incident occurred. Still, she needed to see him one last time, dear, sweet Trajan. She had a graduation gift for him: *Echo of Lions,* a novel that told the story of the *Amistad* slave ship revolt. It was the work that most informed her opinion of President Adams. Trajan needed a hero to emulate, so she thought to give him one of hers.

She'd sat outside the library a couple times the past few weeks, watched Trajan hop into the Service Master van alongside Bunny and his uncle. Another week and she'd miss graduation altogether; her gift would appear out of context offered so long after the fact.

Luscius kept his own vigil. He had Jean-Pierre drive him across the bridge, set up in the shadow of a lazy oak tree awaiting Trajan's return. They, too, watched as Trajan stepped down from the van, lifted two fingers in the air bidding farewell to Bunny and his uncle for the night before disappearing inside the house. They had anticipated a secret engagement with Officer Easy, some clandestine plotting against Luscius and his band of loyal minions. Nothing of the sort would materialize.

The intelligence Jean-Pierre gathered had thus far betrayed them. E-Z arrived a couple of hours later, parked his patrol vehicle in the driveway outside his mother's house, and then vanished inside as well. Luscius and Jean-Pierre drove back to Norwichtown in silence. E-Z could no sooner collect rainwater in a bucket than catch Luscius Brand, a player seasoned in the game, with his hand in the cookie jar.

Past Associations

Rosalie rolled the dice again. She bet Trajan would still recognize a signal from her despite the odds stacked high against her. She paid the library a visit and left John Quincy Adams facing backward to schedule another rendezvous between them. She wouldn't bring Trajan to the house. If she did, they would be careful not to push the bounds of familiarity with one another, rekindling past intimacies. She couldn't afford to let herself slide, couldn't risk falling back on the feelings she had for him, given the renewed commitments she needed to keep.

Trajan nearly overlooked the shelf. He'd encountered the volume resting undisturbed so regularly that his mind was reluctant to see it any differently. He held the book in his hand, felt the weight of its pages pressing into his palm. She'd actually been here. The only other plausible explanation was that Bunny had finally caught on and turned the book inside out to antagonize his friend, Bunny having sniffed out the zigzag pattern in Trajan's routine that started each night with a pass through the biographies.

Trajan consulted his well-honed pattern of scheming. He'd ride home with Bunny as planned, seated facing backward atop a canister of cleaning solution in the back of his uncle's van. He'd tip out again after grabbing a quick shower, head along Rte. 2 to meet Rosalie in her burgundy Volvo. Bunny interrupted him partway through his vacuuming, scattering the details of the timetable he needed to keep as he lined things up inside his head. Carmen was on the phone for him. Her parents had been invited to a retirement party for one of her father's coworkers, no kids allowed. She wanted Trajan to come and see her.

The conversation surrounding when she and Trajan were going to do it had continued within her circle, even though Trajan's friends had long grown bored with the topic. Maria subscribed to the Susie Lindstrom school of thinking on virginity: It was something to get over, like chickenpox.

"He's your best bet," Maria suggested, "if you're ever going to have a first time." It was the least he could do for all the time her friend had invested working to maintain a relationship between the two of them. Carmen couldn't deny the time spent but had serious doubts about their having maintained anything.

292

"I'll leave the door unlocked," Carmen mouthed into the phone, her voice less assured than the time she'd practiced the words in front of her girlfriends while changing after gym class. "Let yourself in," she continued, straining to get through the lines they'd fed her. "I'll be upstairs waiting." She hung up before surprise could settle between them.

Trajan sat at the other end of the line, befuddled. He'd written off any further progression between them as pointless. He'd graduate in another week. Time in the hallway between classes was pretty much all they had left. They would, at best, struggle through the summer together, Mrs. Padilla standing guard at the top of the stairs waiting for Trajan to leave her house. Carmen was sure to find other interests once school resumed come fall. It might be best if they didn't. Plus, Rosalie was expecting him.

He adjusted his plan. If he hustled, he could get by to see Carmen, talk through what the future held between them, then circle back in time to catch Rosalie crossing the bridge from the opposite direction. Provided things went according to plan, he would be home before E-Z finished his shift and set out in search of him.

Trajan gave Bunny that put-upon look boys employ, pretending that the sole purpose behind whatever they're doing is to accommodate their female counterparts. Said he'd catch him later.

❦

E-Z's heartbeat raced when he read Bunny's text message: *Heading home. Trajan's on his way to Carmen's.* (Bunny asked his brother to call if he wanted to hang later, the limits on their affiliation continuing to elude him.)

"It's on," E-Z said, rapping his knuckles against the steering wheel of his patrol vehicle. Mrs. Padilla was legendary for the watch she kept over her daughter. There's no way Trajan could be heading to Carmen's house this late at night. He was no doubt planning to meet up with Luscius again.

E-Z radioed the dispatcher, said he was taking a late dinner break. He fired up his truck and started along Rte. 2 in the direction of Norwich. If they were destined for a showdown, he'd be sure to beat Trajan to the punch.

Hips and Thighs

Jean-Pierre continued to track Trajan's whereabouts after school. "I want to know who he talks to, where he goes if not straight home," Luscius insisted.

Jean-Pierre prepared to drive off, to follow at a safe distance as the Service Master van pulled out of the library parking lot, when a gray-hooded sweatshirt headed in the opposite direction caught his attention. He recognized the slow gait, the sullen disposition lurking beneath the hood. "Bred'ren," he said aloud, putting the Mercedes in drive.

Luscius had eyes posted at every angle leading toward Sylvia Lane, confining the area Jean-Pierre needed to search. He caught a glimpse of Trajan's silhouette as he crossed beneath the street lamp lighting the main entrance to the high school. He crept along a side street. Watched as Trajan climbed the Padilla's front steps, took the knob in his hand, and let himself in. "*Ki sa ki se sa a*—what is this?" Jean-Pierre questioned. A second resting place seemed to confirm that Trajan was undercover, this address a makeshift headquarters, his home in Preston a ruse.

He called Luscius's cell phone seeking further instruction. "Stay put, *mwen frè*. See what develops," Luscius advised.

Competing concerns proceeded to jockey for attention inside Trajan's head. To the untrained eye, he was set to suffer yet another lifeless adventure on his girlfriend's living room sofa, just as he'd assured Bunny. Closer inspection might reveal that he'd left his skateboard at the library, locked inside the janitor's closet with their stash of cleaning supplies in preparation for a long-awaited rendezvous with Rosalie. He climbed the stairs, an opening line at work inside his head. *It might be best if we wait . . . if we didn't.* Waiting implied there was still hope for some future between them.

He pushed open Carmen's bedroom door. She stood in a dim light with hips cocked at an enticing angle, her bra and matching panties handpicked for the occasion. The pecan tan expanse of her skin accented in white lace made him forget what he wanted to say. She pulled him to her, realizing any amount of conversation was bound to drain the little bit of confidence she'd mustered since hanging up in his ear. She engulfed him in a tangle of arms and legs, her mouth loose against his, sucking him in.

A switch flipped inside Trajan's head, transporting him to a place he knew well, had desperately missed. He unzipped his jacket, slipped his shirt over his head. He pressed his bare chest along the exposed length of Carmen's warm thighs, caressing her backside with both hands as he deposited kisses across her trembling belly. Her body tensed as he released her bra strap with a snap of his fingers the way he'd learned to do.

He pushed her panties past her hips, slid them all the way off the way Rosalie had taught him. He was on his way back around hips, down thighs when Carmen asked him to stop, startled by the ease of his fluid movements. It was more than a girl could take. She wanted him to want it like she wanted it, the small hesitations between them highlighting their innocence, their relative inexperience. She had hoped her first time would be his first time too. That could hardly be the case. Maria's instincts were spot on—*a boy will pretend to wait, even though he ain't waiting.*

"This isn't right," she said slipping a nightshirt over her head. "We shouldn't be here like this."

"I want to do this for you," he told her. "I don't mind."

She pushed him from the bed. "If you leave now, it will be for me," she insisted, folding her knees into her chest. "If you stay, we may never recover."

HONEST INJUN

Trajan put his clothes back on: his light gray jacket over top of a dark gray T-shirt, black jeans, and slipped into the night. *I'm sorry* is the last thing he said to Carmen. She couldn't begin to comprehend the magnitude of his *sorry*. *Sorry he hadn't been there. Sorry he hadn't waited, that he'd been someplace else. Sorry he had to leave her this way, that he could never be the person she wanted him to be, someone her mother would adore.*

He had a similar stream of apology in store for Rosalie. *Sorry he'd put her out of her way like that. Sorry things had gotten so mixed up between them. Sorry he couldn't be the man she needed either.* He turned in the direction of the river crossing along Rte. 2, though he was certain she had already returned to Bozrah for the night.

What-Ifs

Rosalie had circled the bridge a dozen times or more, her last pass at slow speed, hoping to see Trajan emerge from the shadows prepared to jump in the seat next to her. She was up to her neck in a hot bath, her tea resting by her side, by the time Trajan began the trek up the bridge's slow incline heading back to Preston.

She donned a pair of comfortable house shoes and a lightweight robe and planted herself at the kitchen table, waiting for life to pass her by. A nervous restlessness surfaced along the back of her neck and settled in her shoulders, her hands at work along the tabletop looking to put themselves to some productive use. She and Trajan had failed to make adequate provisions for the inevitable *what-ifs:* What to do if she found herself suddenly unable to get away? How he would notify her in the event he was unable make it? She was ill prepared to endure another sleepless night. She began dialing before fully contemplating what she intended to say.

The sound of the phone ringing startled Dottie from a light sleep. She sat up, the covers pulled to her chin, waiting for the ringing sound to fill her ears again. Superstition kept the phone resting in its cradle. The phone had never succeeded in bringing Chester home, had proven incapable of sparing Langston. Still, she had Trajan. A phone call might bring him to her. A phone ringing against the night might just as easily surrender him forever.

"Mrs. Hopkins, I hope I'm not calling too late," Rosalie started apologetically, figuring it would be best if she didn't ask for Trajan straight away.

"You're fine. Who is this?" Dottie asked, the voice failing to register.

"It's Mrs. Quigley, Trajan's history teacher. You may remember me from . . . Langston's memorial service."

"I remember you," Dottie replied. "Trajan tells me you retired."

"Why, yes. A couple of years back," Rosalie responded, feeling the conversation gaining momentum.

"Tell me then, why is it you're calling?"

"I was calling to see that Trajan's all right, to ask how he's doing with graduation just around the corner," she explained, laboring to sound upbeat. "He's really quite remarkable. I have every confidence he will do well." She buried her anxiety beneath an uncontrollable stream of meaningless chatter.

A mother who loves her son can detect the slightest uptick in the voice of the woman who loves him too. She is able to read every intention in that woman's tone of voice. "I don't mean to be crass, but do you have any children of your own?" Dottie asked. Mrs. Quigley indicated that she and Gilbert had never had children. "Then you can't know what it means to mother a child, to hold out all your hopes and dreams so that child might have a better life. It means loving your son no matter what."

She curtailed the assault on the off chance her venom was

misplaced. "A mother doesn't need someone else to tell her about her son. I know how remarkable Trajan is."

"Naturally you do," Rosalie offered, already in full retreat. "Excuse the intrusion. It won't happen again."

"I trust that it won't," Dottie responded, placing the receiver back in its cradle.

Dottie ventured a trip across the hallway—a major stride for her. The sound of her sons playing snuck past, escaped into the living area as she ducked her head inside the room Trajan and his brother once shared. She hugged the door frame, searching the walls for some clue of Trajan's whereabouts, what this woman meant by calling. Bunny was the only friend she knew firsthand. Bunny was a hanger-on; she had always seen him that way. He was sympathetic enough in his earnest attempts to be part of the kid collective who used to congregate under her roof. He'd leave something behind anytime he came to the house—his jacket, his hat, his ball and glove—to secure an invite inside when the boys returned. Trajan was bound to tell Bunny only what he wanted him to know.

She'd heard countless stories about BLT's on-field heroics, felt like she knew them from the anecdotes her son related, knowledge that failed to produce a proper name. She eventually came across a team photo propped against the wall at the back of the dresser. She recognized Ben from Trajan's description of him: tall, aloof, possessed of a devil-may-care look in his eyes. You couldn't miss him. The photo cited the boy standing between him and Trajan as Steven Lighty. Recollection of the name came tumbling back to her.

She found the number listed in the telephone directory, was greeted by Brenda, Lighty's younger sister.

"This is Mrs. Hopkins, Trajan's mother." She didn't know what else to say to explain her reason for calling. She was Trajan's mother. That ought to be reason enough.

"Oh, hi, Mrs. Hopkins." The girl spoke with a queer familiarity, as if she knew her son in a way Dottie was reluctant to contemplate. She'd made enough surprise acquaintances for one night. "Let me get my brother," Brenda said, placing the phone down on some hard surface. Dottie listened as the word *STEVE* trailed away from the receiver.

"Mrs. Hopkins?" a voice picked up.

"Is this Lighty?" Dottie asked, getting a rise out of him; adults seldom used his nickname.

"It's okay to call me Steve," he replied.

"Well, Steve," Dottie began over again, "I'm calling to ask when you last spoke to Trajan."

He admitted that it had been awhile. A couple of semesters back was his closest recollection. "We had a bit of a falling out."

"Do you know where he might be?" Dottie persisted.

"Maybe over at Carmen's." That name resonated with Dottie as well. "But the way I hear it, her mother runs a tight ship. I doubt he'd still be over there this late."

Dottie checked the clock on her night table—quarter past eleven. It was too late to disturb the Padilla residence. She was certain to have burdened Carmen's mother enough already. She envied Mrs. Padilla for the hold she'd managed to maintain over her daughter, recognized the benefit she'd undoubtedly reaped indirectly from her militancy.

Lighty asked her to have Trajan call once he got home safely.

"I'll do just that," she said, thanking him for his help.

Dottie picked up the phone again, dialed Tuke's number. "I need you to come get me."

"And take you where, Dorothy?" he asked.

"To find my son," she murmured, hoping the phone would not again see fit to betray her.

Tuke phoned Chester, swung by to get him on the way past his daughter's house.

Canary

E-Z ventured dangerously close to the area surrounding Sylvia Lane, yet failed to catch a glimpse of anything able to calm his curiosity. A glowing red fire engine might have been less conspicuous, the entire village spying his patrol vehicle from a distance, a warning signal darting between buildings to curb activity in the compound.

Luscius responded appropriately to the perceived threat, closing up shop for the night. He called for Jean-Pierre to abandon his post outside Carmen's house, to circle back and pick him up. Bred'ren had witnessed what they'd done to dispose of Mr. Yellow

Goose Down. Now Trajan had turned up again with apparent ties to Mashantucket Pequot Police. Officer Easy was a wrinkle Luscius didn't need, especially seeing how Mrs. Goose Down had survived. She had thus far seen fit to keep her mouth closed. That could change at any minute if Luscius were to come under added police scrutiny. They set out in search of Officer Easy, intent on deciphering his connection to the apparent mole in their midst: his affiliation with young Bred'ren.

E-Z proceeded to travel the full loop, crisscrossing the river along Rte. 2. He made use of the searchlight hanging outside his patrol vehicle, interrogating anything that moved in the shadows. He finally spotted Trajan's hooded sweatshirt taking to the footbridge at the end of Main Street. He appeared to be looking for someone, turning back every so often but otherwise keeping an even stride on the path that led in the direction of the Preston side of the river.

The silhouette of E-Z's massive truck came streaming through the wall of light projected from a rack mounted like antlers to the vehicle's roof. A sudden burst of speed sent high beams running up Trajan's backside. Trajan broke into a light trot that turned to sprinting under the force of the threat bearing down on him. He soon found himself running for his life. He thought about crossing in front of oncoming traffic, jumping the median, and heading in the opposite direction, when the beleaguered raccoon came to mind. He continued charging toward home, determined to evade a similar fate.

He tumbled headlong as he crested the top of the bridge, his sprint faltering with the first few elongated strides downhill. He slid along the asphalt, scraping the side of his face from the crown of his forehead to the end of his pointy chin. He cowered along the guardrail, waiting for E-Z to make the first move, *Moo Duk-Chung-Soo* competing inside his head for which fighting style to employ.

Luscius and Jean-Pierre showed up in time to see Trajan running. He looked more prey than predator. Jean-Pierre sped alongside him, angled the white Mercedes in front of E-Z's patrol vehicle, and pinned it to the guardrail, the truck's high beams illuminating the expansive darkness downriver. Luscius stepped out of the car, motioned for E-Z to follow suit.

E-Z stepped down from his truck, his hand resting firmly against the butt of his handgun. He pushed his badge ahead of him like an amulet meant to ward off evil spirits.

"You think that tin star on your chest will impress me?" Luscius asked, cocking his head side to side to gain clearer comprehension of E-Z's gesticulating. "Luscius is surrounded by your kind *chak jou*— every day. Police, DEA, Tonton Macoutes; they are all the same. Some watch me from a distance through the high-powered lens of a camera trying to catch Luscius with his hands dirty. Then there are those who have their hands in my pocket. They grant me a pass to do what I do. For when I make, they make. Should I fall, they too shall fall.

"There is one I have direct on my payroll. He says he is from my village in Haiti, Petionville, yet I do not know of him, know no one who knows of him. I ask how one would travel to my village, to *our* village, to say what lies nearby, and he stumbles to recall the simplest detail. His Kreyol, it is pathetic, learned from a book no doubt. You cannot learn the ways of my people through any amount of study. You must live *Ayisyen* to be *Ayisyen*. This one I keep by my side for protection. He is my canary in the coal mine. When he goes missing, it means the rest are soon to come with a heavy foot. Luscius is on vacation that day, packs up his work and waits for the feet to pass, for the canary to come singing at my doorstep again. And you think your tin badge will move me, will cause me to change my ways. I regret to inform you, Luscius is not so easily persuaded."

E-Z loosened his grip on his sidearm, lifting his hands in mock surrender. "I wasn't looking to jam you up," E-Z stuttered. "But you've got to understand, I didn't mean for any harm to come that girl's way."

Luscius let a vociferous laugh into the sky, showed his teeth to the moon, his head lolling backward. "The scrawny white girl?" he inquired, his eyes scrambling to gather the full meaning of E-Z's words. "Luscius could care less about a drowned sewer rat," he spat in E-Z's direction, gnashing his teeth on the words. "That is none of my concern."

E-Z's posture again mirrored that of a lunatic discharged early, his hands at work signing to communicate the lies his tongue had yet to articulate. He was overmatched, outmanned, outgunned, arguably more mouse than cat, indoor spoon-fed cat if cat at all. The sway of Luscius's stance was maniacal in comparison, the lunatic having thus far eluded capture. He leaned in, invading E-Z's space full to the brim as his rant caught fire. He let his tirade rage full rail for several hot seconds before fatigue set in, disdain for the persistent nipping at his heels inspiring a calculated retreat.

Luscius despised confrontation. The need to act, to push another being beyond his limits, evoked violent turmoil within him, rumbled inside his gut until the urge to unleash his violence saw fit to escape. He shrugged off the tightness in his shoulders, venom stirring inside his neck to reveal which vein was most vulnerable. He fell backward, fending off the urge to strike. He became tangled in the wind, his skin black as gunpowder, his bulging eyes stained yellow from overexertion.

Trajan rose to one knee alongside the guardrail. His heart was a jackrabbit, pounding inside his chest, his fingertips at work assessing the damage to his chin. Trajan peered across the guardrail. He saw Luscius and E-Z standing in place of Langston and Albert Chu. It was the same foolhardy standoff, only their conflict threatened to erupt in a spray of hot lead rather than a fit of misguided kicks and thrusts and jabs.

Trajan returned to the scene of ketchup in eggs, his grandfather's spirit gods leading the way through Fort Shantok. He saw in those bulging eyes memories of the gun, the finger on the trigger, the lifeless lump of a man buried in snow, struck down with the force of a train. His woman still couldn't bring herself to speak Luscius's name. Luscius was savior by circumstance, by his relative size to the prey that sought to nab Trajan. Things with him could have easily gone the opposite way, Luscius a man with very little space set aside for a soft middle ground.

"Enough!" Trajan shouted to them. "Look at us. Do either of you even know what you're doing here, how we wound up here in the first place?

"I'm not the enemy," he assured E-Z. "No one is out to get you.

"And you," he said flinging a hand in Luscius's direction. "I don't claim to understand all that goes on in your world. I don't belong to that world. I'm a *kid*," he added, resting on the word for emphasis. "This is not the place for me. There's nothing more that I need you to do." He leaned against the guardrail for support.

"We're done here," he said, looking past them. "I'm going home."

Luscius was less sure what to make of Bred'ren. Officer Easy was light dust, a rock in his shoe posing the greatest threat to himself in his flailing attempts to bring down Luscius Brand. But Trajan fell outside the few patterns by which Luscius had come to judge his fellow man: the smattering of Dimitrius Giannakises venturing beyond their mettle, the Yellow Goose Downs looking to gain leverage over him. Neither was he Jean-Pierre Marchand, whose loyalty Luscius could bank on come hell or high water, or another Ned Turner, who despite fond affiliation to Luscius would just as soon see him fall so long as it made news.

Luscius found Trajan's way of seeing the world curious, his uncoerced conviction foreign to him. This mere lad sat at the hands of a pair of certifiable lunatics, each armed to the teeth. Yet he refused to back down with no one outside of himself to lean on. Luscius should call on him in a time of need rather than the other way around.

He passed Trajan a look, his suspicions laid to rest. *Is everything all right, Bred'ren?* he asked with a raise of his eyebrows. Trajan passed him a look in return. *I will be okay,* he said, getting to his feet, standing on his own for the first time in the longest while.

Luscius returned to his Mercedes, climbed into the passenger seat. He eyed Officer Easy one last time. "The business between us is through. *Konprann nou*—understand? Besides, you appear to have other accounts to settle," he said, motioning over his shoulder as Tuke's Cressida wagon pulled alongside them. Luscius and his compatriot sped off as Dottie and Chester swung open the passenger side doors. The Mercedes rested at the end of the bridge, its turn signal blinking in the distance before disappearing into the night.

E-Z should have been made to wait, should have been left to suffer through several swings and misses—working security, night shift, a flashlight, a can of mace his only protection against thieving raccoons, starstruck possum cornered in a deserted warehouse, the power plant, one of the local colleges—a lunatic in training working to dope out what it took to keep the peace without disturbing it in the process. Let time determine the depth of his conviction, the width of his chest. Had he been made to climb the ladder, stuttering, stumbling, making every mistake there was to make, he would have stayed clear of Sylvia Lane, kept to his side of the river, waited to graduate. He should have worked to master more manageable concerns before tangling with the likes of Luscius Brand, learned to appreciate the value in steering clear of that world altogether.

E-Z adjusted the tuck of his shirt inside the waist of his striped pants, completing the look of a crazy man. He spun around, his teeth at work to keep his lip from quivering. He turned to face Mrs. Hopkins and her posse, offering some outlandish excuse about having shown up just in time. He didn't know the men who drove off, but he knew of them, his propensity to bend the truth standing in the way of any meaningful exchange in the things he let past his lips.

He went over to Trajan, helped him over the guardrail. "You get home safe," he said. "And don't let me catch you out here this late at night again," he offered, the subtle threat resting beneath his words lost on no one in earshot. Trajan shook free of his grip, stumbling head down toward his parents, his Grandpa Tuke.

"You have a good night," E-Z said, ambling back to his truck. Dottie annihilated him with one of her stares, ground him to dust while Chester examined the scrapes along the side of their son's face.

Tuke refused to make eye contact, lungs full of held breath—*the devil calls on his victims through the crooked slant of lying eyes*. He thought to call him Chief but figured E-Z would mistake use of the term for flattery, propagating a dreaded sentiment deeper into the universe. Trajan let it be, allowed the universe to do as it saw fit with Ezrah Sessions.

Dottie turned to look at her son. "Whatever you've been up to comes to an end tonight," she advised, placing her arms around him. "Everything you are, I am too. Anyplace you go, I too shall go. I will stand by you come what may." She nuzzled the side of his neck, remembered holding him as a baby, Langston scrambling on the floor beside her feet. "I am your mother and you are my son. And no one is going to take you from me."

Trajan got his mother back that night. Dottie resumed work at the start of the following school year, Mr. Day happy to welcome her back into the fold. She had taken enough time to herself. She needed to inject herself in the world again, place her stamp on things the way her father had instructed her to do.

Dottie had devoted much of the time inside her bubble devising a plan to establish a leadership academy for boys, offering open enrollment across tribal boundaries to avoid competing head-to-head with the other tribes' already-established coed institutions. As a veteran of the mainstream education system, she knows the system from the inside out, understands the good and the bad of it. She recognizes

311

the importance of preparing students to excel in mainstream society away from their separate, set-aside world in order for that world to survive. She plans to name the school after Langston, for the determination he'd shown in making a way for himself despite the obstacles he'd been dealt, the mother in her holding onto the belief that he would have done fine eventually had the heavens only seen fit to allow him a bit more time. She has her sights set on putting the funds the Chu family left in his name to good use. The Langston Hopkins Leadership Academy will be her legacy to the world.

She still suffers the occasional bout with anxiety. She refuses to answer the phone past dark. There are days she finds herself unable to leave her room, a concern she has worked to reserve for weekends or holidays to minimize the impact on those around her, the people depending on her to be their mother, their daughter, their sister, their friend.

Trajan remains in the employ of Bunny's uncle. The Roots played live at The Boom Box on Labor Day, capping off a three-day stand paying tribute to hip-hop's thirtieth anniversary. Public Enemy made a cameo appearance, Black Sheep, Rakim, De La Soul. Connecticut was there when hip-hop first began to creep beyond New York City's five boroughs, made its way to Boston, Providence, Philadelphia, Newark, Jersey City.

Trajan wanted to go but maintains a healthy distrust for the truce brokered between him and E-Z. He heads straight home at the end of the night. You can find him at the library Monday through

Wednesday, eight to ten, earlier as the week winds down. He is enrolled in classes at Connecticut College during the day, majoring in sociology, interested to know how the human mind works. He has plans to try out for the soccer team come springtime, hopes to see his mother rooting in the stands, for no man is an island. We must all stand on our own two feet, yet none of us is destined to walk alone. We rise, we fall, we get up again, the people in our lives a gentle lead, a guy-wire, our tether to a teeming expanse of solid ground.

Trajan wished he could go back in time, take back anything he did to add to his mother's burden. He could start over again with Carmen. Determine from the outset to build something meaningful together or be nothing at all, a fleeting concern, a passing thought. He wouldn't change a thing with Rosalie. He might wish for different circumstances between them, place them at the same point in life with one another. But his feelings toward her would never change.

The next time Trajan walked the stacks at night, he found a new volume next to John Quincy Adams turned wrong side out: *Echo of Lions*. The inside jacket cover was inscribed with a handwritten note: *Never lose your thirst for knowledge; wisdom is a lifelong pursuit.*

EPILOGUE: PERSEVERANCE FOR LASTING CHANGE

The Native American believes that people belong to the land as much as the land belongs to the people. Separating the two is tantamount to taking a mother from a child, ripping the child straight from his mother's arms.

In November 2011, the Eastern Pequot again petitioned the BIA to be recognized as a sovereign state, citing dislocation from their land as central to the concerns for which the tribe is seeking special dispensation. A decision regarding their appeal is pending. Dottie's hopes stand in the way of any cynicism. Her belief that life should play fair for her is no longer a guiding concern.

ABOUT THE AUTHOR

Jedah Mayberry's penchant for storytelling originated in grade school with a short fictional piece about a lone jellybean in search of other jellybeans to play with. He holds degrees in engineering from Georgia Tech and North Carolina A&T, and in the course of his career, he amassed several US 

and foreign patents before returning to his first love, fiction writing. His debut novel, *The Unheralded King of Preston Plains Middle*, is set in southeastern Connecticut, where he spent most of his youth. He lives with his wife and teenage daughters in Austin, TX.